Ameritrash

Linn Parker

Night Books Publishing

First published in Great Britain in 2016
by Night Books Publishing

https://www.facebook.com/linnparkerauthor/
https://twitter.com/linnparkernovel

Night Books Publishing
info@wordnoodle.co.uk

Print ISBN: 978-0-9935523-0-4
Epub ISBN: 978-0-9935523-1-1
Kindle ISBN: 978-0-9935523-2-8

Cover design and typesetting by Emma Dawe
Cover photo by Angelo Sartori

For Krista

'What people somehow (inadvertently, I'm sure) forgot to mention when we were children was that we need to make messes in order to find out who we are and why we are here—and, by extension, what we're supposed to be writing.'

Anne Lamott (1994) *Bird by Bird*

prologue

I actually wanted to write a book about a famous person, as that's all people seem to want to read about these days—a well-known person airing their dirty laundry, letting the skeletons out of the closet and revealing juicy tidbits about all the naughty things they got up to. People like to be voyeurs into someone else's life, but like I say, usually people they know about—like a celebrity, or their sibling, grandparent, or even the next-door neighbor. You may or may not know me, but I am allowing you to peer inside the diary I wrote over one year when I was 20 years old, studying (supposed to be) at a university in France, and trying to turn my life into a novel. The diary served to jog my memory of a time when, to be frank, my brain was so addled that my memories have blurred, faces and places have become fuzzy. It became clear that I didn't know myself back then and that the person I was is still an enigma to me. Why I made some of the choices I did, I do not know. You will probably know me a bit better by the time you finish reading this, and if you recommend it and lots of people buy it, you never know, I could become famous!

So here is the story...

Siobhan Schreiber

The MIJE

The bus spat us and our mismatched backpacks and bags out onto the wet cobblestones in front of the Maison International de Jeunesse et d'Étudiants, or the MIJE (meezh) as we would come to call it. The 17th-century aristocratic townhouse stood on a dark, narrow street in the Marais district of Paris, close enough to the River Seine to smell its dank, sewer-tinged funk. The large wooden doors and window shutters were all firmly shut, preventing even the tiniest sliver of light from escaping into the night. Our leader, Professor Richard Céleste, rang the doorbell while we sat on our bags smoking and trying to blend into the Parisian atmosphere.

A small door within the big doors creaked open and a slight, dark-skinned man emerged. He looked over our bedraggled group of pseudo-hippies, sorority girls, preppies and nerds, and asserted, '*Vous êtes le groupe américain.*' Then he gesticulated for us to come inside.

We dragged our luggage in through the pre-revolutionary doors into an inner courtyard that was surrounded by stone archways and overlooked by French windows and little balconies with curly, wrought iron balustrades and some smaller dormer windows on the floor above. I stubbed out my cigarette and looked around. A wide stone staircase swept up through one of the arches to the left. Yellow lamplight filled the courtyard and the damp cobbles gleamed with the residue of September rain.

I suddenly felt that I had been transported back in time from 1990 to 1700. The faceless strip malls and parking lots of suburban New England seemed to be light years away as I stood, taking in my new surroundings with a sense of wonder.

Richard sauntered to the center of the courtyard, cleared his throat and started to speak in his meticulous French-accented English. 'Gather round, please.' When Richard spoke we listened, especially the female students, who were usually riveted by his sparkling brown eyes and tall, well-toned physique. He was nothing like the other French professors from the university who were mostly elderly existentialists; he was about 35 and preferred wearing tight jeans to tweed suits. 'I'd like to welcome you all to your new home for the next month. You will be taking some cultural acclimatization and language lessons here every morning, to get up to speed before moving in with your host families in Rouen and immersing yourselves in the rigors of French university life.' He ran his hand through a head of thick black waves, and you could almost hear the collective sigh of my fellow females. Too bad he was already married and his heavily pregnant wife, Lucinda, was accompanying him on this trip. 'You are here to learn as much from your individual experiences in France as in the classroom, but please be careful as well. I have heard rumors that this very building was once a brothel and ghosts of disrepute are said to haunt its halls.' A ripple of laughter went through the group.

I couldn't see any ghosts, but I could see a few other people ambling about behind windows and through the courtyard. They looked foreign, their clothes were different and their hair was different. I made a mental note of a couple of good-looking Scandinavian-type guys.

Richard read out the list of who was sharing rooms. Most dorms had four people sharing, but as there were 13 women and only four men, there would be one room with only three. 'Siobhan Schreiber, Lindi Tucker, and Gabriela Ferreira,' he read out.

Our room, we discovered, had French doors and a balcony, and was situated right in the center, overlooking the courtyard. The floor was made of chipped terracotta tiles and there were two sets of iron bunk beds, a rickety wooden desk and chair, and a large, ornately carved armoire. There was a small, open wash area in the corner of the room with a shower and sink. The toilet was down the corridor and shared with the rest of the floor. Gabriela chose one of the bottom bunks, I decided on the one above and Lindi chose the other bottom bunk, leaving the second top one empty.

Gabriela wrinkled her nose. 'The room's a bit shabby, isn't it?'

'It's pure luxury compared to the army barracks I had to live in,' Lindi replied.

'You were in the army?' Gabriela asked, intrigued.

'Well … um, I don't really like to talk about it, but yes,' Lindi said, looking at the floor. 'I'm not proud of it, but it was the only way I could pay for college.'

Gabriela put an arm around her. 'Don't worry, I think it's very admirable.' She smiled.

I watched as Lindi and Gabriela unpacked their things. Tiny, dark-haired Gabriela hung up a few plain blouses and some jeans, and set down a small statue of the Virgin Mary next to her bed. She saw me look at it quizzically and explained, 'My nana from Portugal gave it to me, and it reminds me of her.'

Lindi was emptying a big, worn-out, army duffel bag. She had loads of CDs, a few miniskirts and fishnet tights, some hair gel, and a box of red hair dye for the upkeep of her spiky punk haircut. Lindi saw me lounging on the bed watching, and flashed her big, blue eyes at me. 'Aren't you going to unpack, Siobhan?' she said in her Louisiana drawl.

I jumped from the top bunk. 'I'm too excited. We're in Paris, ladies!' I already felt the shackles falling from my middle-class consciousness, now that I was a million miles away from Connecticut and my neurotic Catholic parents, and I was itching to get out and explore. 'Let's get out on the town,' I suggested.

'But I need to call my parents and Jamie to tell them that I got here safely,' Gabriela whined.

'Do it tomorrow,' I said. 'Let's go.'

Once we had stepped through the huge wooden door, we stopped and looked around us. The river Seine was to our left and a web of crooked cobbled streets to our right.

'Let's go right,' I suggested. I thought it looked like a more promising place to find a bar. Finding a drink was the natural thing to do if you were a 20-year-old American, newly arrived in a country where alcohol was not denied to its under-21 citizens. We wove through the streets, Gabriela clinging wide-eyed to Lindi's arm.

After a while, we heard footsteps behind us. We all looked back. There were three men walking not far behind us.

'I think those guys are following us,' Gabriela said, nervously.

'Just keep walking and look like you know where you're going,' Lindi responded.

'*Eh—les filles!*' one of the men called.

I made the mistake of turning to look. They were gaining on us. We increased our pace but they did too. One of them shouted something else in French that I wasn't sure I understood correctly.

'What did he say?' I asked Lindi.

'Do you really want to know?' she said.

'Yeah, tell me.' We were practically running now.

'He said, "Do you foreign girls want a taste of French sausage?"'

Suddenly I remembered a slang phrase from my street French book, which I had studied scrupulously on the plane before coming to France. I stopped in my tracks, turned around to face our stalkers and yelled, '*Fous le camp, connard!*'

The men stopped and looked surprised. They shrugged their shoulders and backed off. I was so proud. I had spoken my first words in French, to a French person, in France—and they seemed to understand me— 'Fuck off, asshole!' I was glad I had bought that book. It was more useful than all the years of French classes I had sat through in American educational institutions.

We found a little bar and sat down at a table outside, lighting cigarettes and watching the Parisians strut past. We waited and waited but the waiter completely ignored us. I was on my third cigarette and was getting thirsty. 'I think we have to call him over,' Lindi suggested. We were used to the prompt and attentive service that customers received in the States. Even at the cheapest diner, before your butt even hits the seat, a menu is waved in your face. If an American waiter ignored a customer for half an hour, he'd be fired.

'*Garçon!*' Lindi said, finally. An annoyed looking waiter took his time coming over.

Without taking his eyes off a woman walking down the street, he said, '*Oui?*' and stood over us. We didn't know what was on offer, so didn't know what to order.

'*Le menu, s'il vous plait,*' I said, boldly.

'*Il n'y en a pas,*' he said, now looking at a Ferrari that roared up to the front of the café spewing exhaust over the sidewalk tables.

'How can they not have a menu?' Gabriela coughed on the exhaust fumes.

The waiter frowned at us, exasperated. 'You speak Ingleesh?' he said. Then without even waiting for an answer he launched into a list of drinks and snacks—in English.

We ordered three kir royales. It was liberating to order a drink without being asked for proof of your age. Both Gabriela and I were 20 and were used to having to show our fake IDs to get into bars in the US. Lindi was already 23 so it wasn't so much of a big deal for her.

Sipping our kirs, we discussed what we wanted to do during our time in Paris. I wanted to go to Père Lachaise cemetery to see Oscar Wilde's and Jim Morrison's graves, and the catacombs. Gabriela wanted to go to the Louvre. Lindi had already been to Paris as an exchange student in high school, so she'd seen most of it before—her goal was to meet the Frenchman of her dreams.

As we left the bar, feeling happy from the kir, I noticed an elegant old woman sitting at a table. Her companion was an immaculately groomed bichon frise that was seated in the chair opposite her enjoying a croque monsieur from a dainty plate on the table. Only in Paris, I thought. I knew I was going to love this place.

When we arrived back at the MIJE, we were surprised to find someone else in the room. A naked woman was lying on the unclaimed fourth bunk above Gabriela's bed. She didn't seem bothered about covering herself up when we walked in.

We didn't know where to look. A huge muff covered her lower belly and blended gradually into black fur-covered legs, like a 3-D velcro map of Africa. All three of us were stunned. The woman swung her hairy legs over the side of the bunk and reached out her hand, exposing a thatch of sweaty armpit hair. 'Bonsoir, je suis Veronique.' As she shook our hands, she looked each one of us up and down. When she rested her eyes on me she gave me a wink. I quickly turned away and started fumbling in my bag.

Veronique jumped off her perch with a heavy thud and sauntered over to the wash area. There was a knock at the door, so she opened it. Our classmate Mike, stood in the doorway. Mike, usually quite articulate, gaped open-mouthed and then stuttered, 'Um—excuse me... I'm really sorry. I think I got the wrong room.'

'Hi Mike!' Gabriela shouted, jumping up from her bed and blocking the doorway.

'We'd invite you in but it's a bit crowded in here,' I indicated the naked Frenchwoman with my eyes.

Veronique thankfully disappeared behind the shower curtain. Mike shifted nervously from Birkenstocked foot to foot, fidgeting with his watch. 'I got some weed. Anyone want a smoke?' he said, not daring to enter the room.

Leave it to Mike to sniff out some weed within hours of arriving in Paris. Lindi and Angie didn't smoke pot, so I left them behind in the room, which was slowly filling with steam.

Mike already had the joint rolled up, which he produced from the pocket of his orange kaftan. We skulked down dimly lit back alleyways on our way to the Seine, getting pleasantly high as we walked. At the edge of the river promenade, a few dried leaves stuck to the skeletons of trees, rustling lightly. Mike kept turning round to see if someone was behind us, the yellow streetlights glinting off his round, wire-rimmed spectacles.

'It's just the wind blowing the leaves,' I reassured him—my head spinning from the last toke. The immense sky rolled low before us—a soft hue of mauve-orange dappled by blotches of grey clouds. 'It's so beautiful at night,' I said and giggled. 'Is it me, or is the sky closer here?'

'I think it's just the clouds that are closer to the earth, making the sky seem closer,' Mike said, pushing his glasses back up while bringing the joint back to his mouth. There was a comfortable silence before Mike said, 'Can I make a confession?'

'Sure,' I said, intrigued. I didn't know much about Mike and felt flattered that he wanted to share some personal information. There was another moment of silence and Mike inhaled, getting ready to let me in on his secret. Just then someone stepped out of the shadows. '*Excusez-moi. Avez-vous du feu?*' the man asked. Mike exhaled and offered the man a light. We walked on in silence. He seemed to forget that he was about to tell me something and I didn't want to seem nosey, so I didn't pry.

The clouds flew by over our heads and the lamps cast a halo of moisture around the bulbs. We finished the joint, lit up our cigarettes and continued walking through the silent sound of rustling leaves and whispering water. I was lost in my own thoughts, escaping from my head before I could hold them. There was so much that was new, so much to take in that I felt like I might explode. I was like a bird that had escaped from the safety of its cage into the outside world, where it was dazzled and confused by the noise, the lights, the sheer expanse of the never-ending sky. I was determined to make good use of my freedom.

When I returned to the MIJE, I found my roommates all fast asleep. I lay in bed thinking about my boyfriend back home, Toby. I almost didn't come on this trip to France because of him. A week before I was due to leave, we went out to the woods with a case of beer and some weed. Toby was wasted as usual and started to cry. He got down on his knees and begged me not to go. I remember the intense heaviness that gripped my heart. I knew what I had to do, though, and I was going to go to France, even if it meant leaving him behind in the blandness of middle-class suburbia, furtively drinking Red Stripe and dropping acid in the woods.

Then there was my mother, sobbing in the airport, clinging on to me so tightly like she would never let me go. For a second I wasn't sure I could leave her with my obsessive-compulsive father and depressive sister. She needed me—Toby needed me. How would they cope once I was gone? I had all of that holding me back, but I didn't let it.

At the crack of dawn, we were all awoken by Veronique doing her ablutions, once again in all her glory. I lay in bed for a while watching her through half-open eyes. She squatted and stuck a tampon in and, without putting on any underwear, flung on faded dungarees and Dr. Marten boots. She grabbed her backpack, bid us farewell and was gone before any of us even got up out of bed.

Lindi was the first to rise. She stretched and yawned. 'Oh my God, what is that?' she said looking at the top bunk where Veronique had been sleeping. Gabriela and I got up and had a look at the mussed-up sheets on the bed.

'Eeew!' Gabriela scowled, looking away. The sheets were stained with quite a lot of blood.

'God, that's filthy,' I replied. 'She must not have been wearing a tampon.'

No one wanted to touch the bloody sheets so we just pulled the blanket up over them, so at least we wouldn't have to look at them.

When the next girl arrived to stay in our room, a sweet little Israeli called Miki, we warned her that she should ask the concierge to get someone to change the sheets. The poor girl looked like she could use a really good bed. I thought she must have been hitchhiking all the way from Israel without a single day's sleep or a single wash. Her long wavy hair was matted and dirty and her hippy clothes were well worn.

Miki was a good roommate. She stayed with us for a few days before going on to her next destination. She was travelling with her boyfriend Ben, who was due to go into the Israeli army for national service in a few months. She explained that they were doing some traveling and trying to see what they could of the world in case something happened to Ben. They were leaving Europe and going to Laos next as it was one of the only places where an Israeli passport wasn't denied entry without any problems.

We soon realized that, being a youth hostel, there were lots of comings and goings at the MIJE Some people stayed a month, like us, some stayed a week, some stayed only a day or two. The next group to arrive was German. Our next roommate Elke didn't speak any English or French at all. I was the only one who was able to communicate with a bit of German. She seemed like a nice girl but I must admit that I was more interested in her schoolmates and asked her to invite them up to our room for a few beers. The boys were called Hans and Johann and they were perfect German specimens with their shiny blond hair, light blue eyes and lovely white teeth. They told us about a party at the German embassy that they were invited to and asked us to come. There would be kegs of beer and it only cost a few francs to get in. It sounded like fun so I convinced Lindi and Gabriela to come. I think Gabriela really liked Johann, so it was easy to convince her.

All five of us made the metro journey to the German embassy. It was all lit up and there was loud music and voices drifting over the huge iron gates. Then a tall, blond, correct guard stopped us at the gate and asked for passes. The two Germans presented their tickets and said we were their guests. We made our way into the main hall, which was absolutely crammed with people dressed in finery. We jostled our way through the crowd toward the bar where the beer was flowing freely. The boys got us each a big plastic mug full of beer.

We held our plastic 'steins' up and yelled '*Prost*' all together before taking a swig. Smartly dressed men and women were singing and dancing. Germans sure know how to party, I thought. After several steins of beer and a drunken rendition of 'Deutschland Uber Alles' we were the last ones to be shoved out the door by the formidable bouncers. We staggered to the nearest metro draped in German flags and wearing paper fedoras. I just knew I was going to love Europe.

***

Toby was being awkward. I was being nice by calling him and he just had to try to bring me down. 'How's Pierre?' he said.

'Who?'

'You know, some French guy you're probably fucking.' He kept going on about how I was going to meet some Frenchman and cheat on him. He sounded drunk. I loved him, but he had to cut me some slack. I didn't want to spend the rest of my life in small-town New England. I wanted to see the world, learn new languages, and experience new things. Toby was just trapped in his dead-end world of smoking joints in the woods and drinking cheap beer.

'I miss you and think about you every day,' I tried to reassure him. 'It's only a few months until you come over to visit.' His grandmother had given him some money, and together with some money he'd saved up he was going to come over to see me just after Christmas for New Year's.

There were a few people waiting to use the phone in the foyer, so I cut the call short and hung up. Four Australians were setting their backpacks down in the courtyard. I craned my neck to check them out. Two were tall and blond and two were dark. 'Scuse me mate, where do we check in?' the short, dark guy with the glasses asked a Dutch guy who was sitting outside smoking. 'I shink dee guy ish comink,' the Dutch guy said, pointing at the concierge emerging from a door. My ears pricked up. They were cute—I liked their accents.

Anne from our group was also outside having a cigarette and I could see her eyes following the Australian guys. There was a spark in her expression that I had never noticed before. Her eyes bored into the guys, trying to assess what was under their shorts. Anne was always very quiet back at University of New England. She was small and plain looking, with long, straight mousy hair and a conventional, if not outdated way of dressing. She seemed to blend into the woodwork. I never knew she smoked, but by the way she was awkwardly holding the cigarette, trying to look sexy and sophisticated, and trying not to cough with each inhalation, I had a feeling that she had just started. I decided to join her. 'Hey, can you spare a cigarette?' I asked. 'Sure, she said,' grateful for the company. 'Lucky Strike,' she said, pronouncing it the French way, 'Lookie Streek'.

'They're not bad,' I said nodding toward the Aussies. 'Should we invite them out tonight?'

'Really?' she said, following the movements of one of the tall blond ones. They noticed us looking at them and casually sauntered over.

'You ladies stayin' here?' the tall guy asked us.

'We're here for the whole month of September. What about you guys?' I asked.

'We're here for four days. Then we're going to London to work in a bar. Are you Americans?' he drawled.

'Where are you from?' Anne asked.

'Can't ya tell?' he laughed.

'Americans aren't very good with accents,' I said.

'I'm Pete, and this is Tony, Jay and Carlo. We're from Melbourne, Australia.'

Anne was practically drooling over the guy's accent.

'This is Anne and I'm Siobhan. Do you guys want to meet up tonight? We can show you some of Paris.' I thought the short, dark one called Carlo was cute. He wore round glasses that made him look sensitive and intelligent.

The Aussies nodded. 'We'll meet you down here at 9pm? We all gotta take showers and stuff. Do you girls have any more friends?' Pete asked, grinning. 'The more the merrier, you know?'

'My two roommates might want to come out. I'll ask,' I said stubbing out my cigarette.

'See ya later,' Anne said, winking at the tall Aussie.

Back in the room, Gabriela was applying a facemask and Lindi was reading a guide to Paris. 'Hey ladies, how about a night on the town with some gorgeous Australians?' I said.

Gabriela's facemask cracked as she raised an eyebrow. 'Australians? Where'd they come from?'

'Australia, where do you think!' I laughed. 'I just met them downstairs. There's four of them, and me and Anne are going, but we need two more girls to balance things out.'

'I'd feel guilty about Jamie,' Gabriela said. Gabriela never stopped talking about her wonderful boyfriend Jamie. It was, 'Jamie does this… Jamie says this… when Jamie studied in France…' Jamie was in the year above us at university and had done the study abroad program last year. Gabriela pined for Jamie. She was going to stay pure for him, like a good Catholic girl. I had a feeling that Jamie was probably screwing sorority girls in Gabriela's absence.

'Forget about Jamie. He's not here. We're just having fun. You don't have to marry anyone.'

'And what about your boyfriend?' she said, looking me in the eye.

'What about him? He's not here either. I feel like having fun and these Aussies looked interesting.'

Lindi looked up from her book. 'I'll come with you, if only to keep you out of trouble,' she winked at me.

'Now there's a girl who knows how to have a good time! Come on ladies, get ready, we're meeting in an hour.'

Four Aussies and four 'Yanks' as the Aussies called us spilled out from the MIJE onto rue de Fauconnier. We headed toward rue de Rivoli to find a bar. Anne sidled up to Tony right away. She was only about half his height and was craning her neck to talk to him.

We went into a bar and the boys ordered some beers, and wine for the girls. After one glass of wine I noticed Anne put her hand on Tony's thigh as she gazed into his eyes. Jay was staring at Gabriela's cleavage as she talked to him about her boyfriend Jamie and her Portuguese heritage. Lindi was looking confused after listening to one of Pete's Australian jokes.

'Do you want another drink?' Carlo said pointing at my empty glass of wine. I'd already had three, but agreed to another.

He came back with a couple of small glasses of clear liquid. 'Sambuca,' he said. 'My grandfather swears by it,' he said lifting his glass in a toast.

Carlo was Italian-Australian and proud. He looked Italian but sounded Australian. I thought he was cute but quite different from the type I normally go for. Toby was tall and wiry. Carlo was short and quite dark and muscular. I clinked my glass with him and felt the heat of the Sambuca spreading from my stomach into my veins.

He smiled nervously at me and his little round glasses glinted. 'Do you have a girlfriend back home?' I asked.

'No,' he said, 'Do you have a boyfriend?'

'No,' I replied and smiled back. From the corner of my eye I could see Tony towering over Anne and whispering in her ear. She was giggling.

I felt a tap on my shoulder. It was Lindi and her expression betrayed boredom. 'I've had enough of Crocodile Dundee's jokes. I'm heading back to the MIJE.'

I didn't want my friend to walk home on her own, so I said I'd go with her. Carlo said he was a gentleman and would walk with us. The other guys decided to go too, if Carlo was going. So we all headed back together, staggering and swaying along the damp, cobbled back streets of Le Marais.

'We'll never get rid of these guys,' Lindi whispered to me.

'Well there are some of us who don't seem to mind so much,' I said indicating Anne and Tony, who were holding on to each other and kept dipping into shadowy corners to kiss.

I looked over at Carlo. He was looking at me and smiling. 'Let's hang out a bit longer in the courtyard. I don't feel like going back to the dorm yet.'

'No, me neither,' I replied.

We approached the huge wooden doors and buzzed to get in. The North African night watchman creaked the door open and let us in, taking in our drunken state before retiring back to his little office to stare at the security CCTV monitors.

Lindi and Gabriela bid everyone goodnight as they sensibly headed back up to the room.

Pete and Jay looked disappointed as they noticed that Tony and Anne had disappeared into the darkened dining room. They looked at Carlo. 'You coming back up, mate?' Carlo shook his head.

'No, I'm alright. We're gonna hang out for a bit.'

It was 2 am and there was no one else around. The lights were all off. We went into the darkened dining room to sit down at one of the tables, only to discover that Anne and Tony were underneath it, in the throes of passion. We discreetly left them to their furtive groping and slurping, and sat down next to each other outside in the corridor.

We looked at each other and for a split second Toby's face appeared in my head. I immediately erased the image from my mind. My life was here in Paris now, not in a backwoods town in Connecticut. Carlo was cute—too cute. I felt the ghosts of disrepute take over my soul and I lunged at him, sticking my tongue down his throat. I could tell I had taken him by surprise, but he responded and we passionately and urgently kissed.

After kissing for a while I got bored. I needed to take things further, but we were sitting on the steps out in the open. The dining room was already occupied and the dorms were certainly not very private. I had an idea. The ladies' toilet off the main foyer on the ground floor was clean and private. There was no one else around, so I didn't think that anyone else would walk in on us.

As we stood outside the door Carlo looked doubtfully at the lady-shaped symbol on the door. 'Here?' he said.

'There's no one else up and at least the night watchman won't stumble across us in there. Trust me.'

Once inside, I gently took his glasses off that made him look intellectual and sensitive, and placed them on the ceramic washbasin. We laid our jackets on the floor and lay down on them. I started to unbutton his jeans, while he put his hand under my t-shirt to undo my bra.

Stripped down to the bare essentials, I noticed Carlo was sturdy and hairy with short powerful legs, and he wasn't circumcised. I had never seen an uncircumcised penis before and was fascinated. Toby, as most clinically clean American men, was circumcised at birth. We enjoyed a wanton sex session under the harsh neon lights of the MIJE ladies room, feeling the cold terracotta tiles against our skin. We were unfamiliar with each other's bodies, and awkwardly bumped into the exposed pipes and toilet cubicle doors trying to maneuver ourselves around.

Afterwards, we sat naked and shivering against the cold wall tiles, casually sharing a crumpled cigarette. Something in the top corner of the room caught my eye.

'Oh, shit!' I said pointing up at the CCTV camera that was aiming its lens directly at us.

'Bloody hell!' Carlo said as he stood up, frantically trying to pull his clothes on. 'I bet that bloody guard got a right eyeful!'

We dressed and said goodnight to each other outside in the corridor and slunk back to our respective dorms.

The next morning in the canteen, waiting for my bowl of coffee and baguette, I noticed Carlo and the other Aussies. I nodded and smiled but didn't go over to talk to them. Carlo looked down at his bowl, a bit nervous and embarrassed. I couldn't be bothered to make that much of an effort to go over and talk. I knew he would be leaving for London in a few days. The North African came over to my table to refill my coffee bowl. As he poured the hot liquid into the cup, he fixed me with his black eyes and grinned a wide, lascivious grin. I felt sick with embarrassment and quickly turned away to stare into the depths of my coffee.

'What's that all about?' Gabriela asked, bemused. 'That guy's such a grouch. He never smiles at anyone. What've you done to deserve that?'

'I have absolutely no idea,' I said trying to make myself inconspicuous by slouching down into my chair and hiding my face behind my bowl.

I noticed Anne go over and sit down with the Aussies. She waved me over but I slid further down in my seat and pretended not to see her. I wondered if the concierge would give her the grin as well.

Carlo and I pretty much ignored each other for the next couple of days, until it was time for the Aussies to leave for the UK. Surprisingly, Carlo came to my room to say goodbye and tell me he was leaving. 'I had a really great time,' he said nervously, looking sensitive and intellectual with his little spectacles. 'In fact, it was a really unforgettable time,' he smiled coyly.

'It was great to meet you too. Have a great time in England. And don't get led astray into any more public toilets,' I laughed. We hugged each other like good buddies.

'See ya 'round, maybe?' he said tentatively.

'Yeah, see you again sometime maybe,' I said. But we never exchanged numbers or addresses and we never saw each other again. Carlo would be just one amongst many people that would come and go in my new life, unfettered by the moral constraints of the USA. I was in Europe now.

***

The next day I had an acclimatization lesson with my American classmates. We met every morning in one of the meeting rooms at the MIJE while we were staying in Paris, in order to prepare for our real studies at the university of Rouen, which would start in a month. After some intense grammar practice, study of current French news events and research on an assigned arrondissement, our acclimatization would end with a final exam. Richard, being an unconventional professor, announced that the exam would consist of a treasure hunt around Paris. Our group was thrilled not to be subjected to a long written exam and relished the opportunity to explore the city. The group was split into teams and the team that was able to collect the most 'treasure' would win.

My team was lucky to have two of the best French speakers, Lindi and Mike, along with Gabriela and me. We had a week to complete the task and it was meant to get us to explore Paris, learn a bit about the history and culture of the city, as well as use our language skills in real life situations. There were some very odd tasks, amongst them: photographing ourselves in front of the building that Ernest Hemingway once lived in; naming the museum where a pair of stone Lamassus could be found; counting how many steps there were up to the dome of the Sacré-Coeur; listing three interesting facts about the Place de la Concorde; finding out the price of a crêpe from the street vendor on the corner of rue de Rivoli and rue du Renard; finding the inscription written on a plaque in Place des Vosges; taking grave rubbings of the names of five famous people buried in Père Lachaise cemetery; naming the metro stop for the Paris catacombs; listing the current films playing at the Les Halles cinema; finding out the price of a student ticket there; and, the most difficult of all, getting a copy of Moliere's *Les Fleurs du Mal* out of the Sorbonne library.

Our second to last task was to find the exact location of the former Tuileries Palace, which was burned down by the Communards in 1871. We needed to ask someone to take a photo of us at the site, pretending to be shot by the government forces in retaliation. The stunned Japanese tourist who took our picture seemed very amused as we lay down on the ground on the terrace overlooking the Tuileries gardens.

So our team had accomplished all of the tasks and we were confident that we had been successful in obtaining all the information required. There was just one more item remaining: the book from the Sorbonne library. We had decided that it would be best to send Mike into the Sorbonne on his own. It would be easier for one person to get through the security at the entrance of the library than a group, and he had the kind of stoned, confident arrogance that would be useful for talking his way in.

Lindi, Gabriela and I decided to kill some time while waiting for Mike. The sign in a travel agency across the street caught our eyes. It was advertising a 'student special' bus trip to Amsterdam. It included bus travel and two nights in a youth hostel in the center of Amsterdam. I lingered in front of the window. 'Let's do it,' I said.

'Oh I don't know,' Gabriela whined. 'Isn't Amsterdam known for drugs and prostitutes?'

'Exactly! That's why we should go. We're not in the land of the Puritans anymore. Live a little.'

Lindi chimed in, 'I would love to go. There's the Rijksmuseum, the Anne Frank house, canals and windmills. It's not only drugs and prostitutes.'

'OK—why don't we go back and tell the others in the group? I think they might want to come too.' Gabriela said.

I had a feeling that Mike would be up for it, but I really wasn't too sure about anyone else. I couldn't picture who else in the group would want to explore the red light district or trawl the coffeehouses in order to sample different kinds of weed. They were all just too American, with their bouncy blond hair, preppy style, suntans, white smiles and bubbly personalities. I couldn't picture the inseparable sorority girls, Natalie and Sara, toking away on a big joint, looking cool and blending into the European laid-backness; nor Margery, with her Alice in Wonderland hairband and long, straight, carefully brushed hair; nor meek little Sarah who looked like she'd just got out of Catholic school; nor Esther, the studious and serious Puerto Rican, who muttered prayers under her breath while fingering the small crucifix she wore on her neck. Nor could I picture statuesque Fiona, with her porcelain English skin untainted by chemicals, desecrating her perfect body with drugs. And Lulu was just too much of a cutesy airhead; she was dopey enough already. Even Sandra, who was Jamaican, had an outspoken disdain for marijuana and got annoyed when people stereotyped all Jamaicans as pot-smoking Rastas. Maybe Kelly and Penny might be up for a bit of a laugh, but they seemed a bit snobby and didn't bother too much with anyone else. From what I'd already seen of Anne, however, she might prove to be up for an adventure. Or possibly the boys; Bobby was so immature and naïve, but he seemed willing to expose himself to new situations, and Phil, who was a bit of a loner, might be a dark horse. Now Aidan—definitely not. He was a disturbed individual, who must have had some sort of OCD or other psychological problem. Everyone avoided him like the plague. He was just plain weird and I wouldn't want to see him go even more psychotic from drugs. Cathy, the graduate student who was meant to be like our mentor, was straight as an arrow as well. She didn't even drink. But Mimi, now there was someone I thought I could really relate to. I would suggest that we invite her to go to Amsterdam with us. She liked to have a good time. She occasionally smoked joints with Mike and I, and she enjoyed a drink. She was a beautiful, laid-back Jewish party girl, with sultry black eyes, a mane of wild curly hair and luscious, pouty lips, which always had a cigarette hanging from them in a seductive way.

As we meandered back across the street to the Sorbonne, we saw Mike coming out of the library with an attractive Frenchman. He stopped on the steps of the library for a few moments, engaged in conversation with the French guy. He saw us and waved. The young man looked our way. He scribbled something down on a scrap of paper and handed it to Mike. He shook Mike's hand and went on his way. Mike approached us and pulled the book out of his backpack.

'Great, you got it!' said Lindi. 'We must be the first ones to get here!'

'We must be winning! How did you get it?' Gabriela clapped.

Mike casually popped a Gauloise in his mouth and shrugged, imitating the Gallic body language. 'I just asked someone if they could get it out for me. I promised I'd return it.'

***

The next morning, we triumphantly entered the meeting room where the acclimatization sessions were held. As Richard read out the list of treasure hunt tasks he asked each team to give evidence of what they'd managed to find. Our team had correctly completed every task. When he came to the last task of obtaining the book from the Sorbonne, Richard explained that this was actually a trick question and that no one was supposed to have got the book as only students of the Sorbonne were allowed to take books out of the library. Lindi politely raised her hand and pointed out that our team had indeed achieved the last task. Mike produced the evidence from his bag, holding the tattered copy of *Les Fleurs du Mal* above his head. Richard grabbed the book, opening its cover to verify the Sorbonne stamp on the inside. He and Cathy stood staring at us in stunned silence.

'But this is almost impossible. You certainly have not procured the book by the most savory of means?' Richard pried.

Mike smiled enigmatically. 'I just made friends with someone who got it out for me. It's entirely above board.'

'However,' Richard said, pointing at the book cover, '*Les Fleurs du Mal* is actually by Baudelaire, as you'll notice!'

Lindi, Gabriela, Mike and I still ended up getting an A+ for our 'final exam', and to celebrate we decided to book that trip to Amsterdam.

canals, gouda and space cakes

Gabriela had managed to convince a few others to come along on the trip to Amsterdam. Lindi, Mike and Mimi were really up for it, but what surprised me was that Natalie and Sara, the sorority girls, wanted to come as well.

We waited for the bus in front of the Gare du Nord. There was a group of three French guys and their Japanese friend, a few Polish women, and a tour guide also waiting. I got talking to the French guys, who seemed quite friendly. They were staying in the same hostel as us, the enticingly named Big Bob's Youth Hostel. Some of the others were staying in another hostel around the corner.

Once we were on the bus and settled in, our guide briefed us on the safety procedures of the bus, the itinerary and estimated arrival times. She told us all very sternly not to bother trying to take any drugs back into France, as the border patrol would be bringing sniffer dogs on board.

Amsterdam: the city of canals, prostitutes in shop windows, marijuana and seedy sex museums. It was unlike any American city. Even New York, which was once called New Amsterdam, just didn't possess the same type of quirkiness and open-mindedness.

We arrived at Big Bob's and after locking our belongings in the lockers in our sparse dormitory and claiming our bunks, we headed out onto the narrow streets along the canals. We stood outside the first coffeehouse we came to and peered in through the steamy window. Natalie and Sara seemed a bit hesitant, but as the rest of us were going in, they decided it was better than being left out on the street by themselves.

As we entered, a cloud of pungent, overpowering skunk smoke, mixed with the smell of coffee, hit our noses. We sat down at a table, trying to appear as if we'd been there hundreds of times before. A guy wearing an unraveling woolly hat ambled up to the table and handed us all menus. 'The specials are on the board,' he said, pointing to a blackboard above the bar.

Natalie and Sara squinted at the menu. 'I just want some cake or something. Where's the food on here?' Sara said, confused.

I studied the menu. I had never been given the choice of what kind of pot to smoke before. I usually just had whatever stuff Toby got from his brother in Alphabet City in downtown Manhattan. There was Purple Haze, Thai Stick, Malawian, Afghan, Skunk, White Widow, Northern Lights and Hashish. 'What do you think Mike? You're the connoisseur.' I said. 'What about the special?'

'Sure,' he said. 'Go for the Purple Haze.'

I bought a bag of Purple Haze and Mike bought himself a bag of Northern Lights. The coffee shop guy offered to roll up the first one. We watched in amazement as he mixed it with rolling tobacco. With agile hands, like he was making an origami bird, he quickly rolled a perfect, tapered cone, with a filter on the end. I had never seen anything like it. The guy handed it to Mike, who sagely put it in his mouth and leaned forward so the guy could light it for him. He drew deeply and closed his eyes, savoring the taste. I was impatient and wanted to have a hit, but Mike explained that in Europe the culture is to hold on to the joint for a bit, relax, and then pass it on. This was unlike the American custom of rolling up a tiny joint of pure weed, taking a quick toke and passing it immediately to someone else.

I was next. I took a long, deep drag and felt the smoke fill my mouth, then my lungs, and then the molecules of Purple Haze making their way into my bloodstream. Wow. I took another drag and started to feel really relaxed. I could definitely get used to this European custom of savoring the joint. I passed it to Mimi and watched her sensuous lips embrace the joint. She closed her dark eyes and smiled as she exhaled, the smoke curling around her wild hair.

She passed the joint on to Natalie, who wrinkled her nose. 'I don't smoke,' she said disdainfully.

'I don't either,' said Sara. 'I just want some cake and coffee or something.'

'I saw there was some cake over on the counter,' I said to them, feeling a bit mischievous from the weed. I had seen written on the chalk board above the bar that there were space cakes for sale and thought it would be hilarious to see Natalie and Sara tripping out of their heads.

'Oh that's good,' Natalie said. 'Let's get some then.' She waved to the guy behind the bar. 'Could I order the cake please?' she said.

'Make that two,' Sara said.

The waiter brought a plate with a couple of chocolate brownies. 'Mmm, that looks good,' Natalie said, licking her lips. We all watched in amusement as Sara and Natalie wolfed down the brownies, waiting to see the effects kick in.

Gabriela also refused the joint and Lindi only had one tiny, tentative drag. 'Do you want a bit of cake anyone? It's delicious,' Sara said, offering the plate to Gabriela. Gabriela took a small bite and made a face.

'What a weird taste,' she said. 'I wonder what they're made out of?' I burst out laughing, choking and spluttering out the smoke I had just inhaled. Mimi started to snigger and a wry smile played on Mike's lips.

'What?' Gabriela said, indignant. 'Why are you guys laughing? Are you stoned?'

'Those are space cakes,' I said.

'Space cakes?' Sara spluttered, shocked, looking at the remaining crumbs on the plate.

'You know, hash brownies,' Mimi offered, through half-lidded eyes.

'Oh my God!' Gabriela screeched.

'Why didn't you say anything?' Sara said, glaring at me.

'I just did,' I shrugged. 'I thought you knew. Why don't you just relax and enjoy it. You'll be feeling the effects in about half an hour.'

Sara stood in front of me with her fists clenched. I thought for a minute that she was going to hit me.

Mike broke the tension. 'Let's go to a bar and get a drink,' he said, standing up and putting the bag of Northern Lights into his pocket. I pocketed the rest of the Purple Haze.

We walked out onto the street and the cold, damp air cleared the smoke out of my nostrils. The lights glittered on the canal. I felt dizzy and kept having to jump out of the way of cyclists, ring-a-linging their bells. A few times I was dazzled by the lights of an oncoming tram and jumped off the track just before it could plough over me. We walked through the red light district in a stoned haze. I saw a woman with large, cellulite-covered thighs, wearing black lace underwear, sitting on a fluffy pink stool in a shop window. She waved at a group of drunk and bewildered-looking Englishmen. She blew a kiss at Mike, who sauntered along, cool and aloof, not taking any notice.

'I'm just gonna take a walk by myself,' he mumbled to the group. 'I've got to clear my head a little. Mike disappeared into the crowd. My head was spinning and I held on to Lindi for balance. Gabriela clung to Lindi's other arm. Mimi linked her arm in mine as well and all four of us strolled contentedly along the canal. Natalie and Sara were giggling and pirouetting ahead of us.

'These space cakes are amaaaazing!' Natalie sang. 'I feel like I'm flying!' She spun around in circles with outstretched arms, lost her balance and fell into the railing at the side of the canal. Sara laughed hysterically while skipping along joyfully. She decided that it would be a laugh to lay down on the tracks in the path of an oncoming tram to see if it would stop. As the tram approached the driver frantically rang the bell, but it didn't look like it was slowing down.

'Get up, what the hell are you doing?' Gabriela shrieked. Lindi finally grabbed Sara's arm and dragged her out of harm's way.

'That was so much fun!' Sara laughed.

We went into a bar with steamed-up windows and loud music. There were some Dutch guys dancing on a table. 'Hey you girlsh, wan to parteee?' one of them said, grabbing Sara by the hand. Both Sara and Natalie joined the Dutch men in their table dance.

I was conscious that I had a lot of weed to get through in one weekend, so I went to the toilet to roll up a joint. Afterwards, I asked Mimi if she wanted to join me outside for a smoke. We stood outside furtively puffing, as although it was perfectly legal to smoke joints in the coffeehouses, it was still illegal to do so in public. A guy came up to me and asked me for a light. In return he gave me a cigarette, which I thought was a bit odd, but I didn't think too much about it and slipped it into my pocket for later.

Mimi and I walked along a little looking at the houseboats bobbing on the canal. I admired Mimi; she was beautiful and laid-back and adventurous and had a great sense of style. I desperately wanted to be her friend. I gazed at her beautiful face, and without even thinking, I grabbed her hand and then let it go self-consciously.

We were both feeling pretty stoned and thirsty, so we headed back into the bar. We arrived back to total chaos. Sara was still on the table, but she was lying across it, ashen faced, her hair plastered to her face with vomit, and looking fairly incoherent. One of the Dutch guys had slid in the puddle of vomit and was lying on the floor clutching his head. Gabriela was trying to help Sara up and Lindi was comforting Natalie, who was crying, 'I feel sooo sick.'

'I think it's time to go,' Lindi said when she saw Mimi and I come in.

We all trekked back to Bob's Youth Hostel together, Lindi and Gabriela supporting Sara on either side, coaxing her to walk. We had to stop a few times, so that she could lean over a rail and be sick into a canal. 'Is she gonna be alright?' Natalie sobbed.

'She'll be fine,' Lindi said, 'But we just need to get her back and into bed.'

'I need a cigarette,' Natalie slurred. 'I know you smoke, gimme a cigarette,' she said to me accusingly.

I was annoyed by her little miss prim sorority girl putting on the bad girl act. I remembered the cigarette the Dutch guy in the bar gave me and fished it out of the pocket of my leather jacket. She aggressively grabbed it out of my hand. 'Got a light?' she said. I held the lighter to the tip of the cigarette and BANG! The cigarette exploded.

Natalie screeched before she burst out in tears again.

'That was really mean,' Gabriela said, looking at me disapprovingly.

I stopped laughing. 'Honestly, I didn't know that was going to happen,' I tried to defend myself. 'A Dutch guy outside the bar asked me for a light and gave me that cigarette in return. It must have been a trick cigarette, or loaded with a bit of gunpowder or something.'

Secretly, though, I was thanking the Dutchman for finally getting Natalie to shut up.

We climbed the concrete steps up to our dorm. When we flicked on the lights we were surprised to see that there were about six more mattresses strewn across the floor, all occupied by prone bodies, partially covered by threadbare blankets.

'Now I know why this place was so cheap,' I said trying not to step on anyone on the way to my bunk.

Lindi and Gabriela helped Sara to the communal bathroom, so that she could continue being sick into the long metal trough sinks. Natalie was now also vomiting into the trough and they were retching and gurgling in stereo.

I asked Mimi if she felt like having a little puff on a joint before going to sleep. We slipped out the door and stood in the lamp-lit alleyway, savoring the joint in silence. We both felt sleepy and ready to turn in. We noticed some shadows moving in the darkness down at the end of the alley and heard some low whispers. 'We better get back in,' I shivered, when slowly out of the shadows a figure emerged.

The light glinted off wire-rimmed glasses, and a Birkenstocked foot came into view. 'You guys alright?' Mike said in his confident, laid-back New England drawl.

'Oh it's only you, Mike,' Mimi laughed, 'What have you been up to. You missed all the drama.'

'What have you been doing?' I asked him.

'Oh just doing a bit of exploring and thinking,' he said mysteriously.

We went back up to the dorm, stepped over a few bodies on our way to our beds and drifted into blissfully stoned sleep and dreams of canals and space cakes.

***

Next morning, I was surprised to wake up and find no one else around. Even the bodies and mattresses were gone. There was a note stuck to my bunk. 'Wake up sleeping beauty, we've gone to get breakfast. Don't miss the tour. Love, Lindi.'

The bus tour was taking us on a trip to see some windmills, a cheese factory and the tulip fields. I looked at my watch. I had overslept and was going to be late for breakfast.

As I ran out of the dorm, I bumped into the French guys from our bus and their Japanese friend, smoking a joint in the stairwell. They asked me if I wanted to join them. I thought I would just have a couple of quick puffs. It might give me a good appetite for breakfast.

After just one puff on the pungent, musky joint my head was spinning. The Frenchies must have bought some really strong skunk. I excused myself and set off to find the others. Breakfast was served in the main hostel building, which was around the corner from our dorm. I thought it would have been easy to find, but as soon as I stepped out onto the street I lost all my bearings. The brick canal houses all looked the same and loomed over me, and the whole world seemed like it was hidden behind a fuzzy gauze. I walked a bit, looking for the main hostel building or some kind of landmark that I might recognize. But my mind wasn't registering any of it.

A sudden panic gripped me and a nervous sickness welled up in my gut. I felt like I couldn't breathe. I was alone and lost. Where was I? Nothing looked familiar. My heart beat against my breastbone. 'Shit, shit, shit,' I said aloud. The world rocked and careened before my eyes. I was about to give up and sit down on the street to cry, when I saw the yellow Big Bob's sign, right there in front of my eyes all along.

I went in, relieved, and saw that everyone was finishing their breakfast. The table was strewn with empty plates and cups. 'You better get up to the buffet quick, sleeping beauty,' Lindi said when she saw me creep in, 'There's not much food left.'

I filled a cup with some black coffee, hoping it would sober me up. All that was left of the food was a bit of cold scrambled eggs, a dried up sausage and a bit of stale bread. I scooped the chilly dregs out of the metal vats onto my plate. I was so hungry I would have eaten cold maggots at that point.

'Where were you?' Lindi asked.

'I got lost,' I said, ravenously digging into the cold scrambled eggs.

'It's only around the corner,' Gabriela said, 'How on earth could you get lost?'

Natalie, who looked surprisingly spritely, eyed me suspiciously. 'Are you stoned already, at this hour of the morning?' she said in her condescending tone.

How dare she, after the performance that she and Sara put on last night!

'Did you guys manage to get all that puke out of your hair?' I asked. Touché!

Natalie crinkled her pert little nose. 'Why do you have to ask such a gross question?'

'Come on everyone!' Lindi said brightly. 'The bus tour leaves in five minutes.'

She shepherded the group out the door and toward the bus waiting outside the hostel. The other passengers were already on the bus. I noticed the French guys giggling at the back. The tour guide looked annoyed and pointed at her watch as we boarded the bus and took our seats. '*Eh, les filles,*' the French guys shouted from the back, waving at us. I waved back.

I chose a seat next to Lindi and sleepily gazed out the window. As we left the brick canal houses and bridges behind, the land stretched out low and flat, interspersed with water channels. I tried to sleep, but the crimson red of the tulip fields grabbed my eyes and forced them open. Green and red and the sun sparkling off the water—the land was so open, so laid bare. I thought momentarily about the dark wooded depths of Connecticut where I grew up, oppressive and humid and teeming with summer secrets. I wasn't sure if it was the weed or the sight of this flat open land that made my mind feel like it was expanding.

I had read in my *Let's Go Europe* guidebook that in the early days the Protestants had imposed a law of no secrets among the Dutch citizens. Citizens were to remove their shutters and leave their curtains open so that anyone could look in to see what they were doing. The truth was to be out in the open in order to eradicate fear and suspicion. It all made perfect sense, and was perhaps what led to Amsterdam's modern-day tolerance of drugs and prostitution, as long as it is out in the open and controlled. The Dutch don't hide things like sex and drugs; they don't hide the problems, they look at them and deal with them.

I could see the windmill looming. It was a large, wooden cone-like structure with four latticed blades. My fellow passengers got off the bus to take pictures, but I hung back. The bag of weed was weighing heavily in my bag. I needed to get through it before we went back to France and I didn't want to waste any time. Mimi agreed to help me try to finish it off. We found a secluded spot behind the bus and got stoned before going to check out the windmill. It was on the edge of a tiny hamlet, with little cottages and white picket fences surrounding gardens of green grass. There were tourists swarming about everywhere. The cumulative effects of the weekend's pot smoking were starting to take their toll. I was so dizzy that I could barely place one foot in front of the other. Mimi giggled uncontrollably as I stumbled and fell into some shrubs.

The path we were walking on bordered the back of a cottage garden. When I stood up and tried to regain my composure, I saw an old man with a white bushy beard come out the back door of the cottage carrying a bucket. He walked to the middle of the quaint grassy garden and oblivious to the camera-snapping tourists he dropped his pants, squatted and relieved himself into the bucket. I looked around at the other people milling about. Nobody seemed to be paying any attention to the spectacle. The man pulled his trousers back up and hobbled back into the cottage shutting the door behind him, leaving no evidence of the surreal scene I had just witnessed. 'Mimi, did you just see that?' I asked, tugging at her arm.

'See what?' she asked.

'That old guy just take crap in the middle of that garden.'

'No, are you sure that's what he was doing?'

Apparently I was the only one who had witnessed it. I began to doubt myself. Maybe I'd better lay off the weed for a bit. No. We paid for it; there was no way I was going to waste any.

Our next destination was the Gouda factory. It was in a low, dark building with wooden beams and floors imbued with centuries of deep, cheesy aroma. Huge wheels of cheese were stacked up everywhere. I was feeling the hunger creep back in. Luckily, there were plenty of free samples. I savored a triangle of mellow, nutty cheese, enjoying the al dente lusciousness.

A tour guide took us through the factory explaining the process of making Gouda cheese. Then, of course, we ended up in the gift shop stocked full of cheese and wine sets, Gouda wheels of all sizes, and all the accessories a cheese connoisseur would need. I breathed in the nutty, sharp, woody smells, which lingered in my nostrils throughout the bus trip back to Amsterdam.

I loved this country—I loved Europe in general. They made proper cheese here, not like those plasticky, square slices of dyed-orange 'American cheese', or 'Cheez Whizz' aerosol spray. Europeans ate proper food. They were tolerant and open-minded and creative and fashionable. You didn't need to show ID to enter a bar, and you could buy good quality weed from cafés.

Americans—Philistines, I thought, that's what they are—fearful of intellect and culture, ready to just sit impassively in a traffic jam in their huge SUVs, polluting the air, or in front of the television, eating takeout pizza. Rather than being born the wrong sex, I was born the wrong nationality—a transnational. I never felt like I fitted in, in the USA—the ideal for females being the cheerleader type: bubbly, blond, athletic, with big teeth and jaws, and little pert noses. I was an outcast: small, pale and skinny, with crimped dark hair and a penchant for wearing black—into weird music, and art and books. Whereas one of my big-boobed, blond classmates might invoke a cheer of 'God bless America!' when she walked into a room, I would be greeted with odd stares and annoying questions like, 'Do you worship the devil?'

They knew nothing about food, nothing about fashion, nothing about any other countries. When I told my family I was going to study in France for a year, my uncle was stunned. 'They don't speak English over there. They eat snails and horses. They only just started using electricity.'

My mother said to make sure that I packed enough deodorant and toothpaste as I might have trouble finding it in France. I was shocked by the ignorance. They actually believed that people were still going around with a horse and cart!

When the bus got back to Amsterdam we had some free time. Lindi wanted to go to the Rijksmuseum and Gabby wanted to go to the Anne Frank house. My mind was numb and I just wanted to sit on the canal boat tour and float around for a bit.

We had to catch the bus back to Paris that evening on an overnight journey. Everyone wanted to fit in as much sightseeing as possible. I was aware that Mimi and I still had quite a bit of weed to smoke. It would be such a shame to waste it.

I rolled another joint and smoked it with Mimi and Mike. We took a stroll through the Vondelpark over to the museum where we wandered around, being sucked into the shadowy somberness of the paintings, dreaming about the scenes we were witnessing:

rosy-cheeked milk maids bashfully looking out from the claire-obscure; regal, mustachioed men, flashing the whites of their eyes, which followed you wherever you went.

Having been there, done that, we thought we couldn't leave Amsterdam without seeing the Anne Frank house. It was a narrow little canal house, with a steep wooden stairway hidden behind a false bookcase. To think that two families shared that claustrophobic space for the time they did, living in fear, speaking in whispers and not daring to move for fear of being found, made my heart knot up. I didn't want to appear stoned and emotional, so I held back the tears that welled up in my eyes. I rummaged around in my bag for a tissue and pulled out what I thought felt like a plastic Kleenex packet.

Mimi looked at me wide eyed. 'Why are you waving the bag of weed around?' she whispered in my ear. My stoned reaction was a bit slow and it took a minute to register what I was actually holding in my hand. Mimi started to giggle. It was contagious and I started to giggle too. Neither of us could stop and it turned into full-blown laughter, while stunned, frowning tourists looked at us disapprovingly. We quickly made our way out into the sunlight, blinking back tears of laughter and holding on to each other for support.

We had to go meet the others in McDonald's later before getting the bus back to Paris. I didn't know why they had to choose McDonald's. I guess it was like a security blanket for them, something to remind them of home. Nevertheless, we needed to eat before going, so our last parting view of Amsterdam was inside a McDonald's. We were all sitting around a table sipping milkshakes when Natalie jumped up and let out a shriek. 'Someone just grabbed my backpack off the floor and ran away with it!' It must have happened very quickly as no one else had seen it happen. Natalie was in floods of tears and Lindi tried to comfort her. 'We have to report it to the police.'

'But the bus is leaving for Paris in half an hour.' Sara said. 'Let's all go together. The bus won't leave without all of us.'

It was decided that we would all go to the police station. I was hoping to finish up the last of the grass, but now there wouldn't be enough time for that. I felt very uncomfortable about bringing it into the police station and I remembered what our tour guide had said about taking any back into France, and the sniffer dogs that would get on the bus at the border. I reluctantly took the bag out of my pocket and with a heavy heart threw it in the garbage. The bus ride back to Paris was long and tedious and we slept most of the way. I have no recollection at all of any sniffer dogs getting on to the bus at the border. I thought regretfully about the grass that I had thrown away. We arrived back in Paris bleary eyed and disoriented in the early morning sunlight. I got back to the MIJE in a fuzzy blur, only to discover that I had left my handbag on the bus, with my *carte orange* metro travel card and 150 francs. Lindi phoned up the travel company for me, but the bag and its contents were never to be seen again, probably on their way back to Amsterdam to search for their friend, the bag of weed.

La Loco and beyond

Hemingway called Paris a moveable feast, a city with a foretaste so irresistible that once you swallow, you will carry memories of the experience around with you forever after. And this I can vouch for, having gorged myself on its sumptuous and sometimes bizarre offerings. Sure, there were the obvious attractions which left a distinct flavor of France—the Eiffel tower, the immense and impressive Louvre, the winding path and steps of Montmartre and the Sacré-Coeur, the skull-lined subterranean tunnels of the catacombs—but it was the seedy, smelly, Marché aux Puces, the drug addict-infested Père Lachaise cemetery and the rowdy, deafening nightclubs of Pigalle that fed my hunger for excitement.

One day, while Lindi and I were shopping in the marché aux puces, clinging onto each other while the Algerian hawkers tugged at our elbows and tried to yank us into their market stalls, Lindi saw a poster advertising La Locomotive. 'La Loco' was to become our second home in Paris. It was a huge nightclub next door to the Moulin Rouge, full of young Parisians, foreigners, drug dealers, predators and weirdos. It was a throbbing, pulsing living entity that filled the eyes with flashing neon, the ears with an array of deafening euro-pop and the stomach with a cocktail of cheap booze and pills.

For our first visit there we got all dressed up; me in my leather skirt and black fishnets and Lindi with her red hair spiked up. Of course Gabriela wasn't that into the idea, preferring to pine over the absent Jamie.

I went crazy in that place, dancing like a madwoman to the Happy Mondays, the Charlatans, the Stone Roses and euro-pop hits like Gainsbourg's 'Je T'aime'. The metro closed down well before we finished our dancing, so we stayed until it closed at 6 am, often sleeping through the deafening din, hearing prog rock in our fitful, drunken dreams and staggering through the thin dawn light to catch the metro back to Saint-Paul metro station in Le Marais.

Each time I went to La Loco I noticed a maudlin-looking Frenchman wearing a teddy boy suit, with huge rings on every finger and a giant quiff. I couldn't keep my eyes off him and eventually got up the courage to go and talk to him. His name was Frédéric—Fredo for short—that's about all I could get out of him. He shrugged a lot and grunted in answer to my questions. The music was so deafening that he probably just couldn't hear me, or understand my accent. But I didn't care; he was good to look at. We sat side by side on the steps leading to the upper level of the club, staring at the strobing lights, not speaking to each other, just smoking. Lindi sat behind us with her chin in her hands. Then Serge appeared. He was Fredo's friend and seemed to have a lot more charm. '*Bonjour Mesdames,*' he bowed theatrically. 'Who are these lovely ladies?' he asked Fredo, who just shrugged. 'My friend is a man of few words, a deep thinker,' he said, patting Fredo on the shoulder. 'I am Serge and I would be delighted to buy you all a drink.' He gave Lindi a wink and I could see her eyes light up.

After Serge returned with the drinks, he sat next to Lindi on the step. While Fredo and I continued to stare into space, they immersed themselves in conversation.

Fredo really wasn't easy to read—as aloof as a cat and as intense as a lion. He seemed distant and mysterious and that was why I was drawn to him. I was convinced we were the same person. I was convinced that we were similar in almost every way and that we were meant to find each other and crack each other's code. I couldn't tell if he liked me or detested me, and usually I was very good at interpreting the signals.

Lindi and Serge's relationship blossomed. She had found her Frenchman. I was seeing less and less of my friend as she was being swept off her feet. So, I suggested we all go out together one night. I suggested a sort of double date and asked Lindi to ask Serge to invite Frédéric.

Lindi arranged the date with Serge—he thought Frédéric would quite willingly oblige. We were meeting the guys at the square above Les Halles. It was thronged with cool young Parisians, smoking, chatting, laughing and standing in their respective tribes—North Africans, middle-class French and working class French, as well as groups of foreign students and Eastern European immigrants. We saw Serge and Fredo sitting on the edge of a fountain, looking laid-back and cool. Serge got up

and first gave Lindi a kiss and then he gave me a kiss. Serge dug
into a plastic shopping bag and handed us each a beer. Fredo just
stood there scowling, smoking his cigarette, looking around the
square with narrowed eyes.

'*Bonsoir, Fredo,*' I said. He kissed me on both cheeks, European
style, and then went back to eyeing up the other groups in the
square. He mumbled something to Serge and we went off toward
the metro. I had to run after him to keep up with his stride.
Fredo's tall frame sloped alongside me, hands dug deep into his
pockets. He nodded my way nonchalantly. '*Les écrases-merdes sont
cool,*' he said, indicating my Doc Martens with his dark eyes.

Likewise, I complemented him on his 'shit-crushers' too. He
was wearing enormous, thick-soled boots that could have crushed
someone's head, never mind shit.

'*Merci,*' he said exhaling rings of smoke, looking at me from the
corner of his eye. Did I detect a smile from Monsieur Cool? Serge
and Lindi were walking ahead of us, draped all over each other.

I noticed that the train we got on was heading in the wrong
direction for La Loco. 'Aren't we going to La Loco tonight?' I asked,
confused. Fredo didn't say anything. He just threw his cigarette
on the ground and slowly and deliberately crushed it under his
enormous black sole.

'We have a great night planned for you ladies,' Serge said.
'First we go and see some music. Someone Fredo knows is in a
band playing tonight. Then we go for a party at Fredo's place. His
mother has gone away for the weekend. We take you on a tour
of the real Paris tonight.' Lindi stared into his eyes and hung on
every word, as if he was telling her the meaning of life. Fredo
stared out the window of the metro at the blackness speeding by
as we went deeper and deeper into the bowels of the city.

When we emerged from the metro, I didn't recognize where
we were. It was an area of Paris I had not been to before. Fredo
marched ahead, leading the way. There was a crowd of guys with
Mohawks and shaved heads hanging outside a derelict looking
building. Fredo shook the hand of one of them, who looked us up
and down. The gig was in the basement of a decrepit old building
and it smelled of cigarettes, mildew and piss. It was a tiny venue,
packed with punk kids pushing to the front of the stage in
anticipation of the band starting. I could feel Fredo's sturdy body
pressed against my back, he draped one arm over the front of my
shoulder while he held a cigarette with the other. Now maybe
we were getting somewhere. The music started with the beat of
drums and an explosion of guitars. The female singer leapt onto

the stage and started writhing and wailing. The crowd jumped and bobbed like one living, breathing being. Fredo went ballistic. I jumped out of the way to avoid being pummeled. He karate kicked the air with his huge boots and he punched the air with his fists, shouting along with the female vocalist, completely possessed by the throbbing noise. Lindi and Serge had disappeared to the back of the room, probably to paw each other in a dark corner.

After the first band finished playing, Fredo asked, 'Drink?' I nodded. He came back and wordlessly handed me a vodka and orange juice. I thought he looked great tonight. I gave him the eye and said thanks, squeezing close to him in the crowd.

I was surprised and excited to find out that the last band was an American band that I knew. They were a punk, thrash metal group called Prong, and they were one of Toby's favorites. He'd be so jealous, I thought.

After the gig we made our way to Fredo's place. He lived in Villejuif, a suburb about 7km out of Paris. The train ride seemed interminable. I asked about how we would get back to the MIJE. 'Tomorrow,' Serge said. 'Frédéric says we will stay at his apartment tonight. His mother is away.'

We got out at Louis Aragon station and made our way through the concrete jungle. The elegant Parisian Louis the XIV buildings had given way to huge, grey apartment blocks looming over large swathes of concrete. Everything looked dirty, worn out and dull. Suspicious looking characters appeared out of phone booths, and dark, North African faces dominated the grey shadows. A gang of teenagers were shouting and pushing each other. I felt uneasy, but tried to remain cool, making small talk in my stilted, naïve French. Fredo walked up to a traffic cone next to a hole on the sidewalk and sent it flying with a violent kick as he stormed on ahead. I could smell rubber burning somewhere.

We eventually arrived at Fredo's apartment building—one of the monolithic, grey blocks that marred the landscape. The elevator was broken so we stomped up 10 piss-smelling flights of steps to his apartment. When he opened the door we were met with the smell of stale cooking embedded in a cotton candy fluffy 1960s boudoir-style carpet. His mother obviously liked pink. The walls were covered in a 60s rose-hued floral wallpaper and the furniture was all mock renaissance and pink and gold flock. The shelves were adorned with little figurines of ballerinas and fluffy animals. Fredo opened the flowery curtains to reveal a view of Paris glistening in the distance. Then he proceeded to raid his mother's very well stocked bar cart, another relic from the 60s. He poured me a glass of Cointreau and himself a whiskey. Lindi and Serge both had wine.

The apartment was tiny and I could see only one bedroom. I wondered how there was room for both him and his mother in the small apartment, and more importantly, where we would all sleep that night. My question was answered when Fredo pulled out a double bed that looked to me like it was folded up into the pink-flocked wall. To my surprise it was immaculately made up with a shimmering quilted bedspread. It nearly filled the room and we all sat down on it.

Fredo disappeared into the kitchen. I followed him and stopped in my tracks when I saw him cooking up a liquid in a teaspoon and filling a syringe. He saw me watching. 'You want some?'

I shook my head. Even though I was quite experimental with drugs, I drew the line at heroin. I watched Fredo stick the needle in his arm and empty the contents of the syringe into his vein. He then walked past me into the lounge and turned the television on. He fiddled around a bit with the channels, and then put a video on. It was a French porn video. Fredo installed himself on the corner of the bed, right in front of the TV and lit a cigarette.

I hated porn. I thought it degraded and made objects of women; and those who said it was empowering were twisted profiteers or sad losers. This was just too weird. Lindi and Serge were pawing at each other and eventually got up and disappeared into the bedroom. Fredo didn't move. He seemed mesmerized by the moaning and writhing on the screen in front of him. He eventually got up and reclined on the bed next to me, our shit-kicker boots side by side. 'You like it?' he asked indicating the film with the smoking stub of his cigarette. I shrugged. I thought it was disgusting, but I didn't want to appear too 'coincée'.

'I prefer the real thing,' I said, thinking he might get the hint. He seemed not to hear, or maybe he was just too distracted by the multiple orgasms being emitted from the television. I crossed my arms, turned away and instead contemplated the Parisian vista from the window. A few moments later I noticed that the moans were punctuated by snores. Fredo had curled up on the bed, fully clothed, with even his massive boots still on. I tugged the pink duvet out from underneath him and covered him with it. He proceeded to roll over, taking most of the duvet with him. I lay down on the bed next to the frilly pink cocoon, staring up at the ceiling. I remained like this for hours, watching the ceiling become illuminated by the rising sun. I must have fallen asleep eventually and managed to steal a small corner of the duvet from the slumbering Fredo, because Lindi and Serge woke me up. They were looking rosy-cheeked and fulfilled in every way.

'Wake up sleepyheads. Coffee's ready!' Lindi sang cheerfully.

The smell of coffee filled my nostrils. My head was banging from a combination of hangover and sleep deprivation. Fredo rose like a corpse waking from the dead, and still shrouded in the pink duvet, he made his way to the bathroom.

Serge gave me a nudge. 'So did you have a good night?' he asked grinning.

'Not really,' I mumbled.

'What happened?' Lindi asked, looking concerned.

'Absolutely nothing—that's what the problem is,' I said, holding my head. I felt like crying and just really wanted to get back to the MIJE.

'She just doesn't want to tell us anything,' Serge said, laughing.

I don't think he could believe that nothing had happened between Fredo and I—so much for French lovers.

***

I had just spoken to Toby again on the phone. I told him about Prong and left out Fredo, because even though nothing had happened, I knew he would jump to conclusions. Toby was such a downer. He sounded incredibly depressed—because he didn't have class the next day, but had no one to party with, and they had his hash, and he hated his university, it was too boring; because he never did anything fun; it was always the same. What a complainer. He said that I seemed different and that I had changed already—which I supposed was quite possible in the time I had been in Europe. I suddenly thought about what would happen on my return. Would I still be friends with the same people? Would I be able to relate to them, seeing as I would have experienced more and become more versed in the ways of the world? Would the old crowd think I was stuck up, with my newfound European ways? I wondered if Toby and I would still be able to relate. If I had already changed in one month, how changed would I be after a year? I could already feel him slipping from my consciousness. He was no longer part of my reality. All the talk about our future, marriage and children seemed so remote and fading.

That night I wrote a long rant about him in my diary. I was fed up with his attitude and felt a lot better expressing my thoughts on paper—getting it off my chest rather than letting it fester inside.

Sometimes Toby is so shallow. He can never just satisfy himself with reading or thinking. He always has to party and get wasted. He's never happy. Perhaps I shouldn't be so harsh in my judgement. Perhaps his depression is due to me. Great thought. Sometimes I can be a really horrible, critical person, but I guess that's just human nature, because everyone becomes like that once in a while. There's been tension between us ever since I first told him I was going to France. I feel myself pulling away a bit—I don't even want to write it or think it. I try to deny it and wipe it from my mind totally as if the thought did not even exist. But I think it is true. Perhaps I know subconsciously that it won't work out, maybe I'm just unsure. Sometimes I think it doesn't matter and I won't feel upset, but because I do love him, I myself would be devastated by hurting him. What I think right now, though, is that only the future will tell, and I should just take things as they happen. Keep the future domestic plans, but don't remain committed in my mind if things happen to take a different turn.

Little did I know at the time that this passage would be the catalyst that would dictate that turn.

Bienvenue a Rouen

Joan of Arc burned here and Madame Bovary was bored here, and this was the place that was to be my home for the rest of the year. I hoped I would be neither burned nor bored. I said my fond goodbyes to the great city of Paris, and prepared myself for another fresh experience.

I stood outside the grey, 1960s Faculté des Lettres at the University of Rouen waiting for our French host families to pick us up and take us to our respective lodgings. Where was the medieval architecture that I had heard Rouen was famed for? Where was Monet's cathedral, and the half-timbered houses on narrow, cobbled streets? The university campus was in a bland, grey suburb on a hill on the outskirts of the city. Most of the students would be with families who lived in the city center. My heart sank when I realized that I was one of the only students who would be lodging with a family near the university, away from my friends and all the action. I could have just stayed in Connecticut if I wanted to continue the suburban experience. Well, at least I didn't have far to go to get to class in the morning.

Everyone else had been picked up by middle-aged couples in luxury cars and driven down to the historic center of Rouen; I was left nervously waiting on my own with Richard. He looked at his watch. 'The French are not known for their punctuality,' he said sympathetically, noticing my unease. Then, from over the crest of a hill, I spotted a clapped-out 2CV, spewing exhaust fumes, heading toward us. I had never seen a car like it in my life. It resembled a tin can on wheels. The car squeaked to a halt in front of us and a tall man in his early 30s unfolded himself out of the driver's seat. He was wearing a flat cap, a tweed jacket and green corduroys. A young, petite, blond woman with a neat pixie haircut also got out. She was dressed in a twinset with a silk scarf tied round her neck. A newborn baby gurgled in her arms and a girl of about 13 and a boy of about five peered curiously from the rear window, not daring to get out of the car.

'You must be Monsieur DeClermont,' Richard said, shaking the man's hand. 'I am Professor Richard Céleste and this is Siobhan Schreiber, the student who will be lodging with you this year.'

'Ah yes, of course. I am Thierry DeClermont and this is my wife, Sophie, and our three children, Dominique, Antoine and Hélène. I am very sorry if we kept you waiting, we were delayed by some very important church business.'

Thierry precariously strapped my luggage to the top of the 2CV. They let me sit in the front seat and Sophie sat in the back with the three children, who were all chattering, squabbling and crying.

Luckily, we didn't have too far to go. Thierry pulled into the driveway of a fairly new, mock French farm cottage, set in a development of similar buildings on a network of winding tarmac roads and cul-de-sacs, which backed onto a shopping center with a Continent hypermarket and do-it-all store. There was a kennel at the top of the driveway, where a curly-haired dog was jumping about madly and barking.

'That's our dog Laska,' Sophie explained over the din. I thought about my dog, Scooby, at home. He was allowed to run free in the yard and lived inside the house. I always felt sorry for dogs that were left tied up or locked in cages.

The 2CV pulled into the garage under the house. There was a cage full of adorable but strange looking chicks. I loved animals and had had lots of strange pets throughout my childhood. I was immediately drawn to the cage of cheeping, little grey birds and asked what they were. *'Les cailles,'* Sophie said. I didn't know what that word meant, so I looked it up in my pocket dictionary. Quails.

'Oh, they're so cute!' I exclaimed and then I asked, 'What are their names?'

Sophie and Thierry exchanged glances. Then Dominique piped up, 'We aren't allowed to give them names. Papa takes them out to the woods and sets them free to train Laska how to hunt them, so he can shoot them.'

'Poor quails!' I said, not able to contain myself. I hated hunting. I always thought it was a barbaric pastime. But I kept my thoughts on the subject to myself. I didn't want to compromise the relationship with my hosts so early on.

'Don't get too attached to them. They will be on the dinner table soon,' Sophie said, gathering her noisy brood out of the car. My heart sunk even further than it had when I found out I would be living in the ass end of France. I guessed the university hadn't informed the DeClermonts that I was a vegetarian.

Thierry carried my luggage in and deposited it in a room on the ground floor. It had a large double bed, a desk, a huge antique armoire and, curiously, a piano. There was an en suite bathroom, with a separate toilet off the foyer. Thierry shut the door behind him and left me alone to settle in and unpack. I sat down on the bed and my butt was jolted by the impact. The mattress was made of thin foam rubber and the frame was a solid wooden platform. I sat on the edge of the bed with my head in my hands, feeling depression wash over me.

My stomach was rumbling; I hadn't eaten since noon and it was now 8pm. There wasn't any sign of dinner. Two hours later, as I lay feeling faint on my hard bed, there was finally a knock at the door.

'À table,' Sophie sang cheerfully.

I opened my bedroom door and my nostrils were immediately assaulted by the nauseating smell of salty, fatty, gravy laden meat. I made my way to the small kitchen where the family were assembled on benches on either side of a long table covered in a vinyl tablecloth. The children were squabbling and Thierry and Sophie were having a rapid-fire conversation in French. Everyone was speaking far too fast for me to understand anything. My head was spinning with a combination of hunger, bewilderment and sickening smells.

Thierry noticed me standing in the middle of the kitchen and pointed out a place for me on the bench next to Dominique, who flashed her brace-filled grin at me. 'Maman has prepared a special meal tonight for your arrival. We hope you like beef bourguignon.'

I thought there was no better time than the present to explain that I didn't eat meat. I could see a flicker of annoyance on Sophie's face. She smiled a tight thin-lipped smile. 'The university didn't tell us that. We have some salad that you can have and I can put a frozen pizza in the oven for you. It's a vegetarian pizza.' She got up and pulled a pizza out of the freezer. I could see that it was a vegetable and ham pizza.

We started off with noodle soup. I concentrated on avoiding the bits of meat that were floating around in it. This was difficult, however, as the family started firing questions at me. 'What religion are you?' Sophie asked.

I replied that I was raised a Catholic. Sophie nodded her approval. 'Very good, we are Catholic as well. I was hoping they wouldn't send us a Muslim. Not that you look at all like a Muslim. Will you be coming with us to church in the morning, then?'

The truth was that I had renounced religion ever since I was 14 when my father dragged me to confession against my will. When the priest asked me to confess my sins I told him that I hadn't done anything wrong.

This had roused his ire. 'We are all sinners!' he shouted at me.

I decided to make something up and told him that, actually, I had stolen something. He asked me if it was bigger than a breadbox and I told him it was a pair of earrings. He seemed satisfied with this lie and told me to say 10 'Hail Marys' and five 'Our Fathers', and I would be absolved of my sin.

While away from my parents I had absolutely no intention of going to church. 'No,' I said, 'I don't really go to church.'

Sophie's approving smile drooped. 'That's a shame,' she said. Then she brightened again, as she produced a small bottle with a dropper. She put a few drops of a mystery liquid into the food of each family member. 'Would you like some placenta?' she asked me.

My French was a still not up to scratch and at first I thought I had misheard. Sophie went on to explain. 'When I gave birth to Hélène six weeks ago, my homeopath made me a serum out of the placenta. It has incredible health benefits for the whole family.'

My stomach, which was still aching with hunger, did a little flip-flop. I sincerely hoped she hadn't already added this ingredient to the cooking. I pushed my bowl of half-eaten soup away and announced, '*Je suis finis*.' Everyone around the table looked at me and burst into laughter, while I looked from face to grinning face, confused.

Laughing, Sophie explained, 'You must mean to say, *j'ai terminé*, otherwise you are saying that you are dead.'

Dominique suppressed a giggle. Thierry must have seen my discomfort. 'Enough now, Dominique. Siobhan is here as our guest to learn French language and culture and we must help her and not make fun.'

I felt like an idiot.

Sophie suddenly barked like an army sergeant at four-year-old Antoine, who was whimpering and squirming. 'Hands on the table at all times!'

My own hands were in my lap and I, too, quickly put them on the table. I made a mental note to unlearn years of American table manners where having elbows on the table was taboo and it was polite to leave the hands resting in the lap while at the dinner table. I remembered Richard telling our group the history behind the French custom of keeping the hands on the table. There was a French king who was paranoid about being assassinated so at dinner parties, in order to ensure no one could conceal a weapon, he required his guests to keep their hands on the table at all times.

'But Maman, I don't feel well,' Antoine whined. He clasped his stomach and his skin had a waxy pallor.

'No excuses! You will finish what is on your plate!' Sophie commanded.

Antoine started to cry. 'It's not an excuse. I feel sick.'

'Don't be such a cry baby, Antoine. Do as Maman says.' Dominique ordered him.

Suddenly, Antoine projectile vomited. Regurgitated soup and noodles covered the table. Some had even splashed Dominique and I could see brown droplets clinging to strands of her blond hair.

Sophie flew to the sink, grabbed a dishrag and began mopping up the slurry. 'Now look what you have done. Go to your room immediately!' she commanded. The little boy sloped off, eyes on the floor, head hanging, wiping away his tears, but I thought I could sense an air of triumphant relief. I felt a pang of envy—I wished I could do the same to avoid having to face the 'vegetarian' ham pizza. The rest of the family remained at the table as if nothing had happened. I tried not to breathe in the smell of vomit, or look at the little brown rivers that were escaping Sophie's rag and gathering in the creases of the vinyl tablecloth, moving sluggishly toward my hands, which were still placed self-consciously on the table. Dominique and Thierry silently waited for Sophie to finish mopping up so she could serve the next course.

'Here is your vegetarian pizza,' Sophie announced brightly, placing the pizza in front of me. The smell of burnt pizza crust and vomit mingled in my nostrils. Even though I had felt so hungry before, my stomach stubbornly refused to accept what was placed in front of me. I could clearly see the chunks of ham on the pizza. I started to slowly and surreptitiously pick each morsel off and place it on the edge of my plate, biding my time and but not wanting to offend my hosts. Why the French considered ham to be a vegetarian food was beyond me.

Once the beef bourguignon was served up and Sophie was seated, she started to grill me. What did my parents do for a living? How long had I been studying French? Did I have a boyfriend? How long had we been going together? Did we have any plans for marriage? What was he studying? I gave her the lowdown on my parents and sister and Toby, and explained that Toby would be coming over to visit me just after the holidays, so she would have an opportunity to meet him in person.

The conversation was difficult and halting as Sophie corrected my grammar and vocabulary every step of the way. 'I spik leetle Eenglish,' she said in English—in a terrible accent—before turning back to French. 'And I would also like the children to learn English. I would prefer it if you spoke English to them. I don't want them to pick up any of your bad French grammar. I want my children to speak proper French,' she declared in a matter of fact way as she got up to clear away the dinner plates.

I stared mutely, stunned. I didn't really know how to reply to such a rude comment. I wanted to tell her that I wasn't there to be a nanny—my parents were paying *her* for my food and lodging. '*J'ai terminé*,' I said forcing a smile, pushing away the half-eaten pizza, which I had attempted to nibble at.

I sloped off to my room and sat down at the rickety desk to write in my diary about my first day with my host family. Instead, I just laid my head on the desk. The tears came with such a desperate and surprising force that there was no use in fighting them back. I had a terrible sick feeling gnawing away in my gut like writhing termites. How was I going to last a whole year living with these hunting, flesh-eating, placenta-eating, vomit-inducing, religious xenophobes? I was beginning to doubt my decision to come to France but I couldn't face going back a failure—a dropout. Maybe Toby was right. Maybe I should never have left New England.

Just then there was a timid knock on the door. It was Dominique. She said that she needed to do her piano practice. I had forgotten about the piano in my room and was using it as a clothes rack. I realized that I couldn't really say no. I sat at my desk, writing in my journal and listening to Dominique's halting rendition of Beethoven's Fifth.

As the cheerful ditty played in my head, a small encouraging voice rose from the inner depths of my mind. 'Don't give up yet. Tomorrow is the first day at the Fac … and who knows what will be in store—new friends, new professors, new knowledge.'

***

I opened the door to the Fac and was met by a solid wall of cigarette smoke that made me cough instantly. The corridor was thronged with beautiful, fashionable young French people. The girls all seemed to resemble Brigitte Bardot with their sultry eyes and lips and piled-up hairstyles. The guys all looked super cool, leaning against the brick walls smoking their roll-up cigarettes.

I could feel their eyes on me as I waded through the thick, grey atmosphere. I was sure I heard mutterings—'Oh she must be one of the Americans—or is she German? Look what she's wearing.' I met their eyes and smiled—they nonchalantly looked away, disinterested, continuing their conversations.

I was relieved when I saw some familiar faces gathered in a doorway at the end of the corridor. Lindi, Gabriela and Mike were slouched in a doorway, all wearing name tags. Gabriela waved. 'We were wondering when you were going to turn up. You have to go into the overseas students' office and pick up a nametag. We're going to be paired up with our French mentors.'

'What's a French mentor?' I asked.

Lindi explained. 'We're each going to be matched up with another French student who is a member of the English club. The idea is that we help each other with our language skills.'

I went into the office and picked up my nametag. There were a few French students milling about chatting. An excitable girl, clutching a clipboard, came running up to me and held out her hand. 'I am Céline. I am the overseas student social coordinator.' She looked me up and down and declared that she had the perfect match for me. Smiling she led me over to a group of French students and introduced me to a tall guy with spiky red hair, wearing sunglasses, a leather jacket, fluorescent sneakers and a name tag which read, 'Gekko'. 'May I introduce Siobhan. She is going to be your *'filleule'*. I thought you two would be just perfect for each other,' Celine said as she moved on to the next unsuspecting American student to walk in through the door.

I smiled at the man who was to be my 'godfather'. Gekko held out his hand and in perfect English said, 'I'm Gekko—the hottest DJ this side of the English Channel. Do you like to party? As he asked this question he raised his sunglasses and gave me a wink. 'I'm also as gay as they come, so you don't have to worry about me sleazing on you.'

I noticed that Gabriela, Lindi and Mike had come into the office and were talking to their French partners. My eyes were drawn, however, to Mimi's partner, Patrice. He was a real pretty boy with long blond hair that fell over his clear blue eyes. He wore a Stone Roses t-shirt under a fitted leather jacket. Gekko waved at Patrice and suggested we go over so that he could introduce me. As we approached, he patted Patrice on the back. 'Too bad this one isn't gay. He likes the girls too much.'

Patrice laughed and tossed his mane of blond hair. 'Do you girls want to come to a rave on Saturday? Our very own Gekko will be DJing,' Patrice said, indicating Gekko, who bowed deeply.

'Sounds great,' Mimi said.

'Count me in,' I said as well. I didn't have anything else to do but sit around in my room at the DeClermonts'.

We did the rounds, introducing each other to our respective classmates. Céline paired herself with Mike and was babbling animatedly at him in her overly formal English. I could see Mike losing interest as his eyes scanned over the group. Lindi had been paired with a cute guy called *'Gribouille'* or 'Scribbler', because he was good at drawing, and Gabriela was paired with his girlfriend Amélie. I could see Anne looking pleased with herself as she introduced her partner Tony, an athletically built, tall, dark-haired guy. The rave seemed to be the main topic of conversation and by the end everyone was on board, even Gabriela, who looked uncertain when told the party was being held in an abandoned warehouse on a wasteland down by the river.

Gekko made a valiant effort to show me all around the campus, and to introduce me to his friends. He told me that although he was studying English, his passion was music. He was a DJ for a local underground radio station and he played a lot of hip-hop, rap and house; he hoped some day to make it to the big time—DJing at all the big clubs in Europe. He made me promise that I would listen to his program that night and he would send a shout out to his 'little sister'.

In the afternoon I was required to rejoin the group of Americans so that we could attend the afternoon classes and meet our professors. Gekko kissed me on both cheeks. *'À bientôt ma chérie,'* he said cheerily flicking a peace sign. I watched as the ginger head of my very own fairy godfather bobbed away, disappearing into the smoky atmosphere of the corridor.

I went through the afternoon in a cloudy haze, trying to take in all the new information and all the new names and faces but I couldn't stop thinking about the weekend ahead.

Le week-end

Mimi pressed the little white pill into my hand. 'Patrice gave them to me. He said they're *colombes*,' she said smiling sweetly, her beautiful face framed by her curly black hair.

'Doves,' I said, noticing the little indent of a bird on the pill's surface, like on the Dove soap. I knocked it back with a swig from a bottle of cheap Calvados and waited for it to take effect. The joint that Mike shared with us before coming to the party had made me feel mellow and a bit lethargic. The colored lights and blaring beats were lulling me into a trance as I sat against the wall taking regular swigs from my bottle.

I watched the people doing dances that seemed almost tribal, some had their eyes shut, totally immersed in the KLF, 'What Time is Love?' Others waved glo-sticks and whooped and howled to the growing crescendo of beats. I smiled and laughed and felt a slow ebb of love start in my toes and slowly move up to my arms and then my face, making my mouth curve up into a smile. I didn't know all these people, but I loved them. I felt at one with them and the happiness was overwhelming. A hand touched mine. I looked up and it was Mimi. She pulled me up onto the dance floor. She moved like a cat, slinking and slithering to the rhythm. I couldn't take my eyes off her. I had never felt such love for a human being before—she was pure beauty. She reached out her arms and held me in an embrace. I felt her lips on mine and then her tongue flicked its way into my mouth. Enveloped in Mimi's jasmine scented curls I suddenly understood what it was about women that men liked so much: velvety skin, soft lips, warm body. It was a completely different experience to the scraping of stubble against your face in a desperate, crushing clash of lips often experienced when kissing a man.

The beats segued into a French rap tune and everything was lights and shadows and bodies pulsing. Everyone was dancing.

Mike was in a world of his own, standing on top of the speakers with his eyes closed moving like a robot. He hadn't seen us, but Gekko had and I was aware of him giving me the thumbs up from behind the decks.

Suddenly, a house mix of Serge Gainsbourg's 'Je T'aime' started playing. Mimi stared into my eyes and smiled. I could see her mouthing the words along with Jane Birkin's whispery vocals—'*Je t'aime.*' She was driving me crazy and I grabbed her hand and pulled her away into a dark corner behind some crates. I kissed her again, checking her reaction to make sure that I really hadn't just misread her seductiveness. Her eyes were closed and her lips parted invitingly. I tentatively slipped my hands under her t-shirt and into her bra. Her breasts were quite a bit larger than mine and I could feel her nipples as solid as bullets between my fingers. A tingle of excitement coursed through my spine and my hands suddenly felt a bit shaky. I could feel Mimi's hands slipping into my back pockets, squeezing.

Suddenly, a shadow appeared. 'Oh, sorry, I uh…' It was Mike and a French guy. 'I, uh… was just going to roll one up—but I didn't realize there was anyone back here.' Mimi and I looked at each other and giggled.

Patrice appeared as well. 'Ah, you are there. I have look for you,' Patrice said in his terrible English. He sat down on the floor next to Mimi. 'Are you enjoying the party?' He reverted back to French.

Mimi's French was no better than his English. 'Thank you, the doves,' she replied in broken French.

'Do you feel, how do you say, 'loved-up'?' Patrice asked, saying 'loved-up' in his French-accented English.

I wanted to tell him that I was feeling loved-up until he came along, but I decided to leave it. Mimi just smiled her sweet smile at him. They stared into each other's eyes and I suddenly felt like a third wheel. I moved over and sat next to Mike who was putting the finishing touches to his joint. He passed it to me and offered me a light. I eagerly placed it between my lips and inhaled. Through the veil of smoke, I could see Patrice leading Mimi away by the hand. I stared into space and felt the previous excitement of our encounter clunk into a heavy knot in my stomach. 'What just happened?' I asked myself over and over again.

I got up and headed to the dance floor, lost in my own world, dancing out my frustrations of the last few weeks. When I danced I forgot about the DeClermonts, forgot about Toby, forgot about the dreary existence that I was doomed to. The night vacillated between spells of intense dancing and 'chilling out', smoking joints with Mike.

Hours later, through half-lidded eyes, I could make out Gekko's Reebok classics with the iridescent laces sticking out from behind the DJ booth. Attached to them were Gekko's legs, horizontal on the floor. He had finally passed out behind the decks, and the warehouse had become silent. The sun started to peek over the horizon and the birds began their dawn chorus. We left Gekko there, sleeping like a baby.

We all walked home through the cobbled streets of Rouen— me, Mike, Lindi, Gabriela, and Mike's new French friend, Roland. But no one knew where Mimi had gone. She had disappeared hours ago, presumably with Patrice. Mike and Roland were nice enough to walk me to my house, as I lived further away from everyone else. As I approached the back door of the DeClermonts' house in the dim dawn light I fumbled for my keys, my head fuzzy and spinning. It was the kind of door that you had to lock behind you once you were in. I was trying to be as quiet as possible and didn't want to wake anyone, so I didn't turn on any lights in the foyer. In the darkness, I softly pushed the door to, turning the key in the lock. Then I went to my room and flopped down on the bed, with the lingering essence of jasmine scented hair still in my nostrils, and swiftly passed out into fitful, erratic dreams.

I was awoken abruptly by pounding on my bedroom door. I looked at my watch—it was 9am and I had only been asleep for three hours. The knocking became more frantic and then the door swung open. Sophie stood glaring at me, wearing her Sunday best. 'When I came down the stairs the front door was wide open. I thought an intruder had entered. Did you leave the door open?' she demanded, standing over me, while I lay wretched on the bed. She noticed my state and wrinkled her nose. Have you been drinking? It's like a tomb in here.' She began to open the windows so she could fling open the shutters. I squinted and shielded my eyes against the sun's onslaught. 'Did you leave the door wide open last night?' she demanded again.

I harked my mind back to a few hours ago when I came in. I clearly remembered inserting my key into the lock and turning it. However, it had been very dark inside the house. 'I, I, uh... I did lock the door. I remember you telling me to always lock the door behind me.'

'Well maybe you hadn't shut the door properly. It was wide open for any thief to come walking straight in here.'

'I'm sorry. It was very dark inside the house and I, I...' This, of course, was related in halting French.

Sophie interrupted me impatiently. 'Get on with it. I want to know why you left the door wide open, endangering my home and my family. There have been burglaries recently in this neighborhood and you just leave the door open for them to come right in.'

'It was very dark. I didn't want to wake you up by turning on the light.'

'I don't believe this. We're going to be late for church now. But we must talk about this later,' she said slamming my bedroom door behind her.

Well, I thought we *had* just talked about it. Do we have to talk about it more? I thought to myself. I put the pillow over my head and fell back into much-needed slumber.

After dinner that evening, Sophie was very serious. 'Can we have a talk in private, please, Siobhan?' She entered my room and shut the door behind her. She sat on the edge of my bed. Her eyes were suddenly drawn to a small black splodge on the bed cover. 'What is this?' she said rubbing at the mark with her finger.

'I'm sorry, I dripped a little bit of nail polish,' I said guiltily. I had hoped she would never notice it.

'Black nail polish?' she asked incredulously. 'Well this is just another thing. I wanted to talk with you to find out how you find it here?'

I looked at her uncomprehendingly. 'It's OK,' I lied.

'Well, Thierry and I are not so sure. We don't feel that this arrangement is working out for us. We would like to speak to your group leader, Monsieur Céleste.'

I suddenly perked up, thinking that if I could get moved into the university student housing, that would mean I would be a free woman—free from the restraints of the uptight DeClermont household. No more 'vegetarian' ham pizza, no more piano in my bedroom, no more having to sneak around.

***

The next day at the Fac, I entered the smoke-filled corridor and saw Gekko, who doffed his rapper's cap at me. 'It looked like you were having a good time on Saturday, *ma chérie*,' he said, winking, and offering me a cigarette. I lit it up and leaned back against the wall. 'Your secret is safe with me,' he said.

The memory of what happened the night of the rave between Mimi and I came flooding back. I nodded, feeling a bit uneasy, but trying not to let it show. I wanted to appear unfazed and I exhaled the smoke into the space between us, where it hung like a curtain disguising my awkwardness.

Then I saw Mimi come in; Patrice was with her. I was aware that they were talking and then Patrice gave her a kiss and his hand went down to her butt. She giggled. I turned away in disgust, pretending I didn't see them come in. For some bizarre reason I thought about Toby for the first time in weeks and I decided to call him when I got home.

I felt a hand on my shoulder and I turned around, knowing full well who it was. I acted surprised. 'Oh Mimi, I didn't see you come in.'

'Hey, Siobhan. Great party on Saturday,' Mimi purred.

'Yeah,' I said. 'Those "Es" were pretty good.' I looked her straight in the eye, searching for some recognition of what we had done that night.

'Patrice says he can get more any time.' She gave me that sweet smile. 'Do you feel like going out for a drink later?'

'Sure, I'm desperate to get away from my French family. Just tell me where and when.'

'Do you know Big Ben's? It's just next to the *Le Gros*.'

'*Le Gros*' or '*le Gros Horloge*', was a medieval clock built into a gothic archway above a narrow cobbled lane in the center of the old city. Big Ben's was an English-style pub, popular with Anglophones.

'How about eight o'clock?' she said. 'Have you got a spare cigarette?'

I handed her a cigarette, lit it, and watched as she blew sexy smoke rings.

There was no further mention of Saturday night.

***

It was 7.45 pm and there was no sign of any life in the DeClermont house, so I decided that it was a perfect opportunity to make a break for it and head to the pub to go meet Mimi. I quietly turned the key in the lock and opened the door. As I was slipping out, Sophie suddenly appeared, coming in with her bags of groceries, with Dominique trailing behind, also carrying bags.

'Are you going somewhere, Siobhan?' Sophie asked.

'I'm just going out to meet some friends,' I explained.

'But don't you remember, I asked if you could help Dominique with her English homework this evening?'

My heart sunk. I looked at my watch. I would never be able to get away in time. 'I forgot. Can we do it tomorrow? I'm meeting my friends in 15 minutes.'

'Dominique has to hand in her homework tomorrow, so I'm afraid it cannot wait.'

Feeling defeated, I re-entered the house. I helped Sophie and Dominique put the groceries away, trying to get everything over and done with as quickly as possible. I had my eye on the clock the whole time, acutely aware that I was going to be really late. Even after I'd finished helping Dominique, I would still have to wait for the bus to take me to the center of Rouen. I imagined Mimi sitting at the bar and becoming impatient waiting for me.

Finally, I sat down next to Dominique on the sofa in the lounge. Sophie was in the kitchen preparing the dinner, but the adjoining door was open and she was keeping an eye and an ear on what we were doing. There was no chance of me just giving her the answers and going. We plodded through the homework until Sophie announced that dinner was ready.

My stomach was in knots and I didn't feel like eating, so I declined dinner and swiftly made my exit. I ran down to the bus stop. It was 8:45 and the next bus didn't come for another 15 minutes. Then it would be a 15-minute ride into the center and a five-minute walk from the bus stop. I thought I might get to the pub at around 9:30 or so. I could only hope that Mimi would still be there waiting for me.

She was sitting at a crowded table, laughing and smoking. Patrice was seated next to her with his arm around her. Everyone from the group was there too and Gabriela was sitting next to a young man who I didn't recognize.

'You're an idiot,' I whispered to myself, feeling my heart sink again. What a damn fool I was to assume she was inviting me so we could have a quiet drink, just the two of us.

'Hey, what time do you call this?' Lindi shouted, waving me over to their table.

'I'm sorry,' I rolled my eyes. 'The DeClermonts don't eat until 10. It was a miracle getting anything to eat at all.'

'Poor thing,' Gabriela said sympathetically. 'Your family sounds like a nightmare. By the way, let me introduce you to Paul, my French host brother. He's just started at Rouen University as well.'

Paul was a skinny, pale boy with thin blond hair, dark rings beneath his eyes and a hint of a moustache on his upper lip. He smiled and shook my hand limply. '*Enchanté*,' he said.

'Nice to meet you, Paul,' I said. 'I suppose you have to put up with all of Gabriela's weird habits now,' I joked. He looked at me quizzically.

'He doesn't speak English,' Gabriela said. 'He was at a loose end tonight, and my host mother asked if I would mind bringing him along,' Gabriela explained.

'What are you studying?' I asked him in French, trying to be polite.

'Serial killers,' he said, boring his eyes into me.

'Is that a subject?' I asked incredulously.

'Criminology—specializing in the psychopathic criminal,' Paul replied staring at me. I didn't know how to respond and stood in awkward silence for minute.

'You look like you could use a drink,' Lindi got up and went to the bar with me. 'Another beer for you too Gabby … *et toi, Paul, quelque chose à boire?*' They both nodded.

The English bartender took one look at us and could tell we weren't French. 'What can I getcha, Goth?' he asked me.

'What do you mean by Goth?' I asked.

'Ya know, all dressed in black—gothic.'

I quite liked the description and nodded my head in approval. 'What do you recommend?' I asked.

'Well I had you down as a Guinness drinker. How about a pint?'

I had never drunk Guinness before, but decided to be adventurous. 'And two lagers for my friends, please.'

The barman turned away to get some glasses and Lindi elbowed me, giggling. 'Are you flirting with the bartender?'

'No, but he is pretty cute,' I whispered.

'Be careful. I think Anne already has her eye on that one.'

'She's got her eye on anything that's got a penis and a pulse,' I said.

I seemed to be one step behind everyone in the romance department here. Then I reminded myself that I had Toby. And thinking of Toby, I was supposed to call him that evening. Oh well.

'Here you go, Goth,' the barman said, handing us our drinks and winking.

As I approached the table I was aware of Anne frowning at me.

'I didn't realize the whole group was coming out tonight,' I said.

'What else did you think?' Lindi asked.

'Oh nothing,' I said, letting it drop, but looking over at Mimi canoodling with Patrice.

Lindi grabbed my arm and pulled me into the seat next to her. 'Serge is coming to Rouen next weekend.' she said. 'He called me tonight to ask if I was around.'

'After not hearing from him for three weeks, I guess that's something.' I said.

'I know, but he said he's been a bit busy with work and hasn't had the time to talk.'

'He's been acting weird if you ask me. Didn't he hang up on you last time he called and then took the phone off the hook?'

'He explained that he'd been having trouble with the phone line and it had just gone dead that time.'

'OK, if you say so,' I said, taking a sip of my drink.

'He said Frédéric was asking about you.'

'Really, I didn't think that living corpse was capable of speaking.'

Lindi laughed. 'Anyway, don't worry. He's not coming. Serge wants us to have a romantic weekend. He's going to pay for a room in an *auberge*.'

'When it suits him, I guess,' I said sarcastically.

'Don't be so cynical, Siobhan. He's a really nice guy and I like him.'

As she was so hooked on the guy I decided not to push it any further, but I had my suspicions.

'What's going on with your French family?' Gabriela asked.

'They went berserk on Sunday morning because when they came downstairs the front door was wide open. I thought I'd locked it but the wind must have blown it open. They think that I am a security risk but the good news is that they want to speak to Richard about moving me somewhere else,' I said.

'Oh, I heard that Anne was unhappy as well and she asked if she could be moved, but there are no other families and student housing is full,' Gabriela told me.

'Well sometimes I think the street might be a more appealing prospect anyway.'

'I'm sure your family wouldn't put you out on the street!' Gabriela looked scandalized.

'Maybe we could swap families. They're Catholics and they don't like the fact that I don't want to go church with them. They might get on better with you.'

Then I looked over at Gabriela's host brother, Paul, who was intensely concentrating on building a small pyre of matchsticks in the ashtray. 'Maybe that's not such a good idea after all.'

Our conversation was interrupted suddenly when a stranger came up to our table pointing an old-fashioned-looking camera at me, moving around us and trying to get the right angle. I looked at this odd character with bemusement. He looked like a hurricane had blown him in. He was about 25ish, tall and goofy-looking, wearing wire-rimmed spectacles that sat crookedly on his large Roman nose. His mousy, disheveled hair kept falling over his small brown eyes. He wore a dark turtle-neck sweater and he had a hole in the knee of his worn-out corduroys.

'You would make a beautiful picture,' he said in strangely accented French.

Gabriela and Lindi looked annoyed. 'Who is this weirdo?' Gabriela whispered.

'Are you girls English? American?' the stranger said, switching to English.

'None of your business,' Lindi said. 'We don't want our picture taken.'

'Then do you mind if I join you?' the stranger asked.

'Yes, we do mind,' Lindi replied. 'We're having a private conversation.' She turned her back on him.

'Let me guess, you are American?' he ventured.

'Very good Sherlock, now get lost,' Lindi said.

'I am Italian,' he said. 'My name is Bruno Calibri and I am a photographer.'

'Big deal,' Gabriela sniffed.

He continued to stand there, staring at me. 'I noticed you right away when I came in. Do you mind if I take your photo? You have such a classic look.'

'Sure, I don't mind,' I said, vaguely flattered. He spent a lot of time fiddling with the old camera, and moving around trying to get the right angle. Then he started snapping away and I began to feel a little self-conscious. Lindi and Gabriela were looking at me in disbelief.

'We're trying to get rid of this oddball, and now he's hanging round taking your picture.'

I shrugged my shoulders and smiled in defeat.

When he had finished, he approached me again. 'I can give you copies of the photos if you like. If you let me have your phone number, I will call you when they're ready.'

'Nice try,' I said.

'Maybe we could see each other again.'

'I've got a boyfriend already.'

He frowned and looked around him. 'I'm sorry, is he here? I'd like to meet him. Is it him?' he said, pointing to Mike.

'No, he's just my friend. My boyfriend is in the USA.'

'Well, that is a different story then. He is all the way across the ocean and I am here,' and he smiled, a charmingly crooked smile.

I shook my head. 'No, sorry,' I said. 'I'm very faithful.'

'Your boyfriend must be crazy to let such a beautiful woman go away from him.'

I rolled my eyes and tried to get back into the conversation with Gabriela and Lindi. However, the Italian kept standing there, shifting from foot to foot.

'Please,' he said, 'I would like to call you sometime.'

'Don't *you* have a phone number?' I asked.

'No, I have just moved to France from Germany and I don't have a phone.'

I got up to go to the toilet.

'Where are you going? You are not leaving, are you?' the Italian said desperately.

'To the toilet,' I said, and pushed past him.

I was quite annoyed by this invader, but at the same time was impressed by his perseverance. I decided that I would give him my number, not least so he would go away and leave us in peace. If he called I could just say I didn't want to meet him and leave it at that. It's much easier to get rid of someone on the phone. And maybe he wouldn't call anyway.

When I came out of the toilet, Bruno was there waiting for me. 'Please, I cannot leave here without knowing if I will never see you again.'

I shot a glance over at the table where Lindi and Gabriela were sitting. They were laughing at something Mike said and they weren't paying any attention to what I was doing.

'OK, OK. If I give you my number will you go away and leave us alone?' I said, making sure I was out of view of the table. Bruno looked pleased.

'Here, write it on this.' He pulled a crumpled piece of paper out of his pocket. 'Do you have a pen?'

I rummaged in my handbag and found a pen. I leaned the piece of paper against the wall and paused, pen to paper. I thought for a minute about making up the phone number, but a little voice in my head was saying, 'But you would like to see those pictures, wouldn't you, and who knows...' He wasn't blessed with conventional good looks, but he was, after all, Italian, and everyone knows what they say about Latin lovers.

I handed him the piece of paper and he read it out loud with some difficulty. 'See-oban...'

'Siobhan Schreiber,' I said.

He smiled and pushed his glasses back up his nose, looking at me. Then he stuffed the piece of paper back into his pocket. 'I will call you,' he grinned. 'I must go now.'

'Yep, see ya,' I said, heading back toward the table.

As I sat down, Lindi asked, 'How did you finally get rid of that creep?'

I didn't say anything and just shrugged, taking a sip of my drink.

'I can't believe, it. You didn't…?' Gabriela said.

'Did you give him your number?' Lindi asked.

I shifted in my seat and looked at the table. 'No! Of course not.'

A date with the Italian

I was in my room, immersed in Proust, thinking about the essence of time and memory, feeling for poor Swann and puzzling at his masochistic love for Odette when the phone in the DeClermonts' foyer rang.

'Siobhan, *c'est pour vous*,' I could hear Sophie call from the hallway. We still addressed each other using *'vous'*, the formal way of saying 'you', even though we would be living under the same roof for a year and had been sharing meals at the same dinner table for nearly two months. The transfer to another family had not come to fruition, as there were no other families available and the residence halls were full. Sophie was now treating me with an aloof and polite disdain since finding out that she would be stuck with me.

I picked up the phone. *'Allo?'*

'None of that French talk.' It was Toby. 'Why haven't you called me? Have you been too busy with François, or Pierre, or Pepé Le Pew, or whoever?'

Admittedly, I hadn't called him for nearly a month. 'Oh hi, it's you. How have you been?'

'Don't change the subject.'

'I've been so busy with my studies. It's such hard work. Also…' I lowered my voice, 'I've been having a few issues with the French family. They don't like me making phone calls.' I didn't feel like I was lying as it was a partial truth. 'It's hell here. I really miss you.'

'Why don't you come home then? It's so boring here without you.'

'I can't. The term has started now and I'm really getting into my studies. It's important for my future. What have you been up to?'

'Oh you know, partying a lot with the guys, doing a bit of

studying.' He sounded flat.

'Everything OK?' I asked.

'It's just boring here. I can't wait to come over to see you for New Year. My grandmother gave me some money, so I'm gonna buy the tickets soon.'

'Great. Can't wait.' I felt that we were running out of things to say to each other.

'I better go. I'm not supposed to be on the phone for more than five minutes,' I lied.

'Love you,' Toby said.

'Love you, bye.' When I hung up the phone, Sophie suddenly appeared out of the shadows.

'Was that your boyfriend?' she asked.

I nodded.

'There was another phone call for you today. A man who did not sound American. He didn't say who he was.' She looked down her nose suspiciously at me.

The phone started to ring again. I wasn't sure if I should answer it or if I should let Sophie answer. It rang a few more times as we stood looking at each other in awkward silence. Sophie stood rooted to the spot, arms folded. I picked up the receiver. '*Allo?*'

'Good evening. I would like to speak to Mademoiselle See-oban please.' The voice, with its strangely accented French was vaguely familiar.

'*Qui parle?*' I asked, eyeing Sophie who was still standing on the steps.

'Ah signorina, don't you remember me?' the voice said. 'I promised that I would call you. I have developed the photos and they are beautiful as I thought.'

'*Qui parle?*' I asked again, feigning ignorance, although I had already realized who it was.

'It's Bruno. We met last week at the Big Ben's pub.'

For some reason my stomach filled with butterflies. I decided to switch to English so that Sophie would go away. 'Oh, it's you,' I said flatly. I pointed at the phone and mouthed to Sophie, '*C'est pour moi.*' She slowly made her way up the stairs, but I was sure that she was trying to listen in.

'I want to see you again. I'm going to Big Ben's tomorrow night. Meet me there.'

'Um. I don't know. I've got to study.'

'But I have the photos to give to you. I promise you a good evening.'

'No, really, I can't.'

'I cannot take no for an answer. If you cannot meet tomorrow, then the next day.'

'No, I can't do that either.'

'The next day then.'

'Nope, sorry.'

'I am Italian—I do not give up on a beautiful woman.'

I laughed at his over-the-top declaration.

'I am getting somewhere?'

'OK. Tomorrow then—at Big Ben's,' I sighed.

'Good—I see you at 10 pm. *Ciao bella*.'

***

The next evening, I sat at my desk in my room, looking at my watch. It was nearly 10 and I still had a translation to do for class tomorrow. It was a dark and chilly November evening. The last thing I felt like doing was traipsing across the city to meet a total stranger. Plus, my long-buried Catholic guilt had resurfaced and I kept thinking about Toby. I decided not to go to Big Ben's. I returned to my translation assignment and put the Italian out of my mind.

The next evening as I was writing in my diary, I heard the phone ring in the hall. '*Siobhan, c'est pour vous,*' Sophie called.

I picked up the phone.

'Why didn't you show up?'

'Who is this?'

'It's Bruno. I was sad to see that you didn't meet me yesterday.'

'Something came up. I didn't have your number to let you know.'

'Well don't let it happen again. You're going to come out with me this time.'

I really wasn't used to the insistence of Italian men! I felt taken aback but there was something vaguely appealing about his forcefulness. Toby was always just giving in. This guy definitely wasn't a morose shrinking violet—he had a spark to him.

'This time I come to pick you up. I come tonight.'

'No... I—!'

'Tell me where you live.' he interrupted abruptly.

'6 rue des Marayeurs.' It escaped my lips before my brain could even take it in. Part of me was annoyed. Why had I told him where I lived? I felt immediately annoyed with myself. But I also felt strangely excited.

'*Buonissimo.* I see you in half an hour,' he said before quickly hanging up.

'Shit!' I said aloud, running into my room to change my clothes and put on some makeup.

Half an hour later I heard a knock on the front door.

'*Siobhan, il y a quelqu'un pour vous!*' Sophie announced.

I went to the front door where the Italian stood grinning behind the visor of his motorcycle helmet. Sophie was eyeing him suspiciously. 'Would you like to invite your guest inside and introduce him to us?' she asked me accusingly.

'No, that's OK—he's shy. *Bonsoir!*' I said quickly shutting the door behind me. The night was dark, starry and crisp, and the Italian stood out like an otherworldly being against the blackness of the sky. He was dressed head to toe in white—scuffed white motorcycle helmet, white rain jacket, white jeans, white sneakers. Not exactly the type of look that I considered to be cool.

'You look lovely,' he said, placing his hand on the small of my back and propelling me up the driveway toward a battered, old motorcycle. My stomach did a nervous flip as he handed me a helmet. Bruno swung a long leg over the saddle and straddled the seat, holding it still for me to get on behind him. I had never been on the back of a motorcycle before and had heard rumors about Italian drivers. Nevertheless, I gingerly climbed up onto the seat behind him.

'Have you ever been on a motorcycle before?' the Italian asked.

'No, I'm a motorcycle virgin.'

'I will make sure that your first time is a good experience then.'

'Drive slowly. If I fly off and die you're responsible.' The Italian took my arms and wrapped them round his waist.

'Hold on tight,' he said.

'Yes—drive slowly.'

It took him a few tries to get the motorbike started; it finally roared to life and we took off. The cold air grated against my cheeks and the night sky flew above my head. I clung on tightly to Bruno's waist, the roar of the engine filling my ears.

A dream state took hold of me. The scenery passed by like a film on fast forward. Reality was left behind in the dust. I could hear cars honking as we weaved in and out of traffic, leaving a blue cloud of exhaust fumes in our wake. Pedestrians turned their heads to see where the roaring was coming from.

We shot through a red light and we screeched to a halt at a green one. Cars were honking and one nearly went into us. I felt dizzy from the adrenaline rush and my heart was thumping out of my chest. 'What the hell planet are you from? Don't you know what red means?' I shouted over the noise of the engine.

'I'm color blind,' Bruno said, before accelerating again at breakneck speed.

Turning corners was terrifying as well. The Italian advised me to lean into the bend, and every time we did this I felt like the ground was only inches from my head.

We ended up at the funfair on the banks of the river Seine. The Italian parked the motorbike and I got off with rubbery legs. I staggered a few steps and nearly collapsed, steadying myself by holding onto a lamppost.

Bruno bought a couple of tickets for the Ferris wheel. I shook my head. 'You're not getting me on that thing. I'm afraid of heights.'

'Come on, you'll love it!' he said, tugging me along by the hand. The attendant opened the metal gate. I hesitated but the Italian shoved me into the cage. The ride started moving and we slowly rose up and up and up until the lights of Rouen were spread out below us like a glittering blanket. The cold wind whistled around us and I shivered.

The Italian stood up and started rocking the cage. I felt a little queasy. 'Come on, stand up. Look at the lights. You can see the whole city,' he whooped excitedly. He pulled me to my feet. The cage was swinging, my head was spinning, and my legs gave way. I was paralyzed with fear and my instinct led me to grab onto Bruno. He must have taken it as an amorous advance—he held me tightly in his arms and kissed me. It was a long, deep—and extremely good—kiss, which took me completely by surprise. I closed my eyes and gave in to it, imagining I was being kissed by James Bond, or some other dangerous man of mystery. I opened my eyes and saw the reality—a goofy, bespectacled Italian. I couldn't move, so I continued clinging on to him. He must have done this on purpose—scared me into submission—a very cunning tactic.

We got off the Ferris wheel and headed back to the motorbike. I sat on the back with wobbly legs and held on again. There is something about holding on to someone that makes you feel safe and bonds you to them. I began to enjoy that feeling of holding on, and I could tell that Bruno was enjoying it as well.

On the outskirts of town, where the wasteland rolled on forever, we became lost. The Italian stopped the bike for a second to figure out where he had screwed up. The icy wind hurled across the fields and across the autoroute. We started up again and proceeded to speed around the traffic circle five times. At last he chose a route—and yes! I saw the Continent hypermarket. I was almost home and still in one piece.

'Turn this way, and take it easy. The path is narrow,' I shouted over the roar of the engine.

We flew along the dirt path and became airborne several times over some rocks. The bike came to a stop and so did the dream sequence. With shaky legs I dismounted the bike. My ears were ringing and my whole body was tingling.

'Thanks for scaring the shit out of me,' I said handing back the helmet.

The Italian took off his helmet. His hair stuck up at crazy angles and his glasses sat crookedly on his nose. 'My pleasure,' he said, leaning over to give me a short, yet forceful kiss.

'Next time,' he said, 'I want to take nude pictures of you.'

That is how my relationship with Bruno started.

jour d horreur

I felt someone grab my arm as I walked into the grey, smoke-filled corridor of the Fac on my way to class. I spun around and saw Mimi. She looked desperate. Her usual vibrant cherry red lips were pale and her skin was pallid against her dark hair. She looked like she had been crying and her eyeliner was streaked under her eyes. 'Are you OK? You look ill,' I said.

'I need to talk to you,' she said in a wavering voice.

'I've got to go to translation class now, but I'll see you later when it's finished,' I said.

She grabbed my arm again, her dark eyes were pleading with me not to go, and I could see a glimmer of fear in them.

'What's going on?' I asked, suddenly feeling worried.

She looked around furtively to see if there was anyone around. Classes had now started and the corridor was empty. 'I'm pregnant.'

'What? Are you sure?'

'Absolutely sure. I took a test this morning.'

'Oh my God, Mimi.' I gave her a hug and she started convulsing in sobs. I decided not to go to class. I continued to just hold her and smooth her hair as she cried.

'Is it Patrice's?'

She nodded. 'I'm pretty sure.'

'Have you spoken to him about it?'

She shook her head. 'I've been avoiding him. I can't face it.'

'What are you going to do?' I asked.

'I don't know what to do … I … I…,' Mimi sobbed.

I grabbed her shoulders. 'We'll sort this out, Mimi. Don't you worry. I'll come to the clinic with you.'

She pulled back and looked at me, shocked.

'You're not thinking of keeping it, are you?' I asked. It was my turn to be shocked. 'Mimi, you're here in France. You still have another two years of university. You hardly know the father.'

'I'm just so scared,' she said, looking at me with her watery doe's eyes.

'I'll be here for you.' I handed her a cigarette. 'Let's sit down, have a smoke and think about this rationally.'

We went outside the Fac and sat down on a bench to smoke. As she leaned toward me to light my cigarette she put her hand on my knee. I looked at her hand and had a sudden flashback to that night at the rave on Es. I couldn't figure her out. Well, I couldn't figure myself out for that matter.

'Step one is to go to the university medical center and talk to someone there. They can probably make an appointment for you at the clinic.'

'I hate those places. I would fear for my life there.'

'What do you mean? It's a modern medical facility, not some back-room butcher with a coat hanger.'

'No—I mean, from bombs or death threats.'

'This isn't a backwoods Midwestern state. This is France, remember? You're not going to get any religious right-wingers marching around chanting damnation.'

Mimi puffed manically on her cigarette.

'Think about it,' I said. 'Are you really in a position to become a mother? I mean, you'd have to give up smoking for a start.'

At that moment Gekko walked past. He must have seen my serious face and Mimi's tears and he said, 'Not a lover's tiff, I hope?' He winked at me.

'Uh—it's not really a good time now, Gekko. We have something really important to sort out.'

'Has that rogue Patrice got in between you? How do you say… a lovers' triangle? I told him not to come between you two. I thought you were a beautiful couple of dykes—but he just can't resist the ladies.'

I had never said anything to dispel Gekko's beliefs that Mimi and I were an item since he'd seen us at the rave and I sort of enjoyed playing along.

Mimi had started sobbing again at the mention of Patrice's name.

Gekko looked at her and shrugged his shoulders 'I could never understand women,' he said as he walked away.

'I think we should tell Lindi,' I said. Her French is the best. She can come to the clinic in case we don't understand everything.'

Mimi nodded in agreement. 'You're a great friend, you know?'

Later that afternoon I caught Lindi leaving her literature class.

'Hey there,' I said. I'm glad I caught you. I've got a really important favor to ask.'

I could see right away that there was something wrong. Her normally sparkling blue eyes were hard and glowering. Her brow was furrowed and her lips were set in a tight-lipped frown.

'What's wrong?' I asked, taken aback by her angry expression.

'Serge. That's what's wrong. The bastard is married.'

'What? Really?' I was incredulous.

'He came to Rouen last weekend and paid for a room in a little auberge. He paid for dinner and we had a great time. I really thought I'd found the man of my dreams.'

'How did you find out that he's married?'

'His wife must have been suspicious, looked through his wallet, and found the hotel and restaurant receipts along with my phone number. She called me last night to ask who I was and if I knew he was married with a kid and another on the way.'

'I can't believe it! I guess that explains those times when the phone call got 'disconnected'. He probably had to hang up because his wife walked in while he was on the phone to you.'

'I know. I'm such an idiot to be taken in by his charade.'

'Well I wish I had something to tell you to cheer you up. But I'm afraid we've got another problem. It's Mimi. She's pregnant.'

Lindi gasped. 'Oh, poor thing. I feel so bad. My troubles are nothing compared to that. What's she going to do?'

'Well, that's where you come in. I need to take her to the clinic and you need to come too. You speak the best French. She's so scared—she needs us there.'

'Of course I will do that,' Lindi said seriously. 'Let's go find her and get this sorted out.'

***

Mimi, Lindi and I stood outside the door of the clinic. Mimi didn't want us to tell any of the others, especially Gabriela, with her religious convictions, so we all made up lies about why we couldn't make it to class that day.

Mimi was very pale and clutching her overnight bag. 'Well I guess this is it.'

I could see that her hands were shaking. I gave her a hug. 'Don't worry. We'll be waiting for you when it's all over.'

We walked in through the doors and were greeted by a nurse. Mimi was silent as she looked around her. Lindi explained to the nurse that Mimi had an appointment. The nurse nodded and asked Mimi to follow her. Mimi looked back at us desperately.

'Is it OK if we come with her?' Lindi asked.

'Yes, of course. You can come up to her room and wait there for her while she is having the procedure, if you want.'

It was a comfortable private room with views overlooking the cathedral. The nurse handed Mimi a hospital gown to put on. She disappeared into the bathroom and came out wearing the gown. Without her funky, unique style of clothes, Mimi looked pitiful. She was shivering and got into the hospital bed and pulled the stiff blankets over her. 'I'm dying for a cigarette,' she said.

'I don't think you can smoke in here,' Lindi said.

I flung open the window, lit up a Gauloise and handed it to her. Mimi eagerly took a deep drag.

Suddenly an alarm started to go off. I grabbed the cigarette out of Mimi's hand and chucked it out the window. We all started madly waving our arms to try to clear the air.

'You'll get us all kicked out of here,' Lindi said.

Just then there was a knock on the door. '*Entréz*,' Mimi said, feebly. A nurse entered the room with a machine for taking blood pressure. She attached a clip to Mimi's finger, wrote down the number displayed and nodded in approval.

'Are you ready?' she asked. I will send a wheelchair to take you down to the operating theatre.'

We all looked at each other nervously. I went over to Mimi and squeezed her hand. Lindi patted her arm. 'We will be waiting right here for you when you get back,' she said.

The nurse left and returned five minutes later with a porter pushing a wheelchair. Lindi and I watched as they wheeled Mimi away. The nurse advised us that they would bring her back in about an hour. My stomach tightened at the thought of the procedure that Mimi was about to undergo. 'I'm going out for a cigarette,' I said to Lindi who had started to read S/Z by Roland Barthes.

Each minute felt like an hour and I paced back and forth, chain-smoking in front of the clinic. Then I saw Gabriela come out of the bank across the street, with Paul in tow. I didn't want her to see me going into the clinic so I bent down pretending to tie the lace on my Doc Martens, hoping that she wouldn't notice me. When I looked up to see if they were gone Paul was standing over me, with Gabriela hovering behind. 'I thought it was you,' he said in French.

Gabriela looked a little embarrassed. 'Sorry about him,' she said. 'He's always sneaking up on people.' Then she looked around and noticed that we were in front of the clinic. 'What are you doing here?'

I puffed on my cigarette. 'I'm uh… just waiting for Gekko. He said to meet him here.'

'It's a strange place to meet,' she said.

'I know—Gekko is a weird guy,' I said, shrugging.

Just then I noticed Patrice walking past. 'Shit!' I said aloud. Gabriela looked at me in surprise. Unfortunately, he noticed us.

'Hello, how are you?' Patrice kissed me and Gabriela on both cheeks. 'Have you seen Mimi? I haven't been able to find her or get in touch with her for weeks.'

'I think she's been busy writing an important essay,' I said.

'Oh yes, she told me about the essay. I was going to help her with it.' Then he looked at the building. 'What are you doing here?' he asked.

'She's waiting for Gekko,' Paul piped up.

'I just saw Gekko back at the Fac,' Patrice said, raising his eyebrows. 'He mentioned that he thinks you and Mimi are more than just friends. I said this couldn't be true because Mimi and I love each other.'

Gabriela and Paul were both staring at me in disbelief. 'I don't know where he got that idea from,' I said, shrugging again. I thought I was getting pretty good at perfecting the Gallic shrug.

Luckily, Patrice, Gabriela and Paul went on their way and I returned to the room where Lindi was still engrossed in Barthes. 'You must have smoked a whole pack out there,' Lindi said.

'Nearly—and I saw Gabriela, who was curious as to why I was standing there. But what's worse is that I saw Patrice too and he was looking for Mimi.'

Lindi looked alarmed. 'What did you say?'

'I just said I was waiting for someone and that I hadn't seen Mimi for a while either.'

There was a knock on the door and a man in hospital scrubs entered the room. 'I am Doctor Resnard. Mimi is just in recovery. The procedure is finished but she lost a lot of blood. We'll need to keep her in overnight. We'll be bringing her back to the room soon.'

Lindi and I looked at each other, worried.

'That sounds serious. Is she going to be OK?' Lindi asked the doctor.

'It happens to some patients. We just need to keep an eye on her tonight. She will be fine.'

A few minutes later Mimi was wheeled through the door on a stretcher. She was still a bit groggy and two nurses had to help lift her into the bed.

'How do you feel?' I asked.

'They gave me some good drugs. I feel great,' she slurred.

But she looked terrible. Her skin had a yellowy pallor and she had purple rings under her eyes.

'You're great friends,' she smiled wanly at us gratefully.

Lindi and I hung around for a bit until the nurse told us that visiting hours were over. Mimi waved weakly as we said goodbye.

31 october

It was Halloween—the night when the spirits raise themselves from their earthly slumbering places and the Undead walk among the living. In celebration, Bruno was having a party. I guess he knew that Americans were into Halloween and thought it would be a good way to lure me into his web again. He told me to invite whoever I wanted, so I spread the word at the Fac.

I was just putting the finishing touches to my zombie widow costume and listening to the wind outside making the house groan and the shutters shudder. The weather was appropriately gothic; the rain had been on and off, quite heavy at times, gusting in torrents. I could hear the church bells in the distance and I imagined that the spirits of the long dead were ringing them. There was a sudden knock at the window and I nearly jumped out of my skin. I opened the curtain and saw a hollow-eyed ghoul grinning through the windowpane. I opened the window.

'Are you ready yet, Primavera?' Bruno asked. He had taken to calling me Primavera because my birthday was on the first day of spring and he found my real name unpronounceable.

'Give me two minutes,' I said.

I put my shoes and coat on and went to open the front door. Sophie appeared in the foyer and saw Bruno standing on the doorstep in his horror makeup. 'I didn't hear anyone knock on the door,' she said, surprised.

'He knocked on my bedroom window,' I explained.

'In France it is good manners to knock on the door,' she said.

'Signora, in my region of Italy it is customary to knock on the window,' Bruno said, bowing theatrically. I tried to suppress a giggle.

Antoine heard us in the hallway and came running down the stairs. He peered out the door and pointed excitedly at the motorbike parked in the driveway. 'Can I see the moto? Can I see the moto?' he squealed.

Sophie held him back. 'No, Antoine, you cannot. Motorcycles are dangerous.' As we zoomed off, I looked back and waved at Antoine who was still standing forlornly in the doorway.

Bruno's apartment was on a narrow backstreet in the center of Rouen. It was in a building at the end of a central courtyard, accessed through an archway. The building probably would have been a stable block for the grand 17th-century house that faced onto the road. We climbed up a narrow, spiral stone staircase to a one-roomed apartment that overlooked the courtyard. The room was furnished with a rickety wooden table and a couple of folding chairs, which stood in the middle of the small space. A double mattress was pushed into a corner on the floor with a hippy-style throw tossed on top of it.

Bruno lit candles all around the room, which gave it a spooky and romantic glow, and then he put a record on an ancient turntable. Strains of Perez Prado's mambo orchestra filled the air. It wasn't my idea of a cool tune, so I thumbed through the record collection hoping to find some good music. He only had five records. The sleeves were all faded and worn away at the corners, suggesting they had been flea market finds. Along with Perez Prado, there was also an album by Zucchero, Angelo Badalamenti's soundtrack to 'Blue Velvet' and an album called *La Demoiselle* by someone named Angelo Branduardi.

Bruno came up behind me and put his arms round my waist. 'We have some time alone before the others arrive.' He tried to kiss me, but I pushed him away.

'What have you got to drink?' I asked.

'How rude of me. Of course, I should have offered you a drink.' He produced a bottle of white wine from the fridge, opened it and poured some into a plastic cup. I carried it to the window, wanting to avoid any more of his advances.

To my relief, the first guest arrived. It was another Italian called Vincenzo. He was from Naples and was about 40.

Bruno introduced us and I held out my hand in greeting. He looked me up and down and then grinned a toothless grin of approval, patting Bruno on the back and saying something in Italian.

'Hey, that's a great costume,' I said. He was wearing a red hooded cloak and I guessed he was supposed to be a demon. He looked grey and haggard and had a few teeth missing.

'Your makeup is amazing—the rotten teeth are so realistic.'

Vincenzo leered uncomprehendingly and I realized on closer inspection that his skin really was grey and haggard and his teeth were half rotten or missing; it wasn't just part of his Halloween get-up.

The two men gabbled on in Italian for a bit, completely ignoring me.

I was all the more grateful, therefore, when Lindi, Gabriela, Mike and Anne tramped in, in a mass of bandages and fake blood, accompanied by Gabriela's host brother, Paul, who seemed to be hanging around with her all the time these days. Paul was wearing an odd-looking, old-fashioned outfit.

'What are you supposed to be?' I asked him in French.

'Can't you tell?' he asked. 'I am Gilles de Rais, my favorite serial killer. He was a Satanist who murdered 400 children in the 15th century.'

'Well I hope you're not going to kill anyone tonight, Paul,' I said.

I was glad that Mike had brought a boom box and some music, and the party was soon buzzing with some funky reggae.

Over the next half hour, the room started to fill up with an eclectic mix of pirates, skeletons, vampires, ghosts and ghouls.

Bruno had a very international entourage: Takashi, a Japanese art student; a Brazilian couple, José and Cristina; a Mexican, Gerardo; an Irish girl called Elizabeth and her Italian friend, Chiara, who were au pairs; and a French couple, Daniel and Aurélie. People started mingling and as the alcohol flowed so did the conversation.

Mike and some of the other Americans were in a discussion with the French couple about the recent news report of an imminent war in Iraq. It somehow led to a debate about colonialism and languages.

'Did you know that English is the most widely spoken language in the world?' Daniel, the French guy, declared. This seemed to rile José, the Brazilian guy, who had been listening to the discussion on the periphery and decided to actively take part.

'These American colonizers think they can impose their ideas and their language everywhere,' José slurred. 'You are all terrorists!' he said, pointing at me and my American friends. 'We speak English here for you because you are all too stupid to learn other languages,' he sneered. 'I don't understand why you invite the enemy here to ruin the party, Bruno?'

Deeply insulted, I was on the verge of leaving with my friends but in his jovial Italian way, Bruno put his arm around José.

'You need to chill out, *amico*,' he said, handing him a spliff.

José toked thoughtfully and nodded his head. 'This is good stuff,' he said to Bruno, who steered him to the corner of the room where Vincenzo was sitting on the floor, busily constructing something he called a '*chibonga*'. It consisted of a bucket full of water and a plastic soda bottle with the bottom cut off. At the mouth of the bottle, he stuck a piece of aluminum foil that he'd pierced holes in to make a screen, and he placed a lump of hash in it. He pushed the bottle down into the bucket and lit the hash, pulling the bottle up slowly and filling it up with smoke. He then removed the foil and put his mouth over the opening, pushing the bottle down into the water again so that he got a rush of smoke into his lungs. We all gathered round and laughed as he demonstrated. Everyone took turns on the contraption and got steadily more and more intoxicated.

My head was spinning and I was staggering aimlessly around the room, when Gabriela grabbed my hand. 'Can I talk to you in private?'

There wasn't really anywhere private to go, so we went into the bathroom.

'What's wrong?' I asked.

'It's Paul. He's really creeping me out.'

'I noticed he follows you like a shadow.'

'I caught him peeping through the keyhole of my bedroom door last night. And Jamie told me that the other day when he called, Paul told him that I had a new boyfriend so not to bother ringing me anymore. And apparently he's been hiding Jamie's letters from me.'

'Have you spoken to your host mother about it?'

'I feel embarrassed about it. I have to live with him. And Madame Faure seems so pleased that Paul is finally getting out of the house. She told me that he has really started to come out of his shell since I arrived.'

Feeling brazen from the cocktail of alcohol and hash, I offered to talk to him for her. 'Don't worry, I'll set him straight,' I said, flinging open the bathroom door.

I found Paul crouched in the corner by himself, swigging from a bottle of vodka.

'Hey there, Paul. You having fun?'

He stood up. 'Where's Gabby?' he asked accusingly.

'It's OK, Paul. She's in the bathroom. But I've got to talk to you about something important.'

He seemed to relax a little. 'I think you've been acting a little inappropriately toward Gabriela, for a host brother, that is. Jamie heard what you've been doing and he's going to come to France and kick your ass.'

'No he's not!' Paul shouted as he shoved me. I lost my balance and reeled backwards, tripping on the bottle of vodka Paul had left on the floor, and hitting the deck. In the blink of an eye Bruno appeared and grabbed Paul by the collar. Vincenzo stood menacingly at his side.

'You don't treat a lady that way,' Bruno said.

Paul started to shove Bruno but Bruno just laughed at him, which seemed to make him more irate.

'Get out of my party, *stronzo*,' Bruno said.

Paul picked up the bottle of vodka and smashed it against the wall, threatening Bruno with the jagged neck. Vincenzo sprang into action and kicked Paul's feet out from under him. Then he and Bruno picked him up—one grabbed his feet and the other his arms. They took him down the stairs and swung him like a sack of potatoes out the door.

Gabriela came out of the bathroom. 'What's going on? They haven't hurt Paul, have they?'

'The *petit cauchemar* was getting a little drunk and violent. So I threw him out of my party,' Bruno said.

'He knocked me down, Gab. He's crazy. I'd lock your door at night if I were you,' I said.

'You're kidding. I can't believe it.'

Bruno put his arm around her. 'Vincenzo and I won't let anything happen to you girls. If that *pazo* comes back, he will be sorry.'

'Do you think I should go check on him?' Gabriela asked.

'You should just let him calm down by himself,' I suggested.

We poured ourselves some more drinks and carried on partying.

A sudden loud shouting drew us to the window. Bruno's beloved motorcycle was on fire.

'*Porca Madonna!*' Bruno shouted and tore down the stairs into the courtyard.

He shouted Italian obscenities, shook his fists, wrung his hands, gesticulated to the heavens. Thinking quickly, Vincenzo grabbed the *chibonga* and threw the water from the bucket out the window over the motorbike, dousing the flames.

We all rushed outside, like a coven of witches, ghouls and demons surrounding a sacrificial corpse. Luckily, there wasn't too much damage to the motorcycle. The seat was a bit melted and the paintwork was slightly blackened and peeling in places. Ignoring the slimy bong water, Bruno got on the bike to start it. It spluttered weakly and he had to try a few times to get it going.

'I know who did this,' Bruno said.

Vincenzo nodded, looking serious.

'You don't think that Paul did this, do you?' Gabriela's brow furrowed and her eyes glistened with tears.

'The *petit cauchemar*,' Bruno said, his voice taking on a grim tone.

Mike handed Bruno a spliff and patted him on the back. 'Sorry about your bike, man,' he said.

Bruno puffed thoughtfully on the spliff. Then cheerfully declared, 'No one died. Let's go back and have a party.'

After everyone left, Bruno asked me to stay. He poured me what remained of the wine and we both sat down on the edge of his mattress on the floor. He got his camera out and started snapping pictures of me. 'You are a beautiful picture,' he said between shots.

'You say that every time,' I said. 'I'm getting a bit bored of hearing it. How about some music? Haven't you got any EMF or Stone Roses, or anything like that?

Bruno didn't say anything, he just turned on Perez Prado again. Da-da, da-da-da-da-da-da-da-da-da-da. The horns blared in their syncopated rhythm.

Bruno took off his clothes to the Latin beat and mamboed around the room naked.

My eyes popped out of my head as I watched him sway to the beat unselfconsciously. I couldn't believe it, but it was true what they said about the correlation of the size of a man's nose, to the size of what he had downstairs.

I was laughing so hard, I spilt the wine all over the bed. Bruno dramatically pushed me back onto the bed and kissed me, expertly undoing the zips and buttons of my zombie widow costume.

'I can't,' I protested, 'I have a boyfriend!' But as Bruno's hands wandered and settled in all the right places, the need to protest was strongly overtaken by the urge to carry on and see what else this Italian could do. His glasses slipped down his nose and I attempted to remove them, but he grabbed my hand and held it down above my head. 'I want to see you,' he insisted, as he took control of the situation.

We had sex well into the morning. It was probably the best sex I had ever had, although I had only ever had sex with two other people before: Toby and the Australian at the MIJE. Before we got dressed, Bruno produced the camera again and took some photos of me lounging naked on his bed, smoking a cigarette, in what I imagined to be a very 'film noir' pose. My puritanical American inhibitions were discarded along with my clothing on the floor. I reclined, casually watching the smoke from my cigarette catch the sun rays streaming in through the window, as Bruno moved around, searching out the right angles, light and shadows. Here I was—carefree, living the bohemian life that my favorite writers and artists probably lived. I felt so European, with my artistic Italian lover, my Gauloises, my cup of strong coffee. I loved it here, loved my new life. I decided then and there I wasn't ever going back to the States.

Hitchhiking to Paris

About a week after the party Bruno decided that we should go to Paris for the weekend as there was a photo exhibition there that he wanted to go to. I wasn't really that keen on the idea and I declined at first. I didn't want him to get the idea that we were an item. I liked him, but I wasn't sure how much. He wasn't really my type, and besides, I had to write an essay for my literary theory class. But as usual, Bruno would not take no for an answer. He just turned up early on Saturday morning at the DeClermonts', and knocked on the window instead of the front door—for Sophie's benefit I'm sure. As I went to the door to greet him, Sophie appeared in the foyer. Her face was set in stern annoyance when she saw Bruno.

'Going somewhere?' she asked me.

'I'm taking her to Paris,' Bruno announced as he walked into the foyer like he owned the place

'Are you ready, Primavera?' Bruno asked.

'Um—just give me a minute to throw a few things in a bag,' I said. 'Sophie, don't worry about catering for me this weekend.'

'Paris? For the whole weekend? Where will you be staying? I hope it is somewhere safe.' She eyed Bruno suspiciously.

He doffed his helmet theatrically. 'Trust me, Madame. I will look after her.'

We went on Bruno's motorbike, but ever since the fire it wasn't quite the same. When I looked at the charred bike I had my doubts.

'Are you sure we're going to make it on that thing?' I asked.

'No worries. It still goes,' Bruno said, patting the seat. I got on behind him and we spluttered off. But for all Bruno's confidence, we only made it as far as an autoroute service station on the outskirts of Rouen, as the bike was losing power.

'Oh well, I guess we'll have to head back then,' I said, hoping that the crazy idea had come to an early conclusion.

But Bruno decided that we would carry on to Paris without the motorcycle. We left our helmets with the station attendant and Bruno found a piece of cardboard and wrote 'PARIS' on it in black marker. 'We're going to hitchhike,' he said when he saw the doubtful look on my face.

I followed him as he walked confidently around the service station, casually knocking on car windows and showing people his sign. Most people made excuses—they said they weren't going to Paris, or they had a full car; a few just shook their heads and looked away.

A little old lady pootled into the station in an old, clapped-out Renault. Bruno made a beeline for her car and signaled for her to roll down the window. He cheerfully pointed to his sign. 'Mademoiselle, we are trying to get to Paris. Would you be so kind as to take me and my friend in your lovely car?' He smiled his crooked smile and winked at her. Looking at her white poodle hairdo, wrinkled skin, and arthritic, birdlike fingers that clenched the steering wheel, I could tell she was far too old to be a 'mademoiselle'.

'Your car is a beauty, mademoiselle. Only the French could make such a classic as this,' Bruno said as he admiringly patted the hood of the car.

'And the driver, with the classic beauty to match,' he beamed at the old woman.

I rolled my eyes, thinking he was really overdoing it and she would drive away in a hurry. But to my surprise she didn't. She smiled at Bruno, he eyes sparkling as if under a spell.

She apologized. She was only going as far as Louviers.

'That is better than nothing, mademoiselle. We would really appreciate it if you could take us as far as you are going. We can get someone to take us the rest of the way.'

Bruno opened the passenger door and pulled up the front seat for me to get in behind, and he sat in the front. We rattled off in the old Renault. 'Are you Italian?' the woman asked Bruno. 'You have such a charming accent. I love the Italian accent.'

Bruno replied in the affirmative.

'Oh, I so love Italy,' the woman said. My husband and I used to go to the lakes when he was still alive. You remind me a bit of him when he was young. What part of Italy are you from?'

'As a matter of fact, mademoiselle, I come from the original city of romance: Verona, the home of Romeo and Juliet.'

'Oh, I do love it there,' the old lady said smiling fondly at Bruno and giggling like a schoolgirl.

I kept quiet in the back seat, taking note of Bruno's charm offensive.

As she approached the exit for Louviers, the old lady pulled over and dropped us off. It was a very bad spot as most cars were zooming past at 100 miles an hour and wouldn't be able to safely stop. We carried on walking along the hard shoulder, sticking out our thumbs and holding up our sign.

No one was stopping, so in the meantime, Bruno took pictures of me hitchhiking. I was beginning to think that we were never going to be picked up and that we would end up having to walk all the way to Paris, when finally, someone slowed down and pulled over. He was a 'yuppie' type, with a slicked-back hairstyle and expensive-looking wire rim glasses, a leather jacket and reeking of Armani cologne. He drove the French equivalent of a Jeep Cherokee. He opened the passenger door and Bruno got into the front seat leaving me to climb into the back again.

The driver just happened to be from Rouen too and he knew all the same bars that we went to. As we chatted I became aware of him giving me odd looks in the rear view mirror.

I was getting a weird vibe from the guy. I couldn't put my finger on it, but he was really giving me the creeps.

He finally turned right around to look at me and said, 'You're American? And you're up at the university, aren't you?'

How the hell did he know that? I squirmed uncomfortably. Was this guy a spy or something? I just wished he'd keep his eyes on the road.

'And you're a photographer, I see,' he said to Bruno. 'I have a Leica as well. Good cameras. But I'm actually a filmmaker. Documentary films mostly. I recently got back from a stint filming in Iraq.'

'Wow, that sounds amazing,' Bruno said. 'Did you see any combat?'

'Well, I was actually taken hostage for about a month.'

'You must have been really scared,' I said.

'No, not at all. We were treated quite well. There was a swimming pool and we spent the days relaxing and eating.'

There was something that didn't add up about his story. 'You make it sound like a luxury hotel rather than a hostage situation,' I said.

He just laughed and winked at me in the reflection in the rear view mirror. 'The situation changed me as a person,' he said with a smarmy smile.

When I bent down to get a cigarette out of my bag, I noticed some magazines sticking out from under the driver's seat. They were hardcore bondage magazines. I nudged them back under the seat and pretended I hadn't noticed, but I felt an overwhelming need to get out of that car as soon as possible. My imagination started to run wild. What if he kidnapped us and kept us drugged and locked up, using us for his twisted and sadistic gratification— re-enacting one of his 'hostage' situations?

I tapped Bruno on the shoulder and said in English, 'I'm desperate for a pee.'

He asked the driver to pull over.

'There's a service stop ahead,' the yuppie said, giving me another snake-eyed leer. 'I'll wait for you. I need to make a stop myself.'

'Oh that's not necessary. We can make our own way.'

Bruno looked at me quizzically. 'But he said he'll take us all the way to Paris.'

'Yes, of course, no problem,' the yuppie said, looking at us both.

We got back into the car. My senses were on high alert in case he drove off in the wrong direction, or locked the doors, but luckily we were soon at the outskirts of Paris. The guy dropped us off near a metro station and said, 'Great to meet you two. How about we get together next Tuesday at Morrison's?'

As Bruno shook his hand, I was dismayed to hear him agree to meet.

The night of the Beaujolais Nouveau

We got on the metro and headed toward Montparnasse. The exhibition Bruno wanted to go to was a display of Allen Ginsberg's photography at Fnac. I knew Allen Ginsberg as a writer, but Bruno explained that he was also a photographer in his own right. He insisted that I should see his photography.

We walked around the exhibition, studying the black and white photographs. 'Just look at the composition of this one!' Bruno marveled. It was a picture of Jack Kerouac walking past Tompkins Square Park. I couldn't see what Bruno was so excited about; the photo didn't look like anything special. Then, suddenly, I had a flashback of Toby and I walking in Tompkins Square on one of our weekend visits to the city to see his brother who lived in the East Village. I stood and stared at the photo. I remembered that it had been hot that day and Toby had bought me an ice cream from a street vendor.

'Primavera, come look at this one,' Bruno beckoned me out of my reverie. He explained the technique used and how it brought out the drama of the picture but I was lost in my memories of New York, going to gigs at CBGB's and hunting for rare vinyl at Bleeker Bob's.

On leaving Fnac, we noticed that there were fire trucks, police cars and men in strange spaceman uniforms with silver helmets across the street at the Tati department store. We guessed it was a bomb scare—apparently just a normal occurrence here in Paris. Of course, Bruno took pictures of it. He seemed to take forever trying to get the right focus and angle, while I just followed him and hung about behind. After a while, the excitement of the situation wore off and I started to flag a bit.

'Come on, let's go to the Musée Carnavalet. There's another photo exhibition there,' Bruno bubbled, grabbing my arm.

I shook my head. My feet were hurting. I was hungry and frankly had seen enough photography for one day. 'We need to think about finding somewhere to sleep tonight, Bruno, otherwise we're going to be camping under the stars.'

'We stay up all night, no?' He looked at me puzzled.

'No way. I need a bed. I know a good hostel. We can see if they have any beds tonight.'

Bruno was clearly disappointed. 'No more photo exhibitions?'

We headed to the MIJE, that ancient bordello, whose ghosts had once possessed my body to do things I knew I'd always wanted to do. We managed to get beds in the men's and women's dormitories and decided to get some rest before going out but I found it impossible. Bruno said he was going to have a bit of a siesta, but instead I had a cigarette and stared out the window contemplating the sheer bizarrity of life and its little surprises that always lurk around the corner. I asked myself what the hell I was doing in Paris with this goofy Italian who I wasn't even sure I liked. What bothered me was that I found myself attracted to him.

I was on my third cigarette when Bruno turned up at my room with some speed and hash. We did a couple of lines and smoked a joint out the window, as there was no one else in the room.

As it was the night of the Beaujolais Nouveau, we decided that it was time to go out in search of a bottle. We found one in a convenience store and walked along the Seine to the Eiffel tower. It was misting constantly and the light rain spiraled down in little gusts like silver ribbons travelling on the wind, but we shared the shelter of Bruno's raincoat. It was a long walk but we talked and laughed a lot and stopped every now and then to kiss.

As we drew closer, the glowing yellow beacon of the Eiffel tower slowly rose up from the twinkling lights of Paris. Bruno led me to a bench directly underneath the tower. I looked up at the intricate steelwork above us, crisscrossing up and up and up right to the tip. Bruno opened the bottle with his Swiss army knife and offered it to me. We swigged straight from the bottle and watched the tourists passing by. We played a game trying to guess what their nationalities were. Bruno was very good at it. He said it was easy, as each nationality had its own distinguishing style and appearance.

'Do you see them?' Bruno pointed to an older couple who were wearing grey sweatpants and running shoes underneath their plastic rain ponchos. 'Americans always look "comfortable".'

I went up to the couple and asked them if they would take our picture. They had a telltale Deep South American drawl.

A group of young teenagers appeared in the distance. 'Them? Italian. I can tell an Italian from a mile off,' Bruno said cockily.

As the group approached there was a cacophony of loud voices all talking at once and shouting loudly in Italian.

'The Italian tourists all have Invicta backpacks,' Bruno explained. He was right. Every person in the group was sporting a multi-colored, Invicta-branded, canvas rucksack on their back.

A young couple came into view. They looked like they were in their 20s and were dressed like modern-day hippies. I knew that look. The classic American college student hippy. Bruno went up to them and asked if they would take our picture. He struck up a conversation and found out that they were indeed from California!

As the tourists walked past, Bruno continued to pick people out of the crowd, explaining each nationality's distinguishing style and appearance. The French were conservative and stern, yet stylish; and the *'moda inglesi'*, English style, was to wear mostly black, with good sturdy shoes; and the Germans had no fashion sense whatsoever, he declared, and would pair a rainbow sweater with shorts and Birkenstock sandals.

We were pleasantly buzzed on the wine and realized that we had drunk the entire bottle, so we went in search of another. The city was full of inebriated people staggering through the streets trying out each bar's offering of this year's vintage. All the bars were full to capacity so we got a bottle at another convenience store and then went to find somewhere to eat. We found a cute little Mexican hole in the wall and ordered nachos and Long Island Iced Teas. We were ripped! After dinner we walked around the streets with our bottle, catching a few tunes from a street jazz band called The Lost and Wandering Jazz and Blues band. I wasn't ever a fan of jazz, but the alcohol made them seem brilliant.

Walking along the river Seine, we stopped under the Pont Neuf, and Bruno taught me the words to an old Italian partisan song. *'Avanti popolo alla riscossa, bandiera rossa, bandiera rossa!'* We sang it at the top of our lungs, listening to our voices echo beneath the bridge and watching our frozen breath mingle and whirl away into the mist. Suddenly, Bruno pulled me down onto a grass verge and began kissing me. We fooled around a little, until some men saw us and started yelling things, so we stopped and hurried back to the MIJE.

It was after the midnight curfew and the concierge was annoyed with us. He told us that the rules about the curfew were clearly written on the front door. Bruno, whose French was actually perfect, said in broken French, and with a heavy Italian accent, 'I'm Italian and I didn't know. You should have the rules written in Italian.'

I pretended to be Italian as well and said '*Grazie signore,*' keeping my eyes to the ground, when he finally let us in. I was trying to suppress my giggles. It was the same North African concierge who had caught me on CCTV when I was first at the MIJE, and I was hoping he wouldn't recognize me.

There were some Eastern European women fast asleep in my room but I didn't care. I invited Bruno to join me. He tiptoed in quietly and got into my bed. I slid in beside him under the covers. 'I had such a great time tonight,' I whispered as I gently removed his glasses and hung them on the headboard. We quietly made love under the covers. It seemed to be the perfect ending to a perfect day—until we realized that the condom had broken.

'*Merda!*' Bruno swore under his breath.

'How the hell did that happen?' I whispered.

'Italian condoms,' Bruno joked.

'How can you tell jokes at a time like this?'

I could hear one of the Eastern European women stirring.

'You better get out of here now,' I said, and kicked him out of the bed.

In the darkness he fumbled into his jeans and I heard the door click as he closed it behind him.

The next morning, as we sat in a coffee shop, I insisted that we should go to get the morning after pill. I didn't feel like ending up in the same sorry situation as Mimi. It was difficult to find a pharmacy that was open on a Sunday, but we finally found one. I tried to explain to the pharmacist, an elderly man, what I was after. I wasn't sure how to say 'the morning after pill' in French and attempted a crude translation. '*J'ai besoin de la pilule du matin après.*'

The pharmacist looked at me puzzled. '*Qu'est-ce que vous voulez mademoiselle?*' I tried again, in a louder voice, and he still didn't understand.

Then Bruno intervened. He explained that we had sex last night and the condom broke. To my embarrassment I noticed that some customers in the shop looked up at us from their shopping. 'Ah,' the pharmacist said, nodding his head and smiling as he handed Bruno a pack of condoms.

'No,' I shook my head. '*Une pilule?*' I ventured again. This time the man went into a room at the back of the pharmacy and came out with a young woman.

There was now a line of people standing behind us waiting to be served. I tried explaining again to her that I needed the morning after pill. She nodded in recognition, *'Vous voulez dire la pilule du lendemain!'* In French they call it 'the next day pill'. She explained that we needed to go to the hospital to get a prescription from a doctor. Then we could come back and pick up the pill, but we had to be quick as the pharmacy closed early on a Sunday.

After frantically trying to find a hospital, I was at least armed with the necessary vocabulary to explain myself once we got there. Prescription in hand, we raced back to the pharmacy and arrived just as they were about to lock up.

We were both exhausted, feeling shitty from hangovers and coming down off speed, so we decided just to spend the rest of the day hanging out in Montmartre. I just really wanted to go home. The sparkle of Paris at night had given way to a cold, gray day.

I didn't feel much like hitchhiking back as I was feeling sick from the pill.

Bruno said that he understood. 'That's OK. I can come back for the motorcycle tomorrow,' he said, taking my bag so that I wouldn't have to carry it. 'We will get the train. I pay.' He even hailed a taxi to take us to Saint Lazare.

On the train back to Rouen, Bruno held my hand as I fought off the queasiness.

December

Mike sat on a chair under the eaves drinking coffee out of a bowl, smoking and strumming a bit on his acoustic guitar, the light glinting off his glasses. The Italian au pair from Bruno's party, Chiara, lounged on the floor next to him, fixing him in an unfocused and languid stare. I nodded at Chiara in recognition, but my brain registered her as being out of context. I guessed that they might be dating, although Mike hadn't mentioned it. He seemed much more engrossed in his guitar playing and didn't even glance once at Chiara. But there was something out of place about it, and for a fleeting moment it occurred to my suspicious mind that Bruno had sent a spy to check on what I was doing.

Lindi and I had a newspaper open on the desk, scrutinizing the 'lonely hearts' ads and circling the ones that looked interesting. Luckily, Lindi and Mike lived near me and I often went there if Dominique felt the need to practice the piano in my bedroom. Their host family lived in a long converted stone farmhouse. Lindi and Mike occupied their own separate wing of the house and they each had their own bedroom and bathroom. I was jealous of their situation. They had privacy and didn't have to worry about inconveniently crossing paths with their host family all the time.

'Listen to this one,' Lindi said. '*Twenty-six-year- old Polish engineering student looking for an intelligent lady with GSOH to share fun, friendship and maybe more.*'

'That sounds like Pavel, the Polish guy at the university.'

'That's exactly what I was thinking.'

I knew that Lindi had her eye on him even though she had only been introduced to him once.

'Should I call?'

'Go for it. It's probably safer if you meet someone you actually know.'

'But what if it's not him?' Lindi asked.

'Well then you go out on a date with him anyway, right?'

'Will you come with me in case it's a disaster—maybe stand on the other side of the street and I'll give you the nod if it's OK?'

'But what if it's not OK,' I asked.

'Just rush in and pull me away.'

I agreed and Lindi decided to reply to the ad.

'What should I put in my description that will really get his attention and make him want to meet me?' Lindi asked, pen poised over a piece of paper.

'Stunning blue-eyed redhead, measurements 38-28-38, with profound interest in rocket science and stand-up comedy.' I laughed. 'That should certainly spark his interest.'

'No, I can't lie. I've got to be honest.' Lindi looked thoughtful.

She sent in her description and details to the PO box indicated in the ad. Now it was just wait and see.

A week later I got an excited phone call from Lindi. 'Guess what? The guy from the ad sent me a letter. He wants to meet me!'

They were going to meet in the square in front of the Joan of Arc church. I was to sit on a bench, reading, waiting for the signal.

***

I was just leaving my room to go meet Lindi when Sophie knocked brusquely on my door. I thought she must be going out somewhere as she was wearing a smart suit that I had never seen her in before and she smelled strongly of Chanel No.5.

'I want to say you that we will to having guests tonight. The priest and the other members of our church group will to come for a little soirée.'

I thought she was going to ask if I wanted to join them, and I was glad that I already had plans to go out.

'I just want to say you to staying in your room while our guests are here. I will give you something to eat before they arrive.'

I felt like grimacing. I really wished she wouldn't attempt to massacre the English language. 'I'm going out anyway, so you don't have to worry about me getting in the way.'

'Oh—that works perfectly then,' Sophie smiled her thin-lipped, tight smile that made it look like her face would crack.

Thankfully she reverted back to French as she found it easier for more complicated communication. 'By the way, this arrived for you today. A letter from the hospital in Paris? I hope everything is OK.'

I took the letter from her and looked at the logo on the envelope. It was from the hospital where I got the prescription for the morning after pill.

I had to think quickly. 'Oh it must be the bill for the medical certificate that we were all required to get when we arrived in Paris, before starting university.'

Sophie stood over me in the doorway, waiting for me to open it. I put the letter in my bag and looked at my watch. 'I'm late, I better get going,' I said grabbing my jacket and shutting the bedroom door behind me. '*Bonsoir.*'

Lindi was ready and waiting. She was all dressed up in a mini skirt and suede boots, her hair all spiked and her face made up. I was surprised to see Gabriela there too.

'Hey Gabby, are you coming along to spy on Lindi's date too?' I asked.

'I just needed to get away from my host family,' she replied.

'You and me both! How's psycho Paul?'

'He is exactly why I need to get out of there. The other day I looked out the window and saw Paul take a pair of my underwear off the washing line and put them in his pocket.'

'He didn't! What a pervert!' Lindi gasped.

'Ewww. That's creepy,' I said, wrinkling my nose disgustedly.

Lindi nodded. 'So I told Gabby about what we were doing. I thought she could keep you company in case the date does go well.' Lindi winked one blue eye.

'Shall we get the bus into the center?' Gabriela asked.

'No—I've got a better idea.' I suggested. 'I hitchhiked the other day and it's cool. And plus, I don't have any money for the bus.'

'Hitchhike! Are you sure? We might get picked up by a weirdo,' Gabriela said.

'Trust me.' I confidently walked along the road with my thumb out. It wasn't long before a small Renault hatchback stopped. Lindi hesitantly got in the front seat. The man smiled amiably at her. He looked like a respectable, middle-aged man with his tidy grey hair and neat moustache.

'I'm driving into the center, where can I drop you girls?' the man asked cheerfully.

'Are you going past the Joan of Arc church?' I asked.

'Yes I am. I can leave you there if you like. What is your accent? English? Irish?'

'American,' I responded.

'Ohhhh. American. I am sorry for you,' he said, his tone dropping, as if he were offering deepest condolences.

'Why?' Gabriela asked chirpily.

'Well, your president, for one, your army for another…'

'But she's in the army,' I said, patting Lindi on the shoulder from the back seat.

She turned abruptly and shot me an accusing glare.

'But you are too pretty to be in the army,' the man said, glancing at Lindi.

Lindi's cheeks flushed red and she stared at her hands in her lap.

'I only joined because they paid for me to go to university. I couldn't have afforded it otherwise,' she mumbled.

'Oh yes. I understand that is what they do. They recruit people from poor backgrounds with promises of a better life.' He tut-tutted and shook his head. 'I suppose you have come to take advantage of the superior education in France?'

'Yes, we're studying French here,' Gabriela offered.

'Well, you have come to the right place. Normandy is by far the best region in France. Visitors from all over the world come here. I am very proud of it.'

I raised my eyebrows and exchanged a glance with Gabriela behind the driver's back.

We sat and listened to the driver extolling the fabulous virtues of Normandy until we saw the boat-like roof of the church looming.

'Just here is fine, please, Monsieur,' Lindi said.

When we got out of the car Lindi turned toward me confrontationally. 'Hey, why did you have to tell him I was in the army?'

'Well, because it's the truth—you are in the army,' I said.

'I really wish you wouldn't volunteer that information anymore. It's not helpful.'

'Sorry,' I said, 'I won't do that again. Then I noticed a guy in his late 20s hanging around in the square, looking at his watch and scanning the area expectantly. I grabbed Lindi and Gabriela by their arms and pulled them around the corner of a building. 'Hey, I think that's your date, Lindi,' I said pointing out the man in the square. He was of medium height, with closely cut dark hair, dark stubble on his chin and a slightly chubby physique.

We all stared curiously.

'That's not Pavel,' Lindi said, disappointed.

'But he doesn't look too bad,' Gabriela said.

'You don't think he looks a bit out of shape?' Lindi said doubtfully.

'Maybe he's great in bed. Looks aren't everything,' I said, thinking of Bruno.

Lindi nodded. 'OK. I'll go ahead with it. Do I look OK?'

'You look great. We'll wait here until you can get a close-up and an idea of whether or not he's a weirdo.'

'If I need you to rescue me I'll scratch my nose,' Lindi said.

'Good luck,' Gabriela said, squeezing Lindi's arm.

Lindi smoothed her skirt and walked into the square.

We peered around the corner and watched as she approached the man. They both smiled and shyly shook hands. He then pointed across the street to a café. As they walked toward the café, Lindi looked back at us and gave us the thumbs up behind her date's back.

'I'm not too sure about Lindi's date. Let's go for a coffee too,' Gabriela suggested.

We went into the café and saw that they were seated near the window. We chose a table near the bar, a respectable distance away. Lindi didn't even notice us come in as her back was to the door and she seemed very interested in what her date was telling her. She was nodding her head and laughing. They were making good eye contact and I thought it looked like they were both having a nice time. A waiter brought over a tray with a couple of cups of coffee, a glass of pastis for the date and a couple of delicious-looking pastries.

'Wow, let's hope he's paying. They're really splashing out. I think that's a good sign,' I said.

'I'm keeping my eye on him,' Gabriela said, unimpressed. 'There's just something about him that makes me suspicious.'

'So what's happening with Paul?' I asked her.

'It's getting worse. I don't know what to do. I've had to plug up the keyhole in my door because I'm convinced he's been peeking through it. Sometimes I'm sure he's listening at my door. When I'm on the phone with Jamie, I sometimes hear the phone click and think he's listening in on the extension in the study.'

'It sounds serious. You should speak to Richard—tell him you're feeling uncomfortable there.'

'I'm just so embarrassed about it. I can't tell anyone but you and Lindi. I haven't even told Jamie. I mean, I think Paul is harmless—I feel sorry for him.'

'Geezus Gabriela, Paul's a psychopath. There's something not right with that boy. I'd be double-locking my door if I were you.'

I glanced back across the room and suddenly noticed Lindi's date get up from the table and go out the door of the café.

'Hmmm. I wonder what's going on there,' I alerted Gabriela.

'Where's he going?' Gabriela said.

Lindi just sat there patiently nibbling her pastry and sipping coffee. She didn't seem to be bothered. After about 20 minutes, she glanced at her watch and began peering out the window.

'Do you think we should go over to Lindi's table?' I asked.

'Yes, I think we need to find out what's going on,' Gabriela said, standing up.

'I didn't know you two followed me in here,' Lindi said, surprised.

'How's the date?'

'Well it seemed to be going OK. His name is Andre and he is studying civil engineering.'

'Where did he go?' I asked.

'He said he had to go to the ATM and get some money out.'

'There's an ATM right across the street,' Gabriela pointed out.

'He's been gone 20 minutes,' I said. 'I don't think he's coming back.'

There was a moment of silence. Lindi's cheeks reddened, making her blue eyes blaze.

'He hasn't paid for any of this!' she said, indicating the half-drunk coffee and pastis and half-eaten pastry.

'What a prick,' I said, shaking my head. 'Let's go after him and make him pay for what he ordered.'

'No, why don't you two just join me and eat up these pastries. They're delicious,' Lindi said.

Gabriela and I sat down and started digging into the leftover pastries, and I finished off the pastis. Then we all chipped in to pay for absent Andre's part of the bill.

The end of a year

I got up early and headed out toward the bus with my suitcase. It was the start of the winter break and my plans were as follows: Italy for Christmas with Bruno and his family, Paris for New Year with Toby.

It was raining and my bags were heavy, but the DeClermonts hadn't offered to help me. In fact, they barely looked up as I shut the door behind me. I struggled with the bag and had to stop every few minutes. I was beginning to look like a drowned rat and was worried about getting to the train station on time to meet Bruno and catch our train.

Then a man pulled his car up alongside me and asked if I needed any help. I felt so relieved. The man got out of the car to help me with my bag. There was a flicker of recognition. I couldn't place his face. Then I realized that it was the same man who had picked Bruno and I up when we were hitchhiking to Paris—the guy with the bondage magazines under his seat.

I hesitated a moment, but when I looked at my watch I realized that if I was to make the train, I had to accept this lift.

'Ah—I recognize you. I gave you and the Italian photographer a ride into Paris once,' he said as he opened the rear door and swung my luggage onto the back seat.

I had a quick glance to see if there were any magazines in the car but didn't notice any.

'That's right, I remember,' I said getting into the passenger seat. 'I'm sorry, but I'm really late. Would you mind dropping me at the train station?'

'Of course. Where are you going? Not back to the United States I hope.'

'I'm going to Verona.' I didn't really want to give him any more information than necessary or engage in conversation.

'I'm glad I bumped into you again. I'm making a film and I

thought maybe you and the Italian and some of your American friends might like to take part to earn some money. I was a student once and know how tight cash can be. If you give me your number, we can get together and discuss it.'

I had absolutely no intention of giving that sleazebag my phone number or seeing him ever again. I was suddenly aware of how short my leather miniskirt was and I tried to yank it down over my thighs. This only served to draw his attention to my fidgeting legs. 'What is the film about?' I asked in order to try to distract him.

'Foreign students,' he said glancing sideways at me and winking.

I was grateful when I saw the train station looming ahead. 'Thanks for the ride. I can get off here,' I said, eager to cut the conversation short.

He pulled up in front of the station. I opened the car door to get out but he put his hand on my leg and leaned across my lap to open the glove compartment. 'Wait. Take this.' It was a business card, which read *Jean-Sebastien Dufresne—Réalisateur Independent.* 'Give me a call sometime.'

I jumped out of the car impatiently. Jean-Sebastien helped me with my case. 'I hope to see you soon,' he said.

'Must go,' I said dashing away without a backwards glance.

Bruno wasn't anywhere in sight. I waited exactly where we had agreed and I kept looking nervously at my watch. The train was about to leave. Then I saw Bruno rushing through the crowd. He looked just as he had the first day I met him—like he'd been blown in by a gust of wind. His hair was a mess and his shirt was buttoned up wrong. He had a small, frayed duffel bag that could have been a relic from the First World War. I waved at him and pointed at my watch.

'Hurry up!' I shouted. 'The train's going to leave without us.'

We ran through the station, right past the barrier and across the platform to catch the TGV to Lausanne. We leapt onto the train with a fraction of a second to spare just as it was about to move off. We had to pick up an Italian train in Lausanne and then change again in Milan to get to our final destination, Verona.

We found our seats in a private compartment and settled in.

'It's a long journey,' Bruno said. 'I brought some sleeping pills.' He held two capsules in his palm. 'Take one,' he said. 'I also got us some of this for when we arrive,' he said, holding up a Ziploc sandwich bag that was printed with a green marijuana leaf. I saw a caramel-sized lump of hash inside it.

I picked up a pill and we each necked one with a gulp of water. Bruno put his arm around me and I drowsily watched the French countryside fly past until I could no longer keep my eyes open.

I was abruptly awoken by a firm shake. I had trouble opening my eyes and my vision was blurred. I could make out a tall, blond, uniformed guard.

'Passports, please!' he barked. We must have already arrived at the Swiss border. As Bruno dozily rummaged through his pockets looking for his passport, a hashish pipe fell out, clattering to the floor.

The guard picked it up and inspected it with steely blue eyes.

'OK sir, come with me,' the guard said, fixing Bruno with his penetrating stare.

Bruno staggered to his feet, blearily rubbing his eyes and swaying.

I groggily got to my feet as well, feeling the sleepiness dissipate abruptly as the adrenaline kicked in.

'Take your bags with you and exit the train,' the guard commanded Bruno.

Are you travelling together?' he addressed me.

I nodded, gulping back my fear.

'You too, then,' he said.

My legs were quivering and my palms sweating as I carefully hauled my case out of the train. I remembered the little Ziploc sandwich bag that Bruno had shown me earlier, and I started to imagine what the inside of a Swiss prison might look like.

The guard led us to a room in the train station that had a big metal table in the middle and a rickety wooden desk. First, he studied our passports.

'Hmpf. Italian, eh?' he said, narrowing his eyes at Bruno.

Then he looked at my passport.

'You are American?'

I nodded again.

'Why are you with this crazy Italian boy?' the guard said, shaking his head.

'Please open your bags,' he commanded us.

We placed our bags on the table in the middle of the room. A female guard appeared and started to go through the contents of my bag. I had a baguette that I had brought to snack on, and she broke it to bits. She took out my toothpaste and squeezed out the entire contents of the tube. Then she asked me to empty my pockets and she patted me down.

I noticed that the male guard had rifled through Bruno's duffel bag. When he asked Bruno to empty his pockets, I held my breath. I watched, waiting for the bag of hash to be produced for all to see.

But Bruno threw down on the table a packet of rolling papers, a lighter, some loose change … and an empty Ziploc bag.

The guard investigated the objects, opened up the little Ziploc bag with the marijuana leaf printed on it, sniffed it and dropped it on the table. Bruno held his hands up as the guard patted him down.

I was surprised when the guard said, 'OK, you are free to go. But I am confiscating this,' he said, holding up the hash pipe. Then he wagged his finger at me. 'You should think twice about what you're doing with him, young lady.'

We sheepishly slunk back to the train platform, dragging our bags behind us.

'Geez, Bruno, how the *hell* did you manage to get out of that one?' I asked him, incredulously.

'Ha, ha, yes, they are easy to fool with a bit of sleight of hand,' Bruno chuckled. 'I just had the hash right here.' He made to pull it out of my ear and he held it out for me to see.

'Put that away! Are you nuts?' I hissed. 'No really, where was it?'

'It was all along in my mouth,' he grinned. 'I was trying not to swallow it, but if they asked me to open my mouth I would have had a most wonderful hash trip.'

Our train had long gone and we had to wait for the next one to Italy. It was late. Bruno didn't seem surprised by this at all. 'It is the Italian way,' he explained breezily.

As a result of the delay at the Swiss border and the late train, we arrived three hours late in Verona. It was already getting dark by then and no one was there to pick us up. Bruno decided that we should get a bus. While we were at the bus stop a young couple came up to us, attempting to ask directions in Italian. The guy had a vaguely Italian look about him but he spoke Italian with a very broad Anglo accent. The girl, with blond hair and blue eyes and sturdy build, looked very northern European.

'*Scusi, como andare in centro citta?*' he asked. Bruno realized right away that they weren't Italian and spoke to them in English, to their relief. The guy, Vinnie, was English of Italian descent, and the girl, Marietta, was from Berlin. Bruno told them to follow us as we were going into the center of Verona. They seemed like a really cool couple and Bruno suggested that we should meet up again later and go out for some drinks.

When the bus dropped us off in the city center, my breath was taken away. We had emerged out on a cobbled square, flanked by a beautiful and ancient Roman ruin, with columns that loomed up out of the sidewalk, lit by spotlights. Bruno knew someone who ran a cheap hotel, so we all made our way there through the dimly lit narrow cobbled streets, lugging our baggage; our voices and laughter tripping off the stone walls and echoing through the narrow passages. Paris had some of the oldest buildings I thought I had ever seen, but here the buildings looked absolutely ancient, with old stonework emerging from beneath layers of peeling paint, half crumbled walls and fading frescoes. Even the whiff of the ancient sewers told of a time when Romans ruled in this part of the world.

A dark figure emerged from the shadows of an adjoining street. When he saw us he started shouting something in Italian, 'Scemo!'

Bruno dropped his bags and practically jumped on top of the guy. They hugged and shouted, shaking hands and slapping each other on the back. 'This is Matteo, my best friend,' Bruno told us.

Matteo looked us all up and down and then kissed Marietta and I on both cheeks and shook Vinnie's hand. He was the complete opposite of Bruno in appearance. He had dark, hair, cut neatly and parted on the side. He wore a white collared shirt, with a light pink sweater tied by the arms round his neck, casual chinos and leather boat shoes—an archetypal preppy. He joined our entourage and we took the Australian and German to their hotel and waited while they settled in.

Matteo led us to a gleaming black Mercedes. He held up the keys and grinned. 'My parents have let me use their car tonight.' He opened the doors for us and we all piled in for a ride through Verona. We stopped at a pizzeria and ordered some beers and pizza. I finally learned what a true Italian pizza is like—nothing like the rubbery, cardboard-tasting pizza from McGowan's Pizza back home. It was a sensation of flavors and textures that my novice mouth had trouble placing. The tomato was so fresh and succulent, with real, fresh basil leaves, and extra virgin olive oil. I was more used to canned tomato puree, dried basil flakes and Mazola corn oil. I had never before experienced the pleasure of these real, fresh ingredients. That decided it—I was moving to Italy!

Matteo's parents had left a few bottles of champagne in the trunk of the car, so after dinner we decided to take them up to the big castle that perched on top of the cliff overlooking the river that ran through the city. It was another beautiful old ruin lit up by colored spotlights. Bruno and Matteo led us up to a bridge that had once served as access to the fortress and we climbed up to the top of the ramparts and gazed down at the river flowing slowly and tranquilly below us, reflecting the light from the streetlamps, the moon and the stars. Bruno popped open the first bottle of champagne and passed it around. With the first sip I was flooded with euphoria—I was bursting with happiness and contentment—to be in such a beautiful spot, with such beautiful people.

'What do you think of my city?' Bruno asked.

'Beautiful,' I replied, taking another sip from the champagne bottle and passing it along.

'So romantic,' Marietta giggled, squeezing Vinnie's hand.

Vinnie grinned and raised the bottle I had just passed him. 'To Verona, and to good company,' he said.

It was getting late and we had drunk all the champagne, so we parted ways with Vinnie and Marietta agreeing to meet up again the next day. Matteo drove us to Bruno's mother's apartment, where we were going to be staying while we were in Verona. The apartment was on the outskirts of Verona and I was disappointed to see that it wasn't in an old building. It was a postmodern, square apartment block with lots of polished wood and marble in the lobby.

It was 2am by the time we arrived but, surprisingly, Bruno's mother was still up and overjoyed to greet us. Matteo came in with us and while Bruno's mother offered us drinks and food, she talked non-stop. She was a small, chirpy woman with a bouffant of blond hair tied in a bow. She didn't speak English, but she was a schoolteacher and she taught French, so we were able to communicate that way.

Matteo got up to go. He kissed me on both cheeks, and checked me out, sweeping his eyes up and down my body like a customer in a butcher shop hungrily assessing a cut of meat. Then he turned and gave Bruno a hearty congratulatory pat on the back.

Bruno's mother had made up a bed for us. I was surprised that we were staying in the same room and sleeping in the same bed. My parents never would have let me sleep with a boyfriend under their roof. I was also surprised by this because I had always assumed that the Italians were very religious and didn't condone sex out of wedlock.

Bruno's mother grabbed both of my hands as I stood at the threshold of the bedroom. 'I want to welcome my son's fiancée to my home,' she said, beaming. 'The family was so worried that Brunetto would never settle down and find the right girl.'

I flashed Bruno a quizzical look. He smiled and patted his mother's shoulder and said something in Italian. '*Buona notte, Mama,*' he bent over to give his mother a peck on the cheek. She gave Bruno a wink and shut the door behind her.

'Why did she call me your fiancée?' I asked.

'It's her imagination running wild,' Bruno said. 'It is probably best just to play along.'

Verona

The next morning, I was awoken by a huge pink cat kneading my stomach through the duvet. Bruno must have already got up. I rose to go to the bathroom and the cat followed. The bathroom was long and cavernous with marble walls and flooring, and a high, echoing ceiling. The cat sat expectantly in the bidet, staring at me. There was a whirlpool bath in the middle of the room, which was full to the brim with luxurious bubbles.

There was a knock on the bathroom door. 'It's me, let me in,' Bruno said. I opened the door and he came in, with a towel wrapped around his waist. 'Ah—I see you have met Fred the cat,' he said. He turned on the water in the bidet and the cat began to lap at the trickle coming from the tap.

'Mama has gone out shopping, so I have run us a bath,' he said, letting the towel drop from his waist.

'How long is your mother out?' I said, uncertainly. I would never consider having a bath with a boyfriend at my parents' house. Even if they were out, I'd be worried they would come home and catch us in some act of debauchery.

Bruno didn't seem at all concerned. He eased himself in to the bath and turned on the whirlpool. I followed his lead and lowered myself into the hot bubbles. I sank back and Bruno wrapped his arms round me. The feeling of contentment that I had experienced the previous night returned. It was strange—I could not remember a time before arriving in Italy when I had actually felt this happy. I began thinking that maybe the fiancée idea wasn't so far-fetched after all. I could do this whole Italian lifestyle thing—eating pizza, drinking wine, lounging in baths with Italian men in marble bathrooms.

Bruno and I actually did more fooling around in the bath than relaxing. We managed to flood the entire bathroom floor and the whirlpool had frothed the bubble bath up into enormous suds that splashed over the sides of the bath and slid across the floor. As we exited the bathroom, rosy-cheeked and damp-haired, we crossed paths in the foyer with Bruno's mother who was just coming back from shopping. She laughed when she saw the flood of soapsuds in the bathroom and the cat bounding out across the foyer, trailing wet paw prints across the floor. 'Did you have fun?' she asked me in French, smiling. I just smiled awkwardly and ducked into the bedroom.

'Your mother seems very liberal,' I said to Bruno, pulling my clothes on, trying to regain an air of respectability.

'I am her only son and she has not seen me for a while. She indulges me whatever I like,' he said shrugging and laughing.

I thought about that for a moment. So what did that make me? Did she only like me because I pleased her precious son? Was I merely his plaything in her eyes? Even though I had just emerged from the bathroom, I suddenly felt dirty.

After a hearty pasta lunch, Bruno took me walking around Verona. It was a magical sort of place. The buildings were so old and majestic, and the sidewalks were paved with pink marble. I just loved everything about it, and I grabbed Bruno's hand in gratitude for bringing me to such a beautiful place. Seeing the ancient ruins rising up on the side of a mountain like ghostly remains left me speechless. He showed me fortresses, bridges, churches, the arena with its giant sculpture of a shooting star, quiet old streets, Juliette's house, where Romeo would have stood below the balcony, pouring his heart out to his beloved. 'Welcome to the city of love,' Bruno said, grinning proudly.

That evening we met up again with Vinnie and Marietta, and Bruno took us on the rounds of several wine tasting houses. We drank and smoked, told jokes and laughed—just had a great time in general. We ended up at a pizzeria. Matteo and some of his friends were there. After stuffing ourselves with pizza and several bottles of wine, Matteo announced that we should all go back to his house, as his parents were away on vacation and his brother was having a party.

We made our way there on foot. To my astonishment the house was actually a grand old palazzo that sat alongside the castle walls. Its crumbling ancient exterior belied what lay inside. Matteo rang a bell and an Indian servant who was dressed in a white shirt and bow tie opened the huge wooden front door. The foyer rose up around me, all pink and white marble, polished to perfection. In the middle of the room a marble statue stood on a plinth, and in front of us, a marble staircase spiraled upwards. The servant took our coats and Matteo led us upstairs. Chattering voices and dance beats filtered down and reverberated off the marble.

'This is my wing,' Matteo said, taking us down a corridor and opening a door into a room with a large leather sofa and a pool table. The servant brought in some glasses of champagne. We toasted to the good life. My head was already spinning from all the wine I had drunk earlier.

'Let's go to my brother's wing, where the party is,' Matteo said, gesturing us to follow. We trailed behind him along a long corridor flanked by family portraits. The voices and the music grew louder. He opened the door and we all squeezed in. It was hard to move as the room was wall to wall people, all young, all beautiful, decked out in Gucci, Armani, and Dolce & Gabbana. I could feel everyone's eyes on me as we entered the room. I glanced at my Doc Martens and torn fishnet tights and felt like a tramp amongst the glitterati—but then I looked at Bruno who was wearing torn jeans and a faded t-shirt and didn't feel so bad.

A girl with coiffed blond hair and two-inch-long glossy red fingernails, who I later found out was Matteo's girlfriend, shoved a mirror under my nose. It held a few neat lines of white powder and a rolled up lira. I nodded, smiled and snorted.

Bruno went next. 'Go ask my friend Marco over there if he wants a line.' Bruno said to me, pointing to a guy wearing a leather jacket.

'Does Marco speak English?' I asked.

'No—but just say *scopiamo*.'

I was eager to start learning Italian, so I went away with my new knowledge and approached Bruno, feeling a rush of confidence from the coke. I put out my hand and said, '*Sono Siobhan, la amica di Bruno. Scopiamo?*'

Marco's jaw dropped and he looked very uncomfortable. He looked around the area, as if checking to see if anyone else had heard. He waved his hand and shook his head saying '*No, no, no.*'

I shrugged and strode back to Bruno. 'I don't think he's interested. In fact, judging from his reaction, I'd say he doesn't approve of drugs.'

Bruno laughed heartily. 'That is good,' he said, 'because what I told you to say is an expression in the dialect of Verona. It means "let's fuck"'.

'What?' I shouted in disbelief, the humiliation pouring over me like a bucket of ice water. I looked over at Marco, who made eye contact and then quickly looked away. I felt sick. I shoved Bruno out of the way and pushed through the crowd. I bumped into

Matteo as I stormed down the corridor looking for the bathroom.

'Are you lost?' Matteo asked.

'I'm looking for the bathroom.'

'Follow me,' he said. He opened the door for me and then followed me in, closing the door behind him.

'What are you doing?' I asked.

Did you have a little tiff with Bruno?' Matteo asked.

'I need to use the toilet,' I snapped.

'Go right ahead,' Matteo said, grinning.

'In private!' I retorted, angrily.

Matteo stood with his back against the door and he slowly unzipped his fly. 'I've heard American girls are good at blow jobs,' he said, smiling and pointing at his crotch.

I scrunched up my face. 'If you come near me I'll kick you so hard that you'll never be able to use that thing again,' I snarled.

'OK, OK. I didn't think you'd be so prudish, the way you look— all punk and sexy.' He zipped up his pants and left. I sat down on the edge of the bath shaking with anger and humiliation. What was wrong with these guys? What kind of total misogynistic bastards had I got myself mixed up with?

When I regained my composure, I stormed out to go give Bruno a piece of my mind. 'There she is,' Bruno said. He looked at the stormy expression on my face. 'Baby—it was only a joke,' he laughed and put his arm around me. 'It is the Italian sense of humor.'

He introduced me to some other friends. I didn't want to appear grouchy and sullen in front of these strangers so I put a smile on my face. There was Jacopo, who drew cartoons for Italian Walt Disney, and Khaled, the skinhead son of Syrian refugees. When Bruno and I had a second to chat alone, I drew him away and told him what had happened in the bathroom with Matteo.

Bruno chuckled. 'Oh Matteo—he was just testing you.'

'Testing me? Testing what? How good I am at giving blow jobs?' I asked incredulously. I couldn't believe that Bruno could so easily dismiss his friend's disgusting action.

'He is my best friend. He just wants to make sure that you are loyal to me.'

I shook my head in disbelief. I needed to get my head around the Italian male psyche. 'I don't understand you guys,' I said, fiercely.

'I'm sorry, Primavera, don't be upset. It's a beautiful night. The moon is full Let's go out for a walk,' Bruno said soothingly.

We left the party and went for a walk up to the Roman ruins on the hill behind Matteo's family's palazzo. We climbed up the side of the hill until we found a secluded spot to get romantic. It was cold, but Bruno was persistent and I was too wasted to care. We lay holding each other, amid the ruins, with the ancient city of Verona laid out like a carpet below us, feeling the brisk winter air freezing on our skin. Surrounded by Romanesque arches and columns and half crumbling walls with windows framing a river view, I was once again filled with awe and appreciation. 'Am I forgiven yet?' Bruno asked.

He had indeed just made up for humiliating me in front of his friends earlier. He couldn't have chosen a more breathtakingly romantic spot.

I thought of Toby's clapped out Chevrolet, with the torn vinyl seats. Toby would often park up in a dead end or in a parking lot behind a shopping mall and pull his smooth moves on me. I shuddered at the thought of Toby and his redneck car.

Venice

We woke up early Sunday morning to go to Venice. Bruno's mother had already been up for a few hours and had packed us a picnic. Matteo was going to drive us as he had some business to attend to there. He was late picking us up in his Mercedes and drove like a madman through Verona to pick up Vinnie and Marietta, who were coming with us to Venice as well.

Matteo sped along the autostrada trying to make up for lost time, while we all held on for dear life, hoping that we'd actually live to see Venice. We arrived at a mainland parking lot, where Matteo left the car. He opened up the trunk and pulled out a couple of bottles of champagne. 'You need champagne to celebrate your first visit to Venice, he said, handing me the two bottles.

The only way to get to the city from the mainland was either by train, which crossed over the sea via a causeway, or the vaporetto, a kind of ferry bus. We opted for the boat, even though it was more expensive. As we embarked, I could see the city looming out of the shimmering green sea. Hundreds of bell towers rose above red-tiled roofs. The slap of the thudding water on the sides of the vaporetto quickened and then slowed again as we approached.

The moment we stepped off the boat I had a feeling of intrigue. The place oozed mystery, holding millions of secrets hidden safely amongst its solemn canals. I had never experienced a city with no cars and I found the lack of traffic noise to be both powerful and disorienting. I breathed in the unique smell, a mixture of stagnant sea, mud and humans. We followed the other people into the heart of the city, losing Vinnie and Marietta along the way. Every corner we turned, there was another canal. I marveled that the houses were built right in the water.

'Do people really live here?' I asked Bruno, disbelieving that it wasn't just a theme park for tourists, like something from Disney World.

'Si, Primavera, people really live here.'

'But how do they get around without any cars?'

'They use the water taxi, of course!' Bruno said. 'Some people have their own boats as that's the only way they can get into their houses. There are police boats, fire engine boats, even garbage boats.'

I studied the Gothic and Renaissance palazzos lining the canal—many of them had steps to their entrances coming straight up from the lapping water. People moored their boats right outside their front door. I was dumbfounded that the whole city was actually built in the sea.

We wandered along the tiny walkways, losing ourselves in the sound of pattering feet resonating off the walls along the narrow lanes. The 'streets' were laid out like a maze—an intricate network that takes you deeper and deeper into the city's psyche—and it was easy to become disoriented. We finally saw a sign pointing to San Marco square and managed to find our way there.

The square was teeming with people and crawling with pigeons—hundreds of them like ants on a piece of candy. The ground almost looked alive with the writhing mass of feathers and beaks. My phobia of birds made me stop in my tracks, fearful that they might fly at me. Bruno ran over to a street vendor and bought a bag of something, which he then handed to me. Before I could even figure out that it was a bag of pigeon feed, the filthy birds were flapping at me from every direction, landing on my shoulders, my head and my arms. 'Get them off me!' I shrieked, flailing my arms.

Bruno was killing himself laughing, having a grand old time snapping pictures of me freaking out and swatting birds off my head, although I did not see the funny side.

We waited around for a bit after the bird invasion had subsided, and I recovered my composure. We were hoping to run into Vinnie and Marietta again, thinking that the main square might be a likely place to find them, but they weren't there. We figured that we had probably seen the last of them—it's a shame, I thought, but that's how it is when you're travelling—easy come easy go.

'Where should we go next?' I asked Bruno.

'I treat you to a gondola ride,' he said. He went over to a gondolier on the Grand Canal and started negotiating. The discussion was becoming heated. From what I could gather, the gondolier had no intention of lowering his price and found Bruno's offer to be quite amusing. An Italian couple, bedecked in Gucci, who were waiting behind us started huffing impatiently.

Finally, they pushed past us and got into the gondola. Bruno stood frustrated, yelling various Italian obscenities at the gondolier.

'Forget it,' I said. 'Let's just drink this instead,' and I held up one of the bottles of champagne. We decided to wander around, drinking out of the bottle, impersonating the rich people who had gotten on the gondola instead of us. The champagne was beginning to go to our heads and we stumbled about laughing.

We found a quiet spot to stop and rest. It was a magical little corner, empty of people and it was next to a little iron bridge spanning a canal, with a view of the Adriatic Sea on one side and lots of little canal bridges on the other. There was a small courtyard, which was named something like 'the field behind the Pieta', when literally translated into English. There, hidden in a narrow alleyway, carved right in the stone wall, was a miniature version of the Pieta, in a niche in the wall, the white marble contrasting with the yellow brick. It was the most elaborate street sign I had ever seen in my life.

Bruno suddenly smashed the empty champagne bottle. 'What are you doing?' I asked, looking around nervously. 'I make a "*collo*",' Bruno explained, 'an Italian invention.' Bruno stuffed the broken bottle neck with the foil from a pack of cigarettes and some crumbled up hash. We took turns puffing on it. The hash was strong and I felt the acrid smoke burning my lungs as I inhaled. I coughed and Bruno laughed at me. 'Your first "*collo*" is always the hardest,' he said. Suddenly I felt like I was taking off over the church towers—flying above San Marco Square and the Grand Canal and back in amongst the narrow alleyways and canals of Venice. As we walked along, eyeless carnival masks leered and stared at me from the shop windows. The water whispered to me as it slid under the bridge beneath our feet. We stood looking down at our wavy reflections in the water. I glanced up at Bruno and smiled. 'It's such a mystical place,' I said, in awe. He responded by kissing me—the same forceful and persistent kiss that he had planted on me that first night, when I was scared shitless up in the rickety old Ferris wheel at the fair in Rouen. I was still impressed that someone as un-cool and goofy looking as Bruno could kiss like that.

After wandering around a bit, we started to get the munchies, so we sat down in another small square and ate the sandwiches that Bruno's mother had made for us, and Bruno popped the other bottle of champagne. The cork flew halfway across the square and the foam sprayed out wildly, like life trying to forcefully free itself from inside the body of the bottle.

It was beginning to get dark and cold, so we decided that it was time to head toward the train station, becoming temporarily lost again in the maze of little streets. Once inside the train station Bruno practically made me die laughing with his ridiculous antics. He went into the tourist information office, nonchalantly browsing the brochures and maps. The woman behind the desk asked in Italian, 'Can I help you, sir?'

Bruno drawled in what he believed to be an American accent, 'Yeah! Can you tell me where I can find a McDonald's around here?'

I was laughing so hard that I was crying and had to sneak out the door because the woman was looking at me strangely. The poor thing must have thought we were on drugs!

We got on the train, found a private compartment, drew the curtains and the shades, extended the seats, turned out the lights and made love while the train slipped through the darkness. Bruno, or maybe Venice, had put a spell on me.

chr**i**stmas **E**ve

The next day was Christmas Eve. We were going to Bruno's friend Giulia's house, which was near Lake Garda, to collect moss for the nativity later on in Verona. Bruno's mother was using the car and it was too cold for the Vespa so we decided to hitchhike. Bruno used me as a decoy to lure in the drivers. I stood on the side of a deserted road with my thumb out, while Bruno hid in a phone booth, pretending to make a call. The first car that came along stopped. Bruno quickly ran out of the phone booth and jumped in the front, and I climbed into the back. The driver asked us a few questions and Bruno answered, translating for me. Realizing that I was foreign and didn't speak Italian, he said to Bruno, 'You have caught yourself a good prey.'

Bruno translated this for me and I glared at the back of the man's head. Typical Italian chauvinist!

The sexist pig dropped us off near Giulia's house and we walked the rest of the way up a steep, winding dirt track to her cottage. I looked behind me at the vista. There was a large blue lake, fringed by mountainside dotted with villages.

Giulia turned out to be small, with close cropped black hair and brown eyes that twinkled from behind little round spectacles. She wiped her hand on her paint-splattered overalls and extended it warmly. 'Lovely to meet you,' she said before embracing Bruno heartily.

Giulia's cottage was full of oil paintings of landscapes, lakes and mountains, as well as nudes—beautiful, voluptuous women of all shapes, sizes and colors.

'You still prefer the ladies, do you?' Bruno asked. 'Every time I say I will take my clothes off for you to paint me and you always say no. I don't understand lesbians,' Bruno joked.

'You will never change, Brunetto,' Giulia laughed.

'Wow, these are amazing,' I marveled, admiring the paintings. 'You're so talented.'

Giulia smiled modestly, 'Thanks,' she said. 'Would you like some coffee and grappa to take the chill off?'

'Your English is so good. You even speak with a bit of a British accent,' I said, surprised at her fluency.

'Well, I used to live in Brighton, England, for a bit. But you tell me about yourself.' She was very interested in finding out about me—where I was from, where I was living, what I liked reading—who was my favorite artist. She asked me how I met Bruno, and how I was managing to put up with him. 'Good luck,' she said, 'he's a handful.'

We all went outside and smoked a joint together, strolling along the railway bridge that spanned the river that ran by Giulia's cottage. We sauntered along, breathing in the winter air, tinged with the scent of wet leaves and moss—just what we'd come looking for—to place in the crib for the arrival of the baby Jesus. It was everywhere, growing on rocks and trees. We collected a shopping bagful to place in the manger when we returned to Verona.

As we headed back to the cottage, Giulia touched my arm. 'Would you mind posing for me?' she gently asked. 'I'd like to sketch you before you go.'

Feeling giddy with the grappa, the weed and Christmas, I obliged Giulia by taking my clothes off and lounging on the sheepskin next to the fireplace. 'I hope you don't mind me borrowing your girlfriend,' Giulia said to Bruno while she quickly sketched using a piece of charcoal.

'Now why would I mind?' Bruno said, clearly enjoying himself, focusing his camera on the scene. We all laughed and smoked and had a wonderful, relaxing time while Giulia fervently drew, the charcoal scratching briskly around the paper.

When Giulia showed me the finished picture, I was pleased to see that she made my scrawny body look quite mysterious and interesting. 'You should come again and I can do a proper painting sometime,' she said. She pinned it to the wall amongst all the other nudes.

We said our farewells and rushed out to the main road to hitch a ride back to Verona. We had to get back to Bruno's as Matteo was picking us up for their Christmas Eve tradition of going to the movies. We were lucky to get a lift quite quickly with a young couple who were also going to Verona for the Christmas Eve festivities. I was quite excited by the prospect of going to an Italian film and hoped that maybe it would be a 1950s Fellini classic.

Matteo was already waiting for us by the time we arrived back at his mother's building. He was driving his own car this time, a small Alfa Romeo sports car.

'Ciao Matteo,' I said, getting into the car, but Matteo didn't look too pleased to see me. He said something to Bruno, pointing at me and an argument seemed to start. My Italian was coming on a bit and I could understand that they were talking about me but they were talking so quickly, it was difficult to understand everything.

I soon realized what the fuss was about when we pulled up in front of the cinema and I saw the poster out front advertising the film. It was a porno flick.

I looked at Bruno in disbelief. 'Is this a porn film?'

He shrugged and said, 'It's the Christmas Eve tradition.'

I had found the French customs a culture shock, but I now gave up on trying to comprehend the Italians. I resigned myself to this 'tradition' and followed the boys into the cinema, although I was not impressed that this was the kind of film Bruno was bringing me to. Most of the audience were men, but I did notice a number of women as well. Maybe Bruno wasn't having me on after all about the tradition.

We entered the dimly lit theatre and the boys chattered excitedly, waiting for the film to begin. The film starred an actress named Cicciolina, which literally translated as 'little fatty', but loosely translated means something like 'cuddles'. She didn't look particularly fat to me, except for perhaps her enormous breasts. Bruno told me that she was not only famous for her cinema escapades, but she was actually a member of the Italian parliament, who would sometimes give speeches with one breast exposed. Watching the 'plot' of the film unfold, I began to imagine just how the Italian government must be run.

The boys were elbowing each other, guffawing and making comments about the on-screen events. At one point Bruno actually put his hand over my eyes. 'Let's get out of here Primavera,' he said, leading me out of the theatre. He must have thought he was rescuing me from embarrassment, although he looked more uncomfortable than me.

We left the others to their cinematic delights and headed to the city center to take part in yet another Italian Christmas tradition. People were gathered in the square outside the old roman arena and there were huge vats of warm, spiced wine and trays of cakes for everyone to partake of. It was full of light and music and there was a huge white sculpture of a star shooting out from the inside of the arena, brilliantly lit up by spotlights.

I stood wide-eyed, taking everything in, full of wonder and awe, savoring the delicious wine.

'What's next on the list of strange Italian Christmas Eve traditions?' I asked.

'Midnight Mass of course!' Bruno said quite matter-of-factly.

'Church? So first we go to a porn film to get some kicks, then we get boozed up on hot wine, then we go to sing God's praises in church?'

'Naturally,' Bruno said, completely missing the paradox.

We entered into an incense-infused, candlelit world of low mutterings and chanting. The Italian churches were far more beautiful than the ones in France. There was a warmth inside, and lots of light and color. The pink marble emanated an inner life and strength. The French churches seemed grey, austere and forbidding in comparison.

We had brought the moss we had collected earlier near Giulia's cottage and placed it in the manger to prepare the bed for the baby Jesus.

After the Mass Bruno led me through the corridors behind the church, with ancient tombs along the floor. He pointed out the tomb where he had once had a fight with a fellow pupil when he was 10 years old and had subsequently been caught by the priest and expelled from school. He obviously started developing his impetuous character from a young age.

Buon natale

Christmas day was soon upon us. I was to spend the day with the Calibri family and then I was going back to Paris the very next day to meet Toby. I hadn't actually spoken to him for some time, but we had planned to meet at Luxembourg metro station. I hadn't even spared him a thought the whole time I was in Italy. Despite not having seen him for such a long time, I didn't feel any excitement or anticipation now. In fact, I hated to admit it, but I actually felt dread. Not only about leaving this beautiful, magical place for the cold greyness of Paris—but I knew that what I would be facing was going to be unpleasant. I hadn't told Toby about Bruno. I just hadn't had the courage after his enthusiasm about coming over to Europe to see me. I just couldn't face up to telling him the truth, which I knew he would take very, very badly. So I decided that I would just go through the motions, not spoil his vacation, and after I finished my studies for the year and finally went back to the States, I would revisit my feelings about the situation and our relationship and decide then what I wanted to do. Namely, stay with Toby and continue with the boring middle-class American dream, or go back to Bruno and the magic of Europe.

Bruno knew when he met me that I had a boyfriend already. He didn't seem too bothered or threatened by this fact. He also knew that in a day's time I would be going to see Toby.

We had talked about it and he'd asked me if I would tell Toby about us. He wanted me to tell him. In the meantime, I tried not to think about things too much. Bruno was always telling me to just live each day at a time and take things as they come. It was difficult though. I had a knot beginning to tie itself around my bowels in the pit of my stomach.

We woke up late on Christmas morning and Bruno's sisters had already arrived. The kitchen was a buzz with their chatter and delicious smells were wafting through the apartment. I thought that Bruno seemed a little tense, which was so unlike him. I asked him what was wrong.

'My father is coming today,' he said, frowning.

I gathered that some conflict existed between Bruno and his absent father. His father had moved out years ago to go live with his mistress. Mrs Calibri, however, being a good Catholic Italian wife, still considered their marriage to be something sacred. He was her husband and it was her duty to make Christmas dinner for the whole family, including her estranged husband. They were still married after all. I could only hope that he would have the sensitivity not to bring the mistress with him to the Christmas dinner.

'Mama has asked me to go pick up my aunt,' Bruno said to me after breakfast. 'She is lending me her car—let's go.'

We made our way down to the garage behind the apartment building and Bruno unlocked the garage. A red Fiat 500, fringed with rust, sat dejectedly in the dim interior. Bruno opened the passenger door for me and then he squeezed his lanky body into the low driver's seat. He turned the key in the ignition and the engine spluttered and coughed before dying out. He tried again and the same thing happened. After the third try he said. 'I have an idea. Get into the driver's seat and I will push. When I say go, turn the key in the ignition.'

'Are you kidding me?' I laughed at the ridiculousness of the suggestion.

'We do it all the time. It's the best way.' Bruno said.

I got into the driver's seat, shaking my head in disbelief. 'I hope that the brakes work at least.'

Bruno pushed the Fiat out of the garage and I turned the steering wheel so the car was facing toward the road. There was a slight downward slope from the garage to the road.

'Go!' he said, giving a final push and then running along behind the car. I turned the key in the ignition and, after an initial splutter, the engine groaned into life and I careened toward the road, managing to put my foot on the brake just before rolling out in front of another car.

Bruno now took over, and he floored the accelerator, making the engine squeal like a pig being strangled. He navigated the streets at top speed, zooming through intersections with little regard for the stunned pedestrians, and other vehicles, and he swung around corners so sharply I was terrified that the little car would turn over. I groped around for the seatbelt and discovered that it was jammed so I could only cling on to the end of the belt for dear life.

Bruno's aunt lived on a mountain and the roads where narrow and winding, with sharp hairpin curves. Bruno didn't use the brakes or even slow down as oncoming cars bombed toward us around every bend. The drivers blared their horns and Bruno responded by hammering the Fiat's squeaky horn.

I covered my eyes and although I didn't consider myself to be religious, I was praying that I would survive the journey.

We eventually made it to his aunt's house, a charming, traditional old mountain house with green shutters on the windows and a narrow iron balcony at the front. Bruno knocked on the front door. A surprisingly tall, statuesque woman of about 60, with a dyed-black, carefully coiffed hairdo flung the door open and immediately picked up her bag, which she had ready next to the front door. She brusquely kissed Bruno on both cheeks and from what I could gather from her tone of voice, began to berate him.

I looked questioningly at Bruno, hoping for a translation.

'She is complaining that I am late,' Bruno said to me, shrugging.

The aunt seemed not to notice me standing next to Bruno, until he gestured toward me. I understood just enough to realize he was introducing me as his 'fiancée'—that word again!

I shook her hand and she said something, which I didn't understand. Bruno explained to her that I didn't speak much Italian.

'*Lei è tedesca?*' She looked affronted as she asked Bruno if I was German.

'No Auntie, don't worry; she's not German, she's American,' I understood him to say.

Her eyes swept me up and down and then she frowned. '*Però lei è troppo bassa.*'

I smiled politely at her. From my miniscule knowledge of Italian, I thought she was saying I was too short, but didn't actually believe that she would be so rude to me. 'What did she say?' I asked Bruno.

'She likes your haircut.'

We made our way back down to the car, and being the shortest, I, of course, was relegated to the back seat.

When we got back to the apartment, Bruno's father had arrived, thankfully without the mistress. The family all greeted the aunty and the women all went into the kitchen. The decibel level in there soon rose to a deafening cacophony of laughter, chatter and clanking kitchenware. I remained in the sitting room with Bruno and his father, where the tension in the air was so strong you could have cut it with a knife. The two men sat in silence, sipping beer. Signor Calibri was a tall and portly man with dark hair and the same small dark eyes and large Roman nose as Bruno.

In an attempt to break the ice, I commented to Bruno, 'You have the same brown eyes as your father.'

'I may get my brown eyes from my father, but he has brown eyes because he is so full of shit.'

I was shocked and smiled uncomfortably. His father fortunately didn't understand what Bruno had said.

Then his father took out his wallet. He pulled out a few hundred lira notes and handed them to Bruno.

Bruno took the cash and counted it. He looked disappointed as he stuffed the money into his pocket.

'Your Christmas present?' I asked.

'Pizza money,' Bruno said disparagingly.

Mercifully, Bruno's sister came into the room just then and announced that dinner was served. We made our way into the dining room where an extravagant spread was laid out on the table. I sat down next to Bruno and eyed the sumptuous feast. To start with we had minestrone soup, followed by mushroom risotto and a selection of salads. I thought the meal was then finished, but Bruno's sisters and mother reappeared from the kitchen with more food. Just when I thought I was going to burst, they brought out the pasta, meat and fish. Bruno's father kept refilling both my and Bruno's wine glasses. Soon Bruno and his father were laughing and joking like old friends.

The two men pushed their seats back from the table and lounged back in their seats, legs spread apart and patting their engorged bellies. Bruno lit his father's cigar and then proceeded to light one for himself.

Signor Calibri said something to Bruno and indicated me with a flourish of his cigar. Bruno gave me a little nudge with his elbow. 'Papa says you should go into the kitchen with the women now and help them tidy up and prepare the dessert.'

I glared at him uncomprehendingly. Whenever my family had a special visitor for Christmas we would never expect them to have to help clean up. I huffed in annoyance.

'It would show respect to my father,' he said, puffing his cigar, the smoke curling up around his face, filling the room with the foul smell of testosterone.

I didn't agree with the sexist nonsense, but I didn't want to offend anyone, and like they say, 'when in Rome...'

I stood awkwardly in the kitchen doorway, watching the women clattering at the sink. Mrs Calibri beckoned to me, pulled up a chair at the table, and poured me a grappa.

'*Puis-je vous aider?*' I asked.

'We are nearly finished. You sit and relax.' Oddly, she handed me a pen.

'Can you sign the tablecloth, please?'

'Sign the tablecloth?' I asked, looking doubtfully at the pristine, white linen tablecloth that draped the kitchen table.

'You and Brunetto need to sign it, and all your friends that come to visit. I am going to embroider all the names in for your wedding cloth.'

I guess she really believed that Bruno and I were engaged. I took up the pencil and with difficulty managed to write my name on the cloth. It kept bunching up and my signature looked like a five-year-old had done it.

'*Grazie mi amore,*' she said, looking at the signature.

Bruno's two sisters and auntie nodded in approval as they eyed the signature and carried on with their tidying up and drying of pots and pans.

Then Mrs. Calibri handed me the coffee pot. I guessed that I was supposed to take it into the dining room, while the others carried in a variety of cakes they were loading onto plates.

We all settled in again around the dining table and stuffed ourselves even further, on delectable little cookies and melt-in your mouth panettone, and strong coffee with grappa.

Then Bruno's mother got up and came back with a bag full of gifts. She lay a few beautifully wrapped packages in front of me and urged me to open them. I opened them and discovered an Italian/English pocket dictionary, an expensive looking pen and a beautiful diary.

I'm not normally sentimental, but tears formed in my eyes. I just couldn't believe that this family had been so welcoming and accepting of me. It was in stark contrast to the DeClermonts. I suddenly felt really close to Bruno and I reached out and touched his knee under the table. It was a closeness that I both feared and welcomed.

Arrivederci Italia

The dreaded day had arrived when I was to leave Verona. Bruno was staying on with his mother until after the start of the new year, and wasn't sure exactly when he would be returning to France. I awoke in the morning with the winter sun streaming though the slats in the shutters. I wished that my wonderful dream of Italy didn't have to end.

My train wasn't leaving until the evening, so typically for him, Bruno declared that we had the entire day and we would fit as much into it as possible. We started the day with an energetic lovemaking session, and I savored those last erotic moments. I clung onto him like I clung onto my memories of Italy.

Feeling a mixture of fulfilment and anxiety, I followed him to the kitchen and we shared a leisurely breakfast of coffee and Italian pastries before heading out.

'Where are we going?' I asked, intrigued as we drove through the city.

'Hotel Two Lions,' Bruno said.

'Why are we going to a hotel?'

'It's a very special kind of hotel.'

The car drew up to an impressive entry gate, with wide marble steps sweeping up and flanked on either side by two immense reclining stone lions grooming themselves.

'It's a cemetery,' I said. 'I love cemeteries!'

'You'll really love this one,' Bruno said as he opened the car door for me and took me by the hand, leading me through the gate and up the stairs. Above the gate at the top of the stairs stood two shrouded stone figures, welcoming visitors to their world of mourning. The morning sun had given way to drizzle—the only rain I had seen the whole time I was in Italy. My heart felt like the dark, grey sky. The rain trickled like tears down the faces of the statues; I imagined that they were crying over my imminent departure.

Bruno and I walked solemnly amongst the graves, through a vast world of the dead. There was a separate children's area, an area for the rich with mansion-like mausoleums, and an area for the poor, with unmarked plots or simple crosses marking the graves. There were stone courtyards surrounded by columns and cypress trees and even underground tunnels lined with niches and alcoves. Tombs were everywhere—in the ground, in the stone floor, in the walls.

We wandered around, admiring the intricate sculptures of weeping angels. 'I want to show you something,' Bruno said, leading me to a small but ornate mausoleum. I realized why he was taking me there when I saw the name Calibri carved in marble above the iron door. Bruno pushed open the door, which creaked eerily, and led us into a dark and somber space. The stones on the floor were engraved with the names of Calibris from many generations. He knelt down and touched his hand to a stone on the floor. '*Nonno*, I hope all is well with you. Please meet my girlfriend, Primavera. I hope you are still writing poetry in heaven. It's my *nonno* Calibri here,' Bruno explained. 'He was a well-known Veronese poet.'

'You're related to a famous poet?' I asked, surprised.

'Si,' Bruno nodded proudly. 'There is a book published of his poems written in Veronese dialect.'

I was impressed and wondered why Bruno had never mentioned it before.

'Let's go to the children's cemetery to look for my little brother, Andrea,' Bruno said, standing up.

I stopped in my tracks and looked at Bruno in surprise. 'I didn't know you had a little brother,' I said.

'He died when he was a baby. I was five at the time. He would be 18 now,' Bruno said.

The misty rain was beginning to get heavier, dripping down the faces of the angel statues making them look like they were weeping. We searched among the tiny crucifixes but could not find Andrea's grave—so in his honor, and in the honor of all the dead, we smoked a joint.

We were feeling mellow from the weed and we weaved our way through the ordinary graves, until we came to where the wealthiest people had their tombs. Even in death there was inequality. These wealthy dead had their own gated community, with avenues lined by well-groomed shrubbery and lush, clipped lawns. The avenues were lined with house-sized mausoleums, some old and some outlandishly contemporary—mansions for the deceased in their very own classy neighborhood.

A feeling of sadness overcame me. 'Why do the living spend so much money on a stinking, rotting corpse, which just gets eaten by worms, when the money could be better spent on housing a living being?' I said wistfully.

'I know, Primavera. This is the way in the Italian society,' Bruno said, shaking his head.

It suddenly hit me that in a few hours I'd be back in Paris, seeing Toby for the first time in four months. 'We'd better get back to your mother's apartment so that I can pack,' I said to Bruno, anxiously.

Signora Calibri opened the door for us with her usual cheerfulness. 'I have prepared you something for your journey,' she said to me, leading me by the hand to the kitchen like an excited schoolgirl. She explained what each carefully wrapped package was; there was pizza, cake, grapes—I would be taking a little bit of Italy with me, and that thought was comforting. 'You are welcome back to my house whenever you want, darling,' she said, giving me a big hug.

'*Grazie, Signora,*' I said.

'Please, call me Mama,' Signora Calibri said, winking.

Bruno rang the train company to try and make a reservation for me but it was impossible, being that Italy is the land of inconvenience. I would have to try my luck and hope I was able to get a decent sleeping cabin without too many weirdos hanging around.

Once I was all packed and ready to go, we set off in the car.

'This isn't the way to the train station,' I said. 'Where are you going?'

Bruno grinned, 'We have one last outing before you get on your train.'

Bruno drove his mother's Cinquecento up the hill above the Roman ruins to a place overlooking the city below. There was some kind of construction work going on and there was a fence to keep people out.

'Let's go!' Bruno swung open the door of the car and started running toward the blockaded area.

'But shouldn't we start heading to the train station?' I said looking at my watch. A panicky feeling began to set in and I stopped in my tracks.

'This is Italy. I can guarantee that your train will be running late.' He waved me over to where he was standing.

'No, really. We ought to get going,' I called over to him.

He came over to me and grabbed my hand, pulling me toward a narrow gap in the fence. We crawled through it and went out to the edge of some rickety scaffolding. There we were alone and I could hear the wind whistling around us. I looked out upon the city, the river sliding by, the church towers rising above the ancient buildings, the castle, and the roman bridges. The church bells were ringing, a somber, serene sound that made me feel sad again. I wondered if it might be the last time I would look upon this scene. I looked over at Bruno lying stretched out on the ground with his eyes closed and a small smile on his lips. I tried to capture the image in my mind so that I could remember him. He opened his eyes and caught me looking at him. He flashed me his goofy grin. We smoked a *collo* and avoided any talk of the future.

I suddenly noticed the time and prodded Bruno who had settled into a stoned daze. 'C'mon, we have to get to the train station.'

Because I hadn't made a seat reservation, I had to wait around at the ticket desk to see if there were any places available—but no luck. I was going to have to wait two more hours for the midnight train. 'Shit,' I said, kicking my bag. I glared at Bruno. 'If we hadn't wasted time and got here earlier, I probably could have got on that train. Now I'm going to be two hours late getting in to Paris.' I thought of Toby waiting for me and wondering where I was. There was no way that I could communicate this to him, so I just hoped that he would be patient. Thinking about it, I guess he didn't really have a choice. He didn't speak the language and didn't know where he was going. He would be totally relying on me.

As I now had time to kill, Bruno bought some beers and we drove up to a quiet, deserted spot on a hill next to an old church. We held each other, drank, and began fantasizing about the future.

'Maybe when I finish my studies I could come back to Europe,' I said. 'Of course I would need to become a citizen somehow.' OK, I thought, maybe it's a bit irrational and far-fetched, but not impossible, definitely not impossible. 'The best way to become a European citizen is to marry one.' Bruno said, matter-of-factly. 'Our children could grow up speaking two languages fluently— English and Italian, of course,' he added.

These were crazy thoughts, but they made me smile nevertheless. I was jolted out of my dreams of the future when I glanced at my watch and saw what time it was. If we didn't get a move on I would risk missing yet another train.

We returned to the station and I finally got on a train. Bruno took me by surprise when we had our final embrace, he whispered in my ear '*Ti amo, Primavera,*' in his Veronese dialect.

'I love you too,' I said, as he jumped back onto the platform— and then the train took off. Bruno ran alongside the train as far as he could, grinning his crazy grin. As the train pulled away from the platform I watched him grow smaller and smaller in the distance. I suddenly felt bereft, like a child whose favorite toy was just pried out of her arms and taken out of sight. As I turned away from the window and walked down the corridor, I knew that this train was taking me to another phase in my life where the setting, the characters and the plot were different. With sadness, and perhaps a bit of jealousy, I wondered what Bruno would be doing without me—watching porn? Going to the football? Taking pictures? Flirting with other women? I wondered if he would be thinking about me—with Toby.

Luckily I found a seat on the train. It was in a compartment full of Yugoslavian men. They seemed excited to know that I was American and they offered me cigarettes non-stop—all of them, all at once—Camels, HB and some fancy brand that I had never heard of before. One of them could speak French, the other German, but the third could only speak his language—Yugoslavian, I guess.

'You are going to Paris?' one of them asked me.

I nodded.

'Our friend here doesn't speak any French and he doesn't know Paris. My other friends and I are getting off before Paris. Please could you help our friend to find his way?' The Yugoslav produced a crumpled piece of paper that had an address near Châtelet–Les Halles. I really didn't want to become embroiled in someone else's navigational and linguistic problems. God only knew I had my own issues to attend to once I arrived in Paris. However, I agreed purely out of politeness and the fact that I was going to have to spend the next several hours with these guys and didn't want to sour relations.

I was exhausted after the crazy day with Bruno and really wanted to rest and prepare myself mentally for meeting Toby; however, the Yugoslavians launched a flirting assault. They were in competition with each other, as to who could keep my attention longest, who could make me laugh most, and who was going to get in there with a chance. I was on high alert for possible wandering hands and compromising situations.

Eventually the other Yugoslavian guys got off the train and a new person got on. He was a dark-haired, blue-eyed, quite stunningly attractive Argentinian, called Ivan. My attention was suddenly sparked. He was an artist and he carried a portfolio of his drawings and paintings. He showed me a pencil drawing of the Ponte Vecchio in Florence, so delicately drawn, and with such attention to detail that it took my breath away. There were also watercolors of Argentinian mountains and villages, and portraits of somber, dark-eyed people, which I found hauntingly beautiful. We talked all the way to Paris. He told me that his family emigrated from Italy to Argentina during the Second World War, but he still felt a real affinity with Europe. I told him about my studies in France, my desire to leave the USA behind. At one point, when he was showing me one of his drawings, our hands touched and our eyes met and lingered for a moment. I looked away. I couldn't complicate things any more than they already were, I thought to myself. I got out my Italian picnic, which I shared with my two travelling companions, the handsome Ivan and the left-over Yugoslavian, and I never got a wink of sleep.

As we approached Paris, Ivan gave me his address in Italy in case I ever wanted to come and visit—he helped me off the train with my bags and we parted ways. The spare Yugoslavian followed me awkwardly and wordlessly to the metro, like a lost puppy. His presence behind me was becoming irritating, I had my own things to deal with. For one, I needed to get my head together for seeing Toby in a few minutes. I told him which station to get off at but indicated that that was as far as my services would extend, as I was getting off at a different stop. I don't think he quite understood and he exited the train forlornly. I watched him, wide-eyed and lugging his old-fashioned case along the platform. 'Oh well, here we go!' I thought, as the metro train plunged ahead to the next station.

Return to Paris

I got off at Luxembourg station. So, there I was again—in Paris, lugging my bags through the metro, breathing in the aroma of piss and mildew. I was supposed to have met Toby two hours ago. I scanned the people in the crowded metro for a familiar face. Nothing. I went up to the street and had a look around. No sign of him. I wondered if he had got fed up of waiting for me and left, thinking I wasn't coming. I didn't know what to do. It occurred to me that he must have my French family's phone number in case he needed to get in contact. I figured that I should just call them and find out if he had rung them.

As I dug in my pocket, I felt a hand on my shoulder. I spun around and there he was. Toby looked different—older, a bit gaunt. He was wearing a black overcoat and his punk haircut had been shaved off like a skinhead. I realized that I had actually seen him from behind before and had just not registered that it was him.

All I could say was, 'Hi, how are you?' I gave him a small kiss—more like a peck.

His face was taut with stress and worry. 'I've been waiting here for two fucking hours,' he said. 'And no one understands English.'

'My train was cancelled and there was no way of getting in touch to let you know. I'm here now, so what's the big deal?'

We stood facing each other with stormy expressions, my moth-eaten luggage and his brand new luggage at our feet. But then, suddenly, we both relaxed and everything just seemed so familiar—I laughed at us arguing, just like old times, and a smile of relief spread across Toby's face. He gave me a big hug and I breathed in his scent. It was the smell of the Connecticut woods. Maybe things with Toby weren't going to be so bad after all.

'I'm sorry for being angry. I was just so worried when I didn't see you here,' he said.

'I'm sorry too. Welcome to France, the land of delayed trains!'

'Shall we try to find our hotel and then I'll show you a bit of Paris?' I suggested.

He nodded gratefully and we walked back up to street level. We were both so exhausted that we couldn't really muster the energy to talk about anything important—the novelty of the situation just seemed too overwhelming. 'How was your flight?' I questioned lamely.

He shrugged. 'It was OK. It was overnight, so I slept for most of it. I've got killer jetlag though.'

The conversation fizzled out and we walked along in silence. I glanced over at Toby; I felt no longing, no excitement. I wasn't sure I missed him. Where was the love I used to feel for him— that intense attraction that prevented us from keeping our hands off each other and jumping immediately into bed for a wanton lovemaking session? I knew that I used to love him, but something had changed—something inside of me.

The hotel was a shabby and claustrophobic hovel, with a view out over a dark alley. When we opened the window the familiar Parisian aroma of piss and sewage wafted in. We both lay down on the over-sprung bed. Toby fell asleep quite quickly. I watched him as he slept—the man I had been involved with for the past four years. He was like a stranger to me—but perhaps it was because I had turned into someone else.

I dozed fitfully for a few hours, dreaming about stone lions coming to life. When I awoke, it was dark outside and I could hear rain spattering the grimy window. Toby was still asleep, so I went out to buy a bottle of wine, which was also a good excuse to try and call Bruno to tell him that I arrived safely in Paris.

I found a phone booth, and dialed his mother's number, which I had written down on a crumpled piece of paper in my pocket. The phone rang and rang but no one answered.

I trudged back to the hotel room, clutching a bottle of Beaujolais. Toby was finally awake and was sitting on the edge of the bed, his face saggy with sleep.

'This'll wake you up,' I said, cheerfully presenting the bottle of wine. He perked up at the sight of it. I went into the bathroom and took the protective wrapping off the disposable plastic cups and filled them up.

'*Chin, chin,*' I said as we attempted to toast, but there was only a dull slosh of liquid instead of a satisfactory clink as the plastic cups squashed against each other. They were small and didn't hold much wine. We both reached for a refill at the same time. We laughed, and the tension lifted. He reached out and took my hand, pulling me toward him. He kissed the top of my head, and his hands circled my waist.

'Oh my, look at the time,' I said brightly, breaking away from his embrace. 'We'd better go get something to eat before I pass out from hunger.' Toby looked disappointed. 'Come on drink up and let's go, I know of a great little Mexican restaurant. I know how much you love Mexican food.' I jumped up and put on my coat before he could argue.

Once we sat down in the restaurant and ordered our drinks, I had déjà vu. I realized that I had been here once before with Bruno—the time we had hitchhiked to Paris from Rouen.

'What's the matter?' Toby asked. 'You're frowning.'

'Oh nothing, just trying to decipher the menu. How's Connecticut?' I asked.

'Same as usual—boring,' Toby replied listlessly.

'How's the studying going?'

He shrugged and took a swig of beer. 'S'awright.'

I tried to liven the conversation up a bit, 'What's going on with the band?'

'We've been rehearsing some new songs,'

'That sounds great,' I said, putting on enthusiasm.

'What about you? You haven't told me anything about what you're doing. What's it like living and studying in Froggy-land?' Toby asked.

'Don't say that here, Toby. It's racist.'

'OK then, who are you hanging out with? Have you got any frog… uh, French friends?'

'Yes, but I hang out mainly with some of the American girls from home.'

'Anyone I know?'

'No, I don't think so.'

'Have you made friends with any other foreigners, this country seems to be full of them?'

By now we'd drunk two bottles and the wine was starting to go to my head. I thought that getting drunk would help me to relax. I had terrible trouble concentrating on what Toby was asking. I kept having flashbacks to my meal I had eaten here with Bruno, and then to our last sex session, and I suddenly felt my secret, like a little prize fighter inside me punching at my organs, longing to get out and be revealed. I wasn't sure how much longer I could carry on this pretense.

After dinner we bought a bottle of cheap, screw-top wine and walked along the river bank toward the Eiffel tower, like I had done once with Bruno. There was a light but steady rain. I thought about asking Toby if I could shelter under his big overcoat, but thought better of it. I didn't want to risk that kind of closeness at that moment. Sadness filled my heart. Even after the wine, and not seeing each other for so long, I couldn't feel any of the lust I used to have for him—before France. I wondered if he could sense that something was wrong.

Walking back to the hotel, I wracked my brain trying to decide whether it was the right time to tell him how I felt. I figured that maybe I could break the news lightly. But then I thought it might be a mistake to do it too soon. It was going to be even harder than I thought.

'So when are you going to come back home?' Toby asked, jolting me out of my ruminations.

'Toby … I've got something to tell you.'

'Fuck, I knew it, I knew it!' He turned away and shook his head, taking a deep swig from the bottle.

I tried to grasp his hand, but he yanked it away.

'I … I'm thinking of staying in Europe. I might carry on my studies here.'

Tears welled up in his eyes and his voice became cold and quivery. 'And what about us? What about our plans? What about ME?' He stabbed his finger several times into his chest.

'Well what about ME?' I said. 'I feel I've got a right to further my education.' 'I knew this was going to happen. Why did I spend all my money to come over here to Europe, to see the girl I love, and who I thought loved me?'

I remained silent. My heart was wrenching.

I gingerly felt for Toby's hand and he accepted it, and that seemed to calm him down. I knew what was inevitably going to happen when we got back to the hotel, and I tried to brace myself mentally.

As expected, as soon as we got in, Toby became amorous and kissed me tenderly. 'I've missed you so much. To think of you not coming back makes me crazy,' he whispered. He put his hands on my ass and pulled me close. 'God, I've missed you,' and then he kissed me passionately.

I felt no reciprocal passion, and was so tired I really just wanted to go to sleep. 'What's the matter?' he asked.

'I'm just really tired.'

'But we haven't seen each other for four months, come on,' he started to sulk. Toby had that sullen look that I remembered always used to upset me. When he was like this he was like a petulant little boy.

I knew what I had to do. I automatically started undressing and got between the covers, waiting for him.

'I've been wanting you … thinking of you,' he said, unbuttoning his jeans. He slid into bed and he began to caress my thighs. I winced at his touch. His hands felt inept and awkward, so unlike Bruno's passionate touch. My whole self seemed to revolt. I really had trouble bringing myself to do it. I couldn't bear to have him touch me there and I pulled away.

'What's the matter?' he asked.

'Nothing, your hands are just cold,' I said. I wanted to get the deed over with, so I closed my eyes, gritted my teeth and let him have his way.

Afterwards, I turned on my side away from him and cried silently to myself.

Hell is other people

The next few days I wandered around Paris on autopilot, with Toby in tow. Drifting from one tourist attraction to the next. The times in between were filled with superficial conversation. Everything was fine on the surface—but underneath, something foul was brewing. Whenever I could, I called Bruno. I even stooped so low as to call him once with Toby standing right outside the phone booth. I pretended that I was phoning my French family and I spoke in French so that Toby wouldn't be able to understand me.

'Primavera, it is good to hear your voice. Mama is asking after you.'

I suddenly had a flashback to Bruno's mother's kitchen table laden with Italian cakes and coffee, and a warm feeling filled my heart.

'How is it going? Have you told him about us yet?'

I squirmed. 'It's not been so easy.'

'You know we agreed that it is best.'

'I know.'

'I'm coming back to France in a few days and I want to see you. I've been missing you, *ti amo*, Primavera.'

I looked at Toby standing outside and said goodbye to Bruno. We were going to Rouen in a few days to meet my French family. Now that I knew Bruno was going to be back, that changed everything. I had to come clean.

On our third day in Paris, all hell broke loose. We had to lug our baggage around with us because we had to move out of our hotel and hadn't yet found anywhere else to stay. We spent all day looking for a hotel, with no luck. As it was the day before New Year's Eve, everything was fully booked. The weather was miserably cold and violently windy and rainy. The icy rain was being blown down my collar making my neck feel stiff and tense.

To escape the torrential rain, we sat in a café drinking cheap booze. My heart felt black and heavy and I sat staring moodily out the window.

Toby glowered at me over his glass of beer. 'Some vacation this has turned out to be. Why couldn't you have booked somewhere?'

I turned slowly to eye him. 'I could ask you the same thing.'

Then Toby began his prying, pounding, interrogating.

'What's wrong with you? You've been acting really fucked up.'

I shrugged and took a sip of my wine still staring out the window. 'Nothing. What do you mean?'

'I mean you're acting cold. It doesn't seem like you're very happy to see me.'

I didn't reply.

'And you keep making these secret phone calls. You flinch when I touch you. You were like a cold fish when we had sex. I've figured it out. I know you've been seeing someone else.'

I couldn't take it anymore. I lowered my eyes. 'Yes,' I said dryly, with no emotion.

He glared at me with complete and utter hatred. I thought for a second that he was going to hit me. 'I knew it! I fucking said I knew it, didn't I? How could I be such a fucking idiot? Coming out here, spending all my money—for a damn whore.'

'I'm not a whore.' I replied angrily. 'I'm in love.'

'Love? You don't know the meaning of the word. You're a cold-hearted whore.'

'If you call me a whore one more time this glass of wine is going to end up on your face.'

'You could have told me before I wasted my time and money coming over here that you were fucking someone else.'

'I know. I should have told you.'

'Geezus—I fucked you too. I've probably got some foreign disease now.' His face twisted up in disgust.

I dashed the contents of my wine glass in his face. The sneer disappeared off his face; he gasped and wiped his eyes with his hand. Then suddenly his eyes welled up and his bottom lip began to quiver. His tears had no fear and pushed everything aside. 'I thought you loved me,' he sobbed like a little boy.

I looked at my hands resting in a puddle of wine on the table. I couldn't meet his eyes.

'I thought you loved ME,' he shouted, getting up from the table, grabbing his rucksack and running out into the darkness, the coldness and the rain.

The other customers were staring at me. I quickly threw some francs on the table and went out to find Toby. The rain was pounding down, soaking me and my already dampened spirit.

How could I do this to another human being—someone who I had loved? My heart started to thump as I began to panic. I saw Toby standing on the Pont Neuf just across the street, looking down into the swiftly moving current. I ran to him and grabbed his arm, and we both stood looking at each other like a couple of drowned rats. Below us, the river Seine flowed—a river of tears of broken-hearted lovers.

I knew I had to at least temporarily patch things up with Toby. His flight back to the States wasn't for another week and I couldn't just leave him to fend for himself.

'Hey, I'm sorry, I really, really am,' I said.

He turned to me with a hangdog expression, misery glistening in his eyes. He swallowed and said, 'OK, if you leave him and never see him again, I can learn to forgive you. When you get back we can start over and forget all about it.' Trickles of water coursed down his nose. He stood there on the bridge, looking forlorn, with his rucksack in his hand, his eyes pleading.

My heart melted and a queasy feeling of guilt lay in my gut like a greasy meal.

I gently put my hand on his arm. 'C'mon, you. We better find somewhere to stay. It's getting late. I know somewhere we can try,' I replied. The only place I could think of going to was the MIJE, so we trudged through the rain to Le Marais.

When we arrived, exhausted and bedraggled, looking like a couple of street urchins, the concierge took one look at us and shook his head. 'No more room,' he said.

Toby kicked his rucksack. 'Fuck!' he said. 'What a stupid ass I've been to come all the way over here.'

'Listen, your attitude isn't going to help find us somewhere to stay,' I said.

Toby glared at me—a glimmer of hatred returning.

We quietly left the concierge's office. I had an idea as we passed through the darkened foyer. The dining room to the left was empty. If there were no rooms I figured we could just sleep on the floor in there. At least it was shelter from the rain, if not very comfortable.

I held my finger to my lips and gestured to Toby to follow. We sneaked into the dining room and I took my wet coat off, spreading it on the floor under a table in a dark corner of the room. Toby copied me and we stretched out, using our packs as pillows.

Toby crossed his arms and turned away from me. I lay damp and shivering, feeling utterly miserable, mulling over the events of the day. It was all just too much and I found myself crying.

Suddenly, I heard a noise and the door opened. There was a flash of light in my face and a boot nudging me in the back.

'What are you doing here? You can't sleep here.' The concierge said in French, shaking my shoulder. We both shot upright.

'But we don't have anywhere else to go, and it's cold and raining outside,' I sobbed.

'*Bien*—maybe there is something I can do,' the concierge softened. 'Come with me.'

We followed him back to the office and he looked in his book. 'There is one bed available for one night only in the men's dormitory. At the moment there is a group of Swiss in there. I will have to ask them if they mind you staying there, and you two will have to share a single bed.'

The thought of an actual bed, even a single one was heaven to me. I translated for Toby, who looked unimpressed. 'A single bed in a roomful of yodelers—great,' he said sarcastically.

'Well if you can find something better go ahead,' I challenged him.

He turned cold and sullen again, and walked away, lighting up a cigarette. The concierge disappeared to go ask the Swiss guys if they minded us crashing in their room.

He returned five minutes later, giving us the nod. He gave us a key and we headed up the stairs, lugging our packs. The dorm was full of men in various states of undress, lounging on beds, clowning around, reading and leaning out the window smoking. All eyes turned to us when we walked in. I spotted an empty bunk and dropped my pack on it. I smiled awkwardly at the guys, took my Doc Martens off and slipped under the stiff blanket without taking my clothes off. Toby looked uncertainly at the narrow bed with me in it.

One of the Swiss guys sitting on the edge of the bunk opposite said, 'You look like you could use some pills, man.'

Toby suddenly perked up. 'What have you got, dude?' he asked.

'Ecstasy, coke, downers, hash, skunk.' The guy was a veritable drug store.

Without hesitating Toby slapped a wad of francs on the bed and was handed a plastic baggie full of pills and powder. He selected a downer and swallowed it, and stuffed the rest in his pocket. He sat moodily on the edge of the bed until the pill kicked in. He collapsed on top of the covers, trapping me under them, with my face pressed up against the cold, grimy wall.

Within minutes he was snoring. Well at least one of us was going to sleep that night.

New Years Eve

I woke with a start, jolted into consciousness by the dormitory door slamming. I looked around the dorm and all the other beds were empty. The Swiss guys had all gone out. Toby was still comatose next to me. I gave him a nudge and he groaned.

'Get up, we have to leave.'

I shook him and tried pulling the cover out from underneath him. He eventually woke up when he rolled off the bed and hit the floor. Groggily, he wobbled to his feet. He looked like absolute shit. I looked at myself in the mirror and realized that I looked like shit too.

It was New Year's Eve and we had to go in search of a place to stay. We gathered our things and set off. The rain had stopped but the cobbled streets were full of grey puddles and there was a damp chill in the air. We made our way to the nearest tourist information center, which was teeming with jostling tourists. Toby looked pissed off when he saw how long the line was and went outside for a cigarette, while I resolutely waited my turn. After half an hour I finally made it up to the counter.

'I'm looking for a hotel for tonight,' I said to the adviser.

Without even glancing up, she shook her head and pursed her lips. 'You will be lucky,' she said. 'Everything is fully booked for tonight.'

'I'll take anything,' I said desperately.

'There is only one place that is available but I think it is probably not in your budget,' the adviser said, looking down her nose at my torn fishnet tights and muddy boots.

'I'll take it,' I said. I remembered that my parents had given me an American Express card to be used in 'emergencies'. I considered this to be an emergency.

I slapped the card down on the counter and stared challengingly at her.

'Hmpf,' she said. 'You wish to pay on American Express. I'll reserve a room for you. That will be 4,000 francs, for one night. You pay at the hotel when you check out.'

I gulped but tried not to let my shock show. I hoped that my parents would understand this *was* an 'emergency'.

Once the reservation had been made I went outside to get Toby. He was staring listlessly into space. I guessed that he must have popped another pill. I led the way to the metro to find our hotel.

It was a nice four-star establishment near the Arc de Triomphe. Toby and I got a few stares from the staff and other guests as we went through the revolving door. Our feet left muddy tracks on the polished marble floor. I caught sight of myself in one of the mirror-clad pillars. I looked like a heroin addict. My hair was greasy, and days-old makeup caked my face in patches, emphasizing my pallor and zits. There were dark circles under my eyes and my lips were dry and cracked. Toby just looked like a zombie. I felt all eyes upon us as we walked across the vast lobby, dragging our bags with us.

We were on the fifth floor and the porter attempted to help us with our bags. I smiled politely and said we could manage. I couldn't afford the tip. The room was small and had a double bed that took up most of the room. With our suitcases on the floor there was actually no space to walk around. But there was an en suite bathroom and it was *clean*. I flopped down on the bed and breathed in the fresh detergent smell of the pillows. The bed was so comfortable and for a fleeting moment I experienced a pure and simple happiness that I had not felt since I'd left Italy. Toby immediately started rolling a joint. I went into the bathroom to take a shower. I stood under the soothing spray of hot water. It felt so good—I had forgotten how therapeutic a hot shower could be, and I found myself thinking of Bruno. I wondered what he was doing for New Year's Eve?

When I emerged, feeling clean and refreshed, Toby was reclined on the bed, still toking on the final dregs of his joint. He handed the roach to me.

'You didn't leave me much,' I said. 'You must be absolutely baked.'

He narrowed his bloodshot eyes at me. 'Fine—I'll finish it then,' he said while exhaling a cloud of pungent smelling skunk.

'You going to have a shower?' I asked him. 'You could do with it.'

'Nah, can't be bothered,' he replied squeakily, trying to hold the smoke in his lungs.

I got ready to go out while Toby just lay on the bed staring at the ceiling. When I was dressed and finished putting on my makeup I tried to persuade Toby to get up and sort himself out. I suggested we start the night by buying a bottle of wine. This seemed to motivate him and he put on his ratty old sneakers and peeled himself off the bed. We both popped a pill before leaving the room. As we made our way back out through the hotel lobby, the staff and hotel guests, all dressed in their glamorous finery, stopped and stared at us.

Once out on the Champs Élysée we got swept up in the sea of people. The streets were already teeming and there was a huge crowd forming down the avenue at the Arc de Triomphe. We went to Monoprix and bought a couple of bottles of wine and walked around the streets drinking, soaking up the buzz. The crowd was dense and it was becoming more and more difficult to move freely along the sidewalk. People were shoving and jostling each other and overflowing into the road where the traffic was at a virtual standstill.

I felt intoxicated by the wine, the pill and the atmosphere. The people drifted past as if in slow motion, the cars' yellow headlights imprinted tracer on my retinas, and swooshing lights seemed to swirl around me. I thought I heard a woman screaming and tried to figure out where it was coming from. I noticed a young woman surrounded by a group of what appeared to be Algerian men, all grabbing and pulling at her. She was screaming and trying to push them away. The crowd ignored them and as I was swept past the scene, I thought I saw one of the men wrestle the woman to the ground. Why wasn't anyone helping her? I had an uneasy feeling and held my handbag close, feeling for Toby in the crowd. I noticed he was in front of me and I grabbed on to his waist, trying not to lose him. His familiar warmth made me feel safe.

Midnight was imminent and we managed to squeeze up near the Arc de Triomphe. At the stroke of 12 a great cheer rose up and car horns started honking.

'Here's to a brand new year,' Toby said raising his bottle, beginning to look a bit more cheerful. Just then a strange man grabbed me by my shoulders and planted a big, wet slobbery kiss on my lips. I instinctively pushed him away. I looked down and realized that my bag had been opened. I checked inside it to see if anything had been taken, and sure enough someone had lifted my wallet. The kissing man must have been part of a team—when I had taken my hand off my bag to push him away, his accomplice must have pickpocketed me. I suddenly felt overwhelmingly depressed.

'Someone just stole my wallet,' I said to Toby.

'Shit! What did you have in there?'

'About 100 francs, my bank card, my credit card and my student ID.'

'Oh fuck,' was all he could say.

'We better find a police station to report it,' I said.

'Are you crazy? You're on your own. I've got a pocket full of drugs. I'm not going inside any police station.'

'You're the one who's crazy. I just got mugged and you won't come with me to the police station?'

He just stared blankly at me and shrugged. 'Fine,' I said thrusting the hotel key into his hand. 'I'll see you back at the hotel,' and I stormed off.

There was already a crowd of people at the police station who had been victims of crime. I overheard a woman in a fur coat, who was standing in front of me, telling the police that her Mercedes had been stolen. When it was my turn, I explained what had happened and I was told that my complaint was only minor. A harassed, yet smug looking officer pointed to a crowded bench and told me that I had to wait my turn for someone to take a statement.

I sat and waited, hoping to God that Toby had enough money to pay for the hotel. The police station was filling up and I kept having to budge up on the bench as more and more people sat down. I could swear I saw the woman who I thought was being attacked earlier; she was crying, her makeup smeared down her face and blood was streaming from her nose. I looked at my watch. An hour had passed and the line was getting longer. I began to realize that the police were not going to do anything and that there were other more serious problems they had to deal with. I decided there was no point in waiting any longer.

I got up and headed dejectedly back to the hotel. The streets were still full of revelers having a good time and celebrating. I wished that a nuclear bomb would fall and vaporize every single one of them. I spotted a phone booth on the way and decided to try and call Bruno. Luckily my phone card was still in my handbag. I dialed his number and listened to the odd foreign sounding tone that you get when calling an Italian number. Signora Calibri answered the phone and I asked her if Bruno was there in mixed-up French and Italian.

She seemed surprised that I didn't know that he had already left for France.

When I got back to the hotel Toby was sitting in the bar having a drink. He narrowed his eyes at me, trying to focus through the alcohol and drug blur. 'I'm going up to bed,' I said. I noticed the room key was on the bar, so I snatched it away and sloped toward the elevator.

There were some Italian people in the elevator, all laughing and chattering animatedly and I was reminded of Bruno. I wondered what he was doing in France already. Was he in Paris too? Or maybe he was in Rouen celebrating the New Year back at his apartment. I had to admit to myself that I was really missing him. An image came to me of him at some party, engrossed in taking pictures of the festivities, completely oblivious to his crooked glasses and flyaway hair. I would have given anything to be with him on that night instead of Toby.

I got into bed and started to fall into a fitful slumber, when I heard Toby creep into the room. I could tell he was trying to be quiet but he crashed into something and he shouted 'Aw fuck!' I heard him stumble into the bathroom and a moment later I heard a glass shatter. I pulled the blanket over my head to try and muffle the racket.

Then I felt him collapse into bed next to me. He put his arm round me and pressed himself against me. He was naked and aroused. He slid his hand under my top. I pushed it away.

'Come on,' he said. 'Let's forget about everything. Let's make a new start to the new year. I need you so bad.'

I turned my back to him and pulled the cover tighter over my head. 'I'm tired and I'd like to sleep now.'

Toby sighed and got up and switched on the light. He sat on the side of the bed with his head in his hands. 'I don't get you,' he said.

'I'm fucking tired!' I sat up in bed. 'Can you please turn off the light so that I can get some sleep?'

Toby lifted his head up and his face twisted into a snarl. 'You know what you are? You fucking ice queen bitch!' he stood up and shouted. 'I bet you'd do it with fucking Pedro or whatever his name is.'

I tried to pacify him. 'Toby you are drunk and drugged-up. I just got mugged. I am really not in the mood for your amateur dramatics right now.'

He shut up, grabbed the bedside lamp and smashed it against the wall.

Someone in the room next door started banging on the wall.

Toby picked up his battered suitcase, which was half open and ran out into the corridor stark naked.

'Oh my God—where are you going?' I ran to the door. He was halfway down the corridor with his suitcase hanging open, leaving a trail of socks, underwear and t-shirts.

'Toby, come back,' I called after him.

A door opened and someone peered out with a startled expression before withdrawing instantly. I could hear the door chain being fastened inside.

'Toby, you're going to get us kicked out. Just get back in here, please. Before someone calls the hotel security.'

He must have had a moment of lucidity and he stopped in his tracks. He let me lead him back to the room where I got him a glass of water and tucked him in. I went back out into the corridor to pack the case and when I came back Toby was crying.

'It must be a bad come down,' I said to him, patting him on the shoulder. 'I think we both just need some sleep.' I fell heavily into bed beside him, longing for sleep and a new tomorrow.

A new tomorrow

When we got to the reception desk to check out, I saw Toby turn white at the sight of the bill. Seeing as my credit card was now in the hands of a thief, Toby begrudgingly got out his and unquestioningly paid the bill. I braced myself for an argument but I think he wanted to get out of there as quickly as possible before they realized about the smashed lamp, or before someone in the lobby recognized him as the naked madman from the night before.

We made our way to Gare du Nord station and got on a train to Rouen. I stared out the window, wondering what Bruno was up to. I tried to avoid conversation with Toby, as it all seemed to focus on us patching things up.

'Hey,' he said. 'I was thinking. This is just a stupid blip. I know we can sort this out.'

He seemed to think that after everything that had happened our relationship could be put back the way it was. Just like that. That all it would take was for me to say OK and everything would be forgotten.

'OK,' I said, still staring out the window.

He put his hand on my leg—laying claim. I had the urge to push it away—but I let it stay, closing my eyes and gritting my teeth.

On arrival in Rouen, we got a taxi up to the DeClermonts'. As the car drew up to the driveway my heart leapt into my throat. There was Bruno, dressed head to toe in white, just as he had been on that first crazy motorcycle ride. He was standing at the top of the driveway next to his motorcycle and holding a bunch of flowers and a heart-shaped box of chocolates, grinning his goofy grin.

'Who is that?' Toby asked, craning his neck to get a better view.

'Oh just a friend from the university,' I said. 'I have no idea what he's doing here. I better go see what he wants, just stay here with the bags a minute.'

I jumped out of the taxi and hurried over to Bruno. He bent down to give me a kiss and I ducked out of the way.

'I brought you these,' Bruno said, offering me the flowers and chocolates.

'Now's not a good time, really, Bruno.'

'Want to go for a ride later, Primavera?'

'Bruno, I can't tonight, I've got someone with me. You know.'

'Did you tell him about us?'

'Yes. He didn't take it well.'

'Well then it should be OK—you forget about him and come out with me.'

'You don't understand, Bruno. I can't right now.'

'You prefer him to me—I understand.'

'No—it's not like that at all. Things are just still very delicate and I'd prefer if you just kept a low profile right now. He'll be gone in a couple of days.'

'I call you then,' he said thrusting the flowers and chocolates into my hands. He started up the motorbike and whizzed off in a cloud of smelly blue smoke.

I went over to Toby who was having trouble working out the French money to pay the cab driver. I helped him to count out his francs.

'That was him, wasn't it? Couldn't you do better than that? That dude looks like a real nerd. I'm not so worried anymore,' Toby said, laughing caustically.

'It was just a friend giving me a late Christmas present.'

'You never were a good liar—wait till I tell the guys back home about that wally—what a laugh!'

I ignored the taunts and braced myself to face Sophie as we entered the house.

As predicted, Sophie was there at the door, smiling her fake smile and holding her hand out to Toby. 'I am Sophie—Siobhan said me about you,' she said in her awful English.

I introduced them and Toby shook her hand awkwardly. 'What subject do you study?' she asked him.

'Computer programming,' Toby explained. I didn't know if Sophie actually understood what that meant, but she nodded appreciatively. Then she turned to me with that familiar disapproving stare and said in French, 'That bad-mannered Italian was here to see you before.'

'Thank you for letting me know,' I smiled a false smile back at her. 'Is it possible for Toby to stay here tonight?' I asked hopefully.

'Oh—I don't think so. We must be up early and it wouldn't be convenient to have someone sleeping in the living room.'

I relayed the message back to Toby, who looked annoyed. I had told him it might be possible for him to stay there, as he hadn't made any hotel reservations in Rouen.

Sensing his concern, Sophie jumped in, 'I have a friend who runs a little pension in the center of Rouen.' She turned to get a little piece of paper off the side table in the foyer, scrawled down a number, and handed it to Toby.

Toby smiled politely and nodded. 'Is it expensive?' he asked. He always was incredibly cheap.

I asked Sophie in French if she thought it was expensive and she shook her head. 'Very good value,' she said. She even offered to call up and make the reservation. 'I hope you have a good impression of France and French people,' she said, smiling at Toby as she picked up the phone to call her friend at the hotel.

Toby and I went to my little room. 'She seems nice,' Toby said. 'You made her sound like such a witch.'

I wanted to unpack and have a bath before heading out right away to book him into the pension.

He sat down sullenly at my desk and didn't say a word while I emptied my rucksack and started putting things away. I put my diary in the desk and went into the bathroom to take a bath. I locked the door behind me and sat on the edge of the bath, the roar of the water drowning out my thoughts and the steam clearing the fog from my brain. I breathed a sigh of relief. Finally, I had some time to myself away from the burden of a betrayed boyfriend following me around like a bad smell. I eased myself into the hot water and shut my eyes. I didn't care about Toby waiting—he could wait. I was going to relish every moment of time to myself.

Things seemed unusually quiet out there in my bedroom. I didn't hear any movement, no shuffling, no music. Maybe he'd decided to take a nap.

I got out of the bath, dried myself off and got dressed. I slowly opened the bathroom door to go back into my bedroom. Toby was sitting at my desk with his shoulders slumped and his head bowed over my diary, open in front of him. He turned to look at me. Pure hatred emanated from his narrowed eyes. 'So now I know what you thought of me all along,' he said flatly. 'You think I'm a shallow waster who is dragging you down. And you're quite happy to go on stringing me along that we have a future together. You are a deceptive little cunt. I wasted my time coming out here to see you. You ruined my life. I hate you.'

'You read my diary? How dare you!' I snatched the diary from under his nose. 'These are my most private thoughts. You have no right to go poking around in my desk.'

'Don't pretend you didn't put it in there, right in front of me on purpose—to torture me even more than you already have done. You left it there because you didn't have the guts to tell me to my face—you did this to stick the knife in even further. You are devious and evil. I wish I never met you.'

He began to sob and I hung my head, feeling the weight of misfortune fall upon me. I wished that he would just get up and go, but his neediness was too overwhelming.

'Take me to the hotel. I just need to spend some time on my own.' He glared at me. Even in his hatred he relied on me. That's how it always was. I always did everything—he was too much of a drip to do anything for himself.

'Why don't you take yourself there if you hate me so much? Why do you have to rely on me all the time?'

He stared at me blankly, his whole body slack and hopeless. I looked at his tear-streaked face and felt a stab of guilt. He was right. I really did think those things about him; I had been stringing him along. I probably had ruined his life. I was being evil and I needed to do penance, just how it had been rammed down my throat at Sunday school. You must suffer for your sins. The horrible wrenching feeling in my heart was my penance for treating another human being with such disregard.

'OK—I'll ask Sophie if she can drive you there.'

Unusually, Sophie was very obliging. Toby got into the back of the tin can of a 2CV like a zombie. 'Are you two having a tiff?' she asked me chirpily, with a sly smile, as I slipped into the front seat next to her. 'We're both just a little tired from travelling, Sophie. Thanks for offering to drive him. He's really exhausted from Paris.'

'He seems like such a polite, serious and smart young man. I hope you hang on to him,' Sophie said.

She drove us down into the old town and stopped in front of the pension. It was in a really ancient half-timbered house with a large crooked beam over the entrance. The owner greeted us smilingly at the door and started chattering away at Toby, who just stood listlessly mute.

'He doesn't speak French,' I said. 'I can translate.'

The man explained about the 11pm curfew, about not leaving wet towels on the floor and about breakfast in the morning. Then he handed Toby an old-fashioned skeleton key and led us up a creaky wooden staircase to the very top of the old house.

The room was a cozy little nook under the eaves, with a tiny latticed window and a beamed ceiling, and was cluttered with antique furniture. The man left the room and I stayed with Toby to help him settle in.

I sat down on the lumpy bed, covered in a musty-smelling red brocade bedspread. 'Listen, I'm so, so sorry about this. I do love you Toby, and it breaks my heart to see you like this.'

Tears welled up in his eyes again, which caused me to well up too.

'We've shared so much together. I can never forget you. I won't be able to forgive myself.'

He sat on a chair with his back toward me. 'I think you should go. I don't want to see you ever again.'

'Toby—honestly. I hate seeing you like this. I feel so bad.' I went over to him and placed my hand on his shoulder. He shrugged it off.

'Don't touch me!' he snapped.

'Don't treat me like this Toby. I know you still love me.'

He raised his head out of his hands and looked at me. 'Go to your Italian stallion and get fucked,' he said.

I was crying again. 'Toby, can't you see? This is the problem. The way you treat me. The way you speak to me. You make me feel like shit and I needed to get away from that.'

'Just go—it's over.'

I walked over to the door to go. I was worried about leaving him in the state he was in. 'Ok—bye. Shall I come back to see you tomorrow, maybe once we've both slept on it?'

Toby didn't say anything until I opened the door and stepped out onto the landing.

'Wait,' he said.

I went back into the room and he was getting into the bed. 'Please,' he said.

Once again, I knew what I had to do. Maybe it would be the last time—one last sympathy fuck. A final farewell to my former lover.

The sex was cursory, but tender—so unlike the wild, wanton, fucking sessions we used to have for hours in his dorm room. We both cried and held each other afterwards. Then I got up and dressed. Toby lay in bed staring at the wall and I slipped soundlessly from the room to disconsolately walk it off on the way back to the DeClermonts'.

crash and burn

I was dozing in my bed back at the DeClermonts', relishing not having to share it with anyone else. I smiled to myself, stretching out my arms and legs, enjoying being able to lie in and not have to vacate another hostel or hotel room *tout suite*.

The pleasant feeling dissipated quickly when there was a brisk knock at my bedroom door, and Sophie's brittle voice called to me. I put the pillow over my head, hoping she would go away. Then she just opened the door and burst in.

'Siobhan. I just had a call from the pension owner. He says your friend didn't go down for breakfast this morning and he is not getting up.'

I didn't see what the big deal was. Toby was probably just having a lie-in as well.

'I think you should go and get him. My friend at the pension would like to clean the room. It is already noon.'

I huffed loudly and swung my legs out of bed. 'OK,' I said, resigned. 'I'll just get ready.'

I took my time and I made myself some toast before heading down to Rouen center on foot.

I arrived at the pension and the owner met me at the door, looking flustered. He rushed me up the narrow, creaking staircase.

The man stopped outside Toby's room and then explained. 'I knocked on the door several times, as I wanted to get in to clean the room. When no one answered, I unlocked the door and went in, as I had assumed your friend had gone out. As usual, I announced myself loudly, in case your friend was in the bathroom. But I was surprised to see him still in bed, and well ... there seems to be a problem. He doesn't answer.'

My heart leapt into my throat. Wearing only his y-fronts, Toby was sprawled across the bed, his head dangling off the side. He was as white as the twisted sheets he was lying on. I ran to the bedside. I couldn't tell if he was breathing or not. On the bedside table was an empty bottle of whisky, lying on its side, and a plastic Ziploc bag of pills next to it. 'Shit, he took half those pills,' I whispered aloud to myself.

'TOBY, TOBY!' I yelled at him. He lifted his head weakly and groaned before flopping back down onto the pillow.

'TOBY, wake up, you fucking asshole. Stop joking around!'

'Gon' be sick,' Toby moaned, before leaning over the side of the bed and vomiting on the floor.

'Toby, we're calling an ambulance.'

'No … no amblince,' he raised his hand weakly in a stop signal.

'He's sick?' the pension owner said, his face grimacing in disgust.

'He must have drunk too much,' I said, shaking my head. 'I'll take him for a walk so you can clean the room. Sorry about the mess, I'll pay for any extra cleaning.'

The man nodded and quietly shut the door.

'Toby, what the hell are you playing at? Let's get you sobered up. Up you get. We're going to walk it off.'

He managed a few steps toward the bathroom and stopped. 'Gon be sick.' I grabbed the garbage pail and shoved it under his face, just in time to catch the splash of whisky-smelling vomit.

I helped him to the edge of the toilet. 'It's best to get it all out of your system.' He heaved until there was nothing left inside him.

'Come on, you need to clean yourself up.' I helped him to the sink so he could splash some water on his face. Then I threw his jeans at him. 'Let's get you dressed and out in the fresh air.'

He pushed me away, as I tried to help him to dress. 'Leave me alone. I'm not a retard,' he slurred. He was definitely getting his wits back.

I sat on the bed and waited for him to get dressed, trying to breathe out of my mouth, as the vomit smell was making me feel queasy.

He finally staggered out, still swaying and looking a bit green. 'I feel like shit, I'm going back to bed.'

'No you're not, the fresh air will do you some good. Plus, the pension owner needs to clean up the disgusting mess you made.'

Toby rubbed his hand over his face and looked at me blankly. He didn't have the strength to resist and he followed me out of the room. We sheepishly made our way past the reception desk and out the door.

Outside, it was a cold, brisk day with snow flurries sprinkling from sky. We made our way through the town center toward the cathedral.

'Toby, what the hell were you trying to do? You could have killed yourself taking all those pills and drinking a bottle of whisky.'

'No shit, Sherlock,' he replied with a challenging stare.

'How woulda that made you feel if I topped myself?'

'You can't tell me that performance was for my benefit.'

Toby shrugged and continued shuffling along. 'Or maybe you wouldn't have given a shit. Good riddance to old garbage, eh?'

'Toby, don't say that. Look I'm here aren't I? That means I care. I really do care. How do you think this whole situation makes me feel? It really hurts me that things have to be like this.'

'Well forget about the Italian dude, forget about France. Come home with me. Let's pick up where we left off before you came out here.'

'You know I can't, I've got to finish the year here. We'll talk about it when I get back in the summer, OK? I promise.'

As we walked along a narrow cobbled street, I was trying to keep Toby from staggering into the road. From behind us I could hear the sound of a motorcycle approaching. The roar of the engine made us both turn around.

Toby's face suddenly transformed into a mask of anger. 'It's that asshole!' he yelled. As he spun round in his rage he tripped over the gutter into the street.

I drew in a sharp breath, 'Watch out!' I screamed, as I saw the bike try to swerve at the last minute. The handlebar must have caught Toby's arm and the rider fell off.

There was a horrible screech of tires and the sound of plastic and metal crunching as the motorbike hit the cobbles. I stood, mouth agape in a silent scream, as my eyes focused on the carnage: two bodies lay crumpled in the street amongst the debris of mangled motorcycle, each in its own blooming puddle of blood.

Back at the Fac

The fog was incredible. I saw it roll in and conquer everything as I stood at the bus stop. It enveloped me and the other people waiting. The trees were draped by layers of the finest gossamer veil. I looked up at the white sky and saw a brilliant white orb. At first I thought it was the moon but then I realized it was the sun valiantly trying to burn its way through. When I arrived at the campus, I walked shrouded by the winter mist and my breath became one with the atmosphere. I could see the outline of the Faculté des Lettres, like one of Monet's impressionist paintings, all muted blues, pinks and silvers swirling together.

I shivered as I walked along the leaf-strewn path, the damp fog chilling my neck. The temperature had plummeted—it felt cold enough to snow.

Inside the building, the corridors were filling up with students pouting and posing, wrapped in an acrid haze of Gauloises smoke. Some students seemed animated, swapping stories about how they had spent their winter break, and others just looked plain depressed to be back to the old grind.

I went straight to the overseas student office to see if Lindi, Gabby, Mike and Mimi were there. A lot of the American students had been back to the States to spend Christmas with their families or had been travelling in Europe, so there was a lot of catching up to do. Lindi was standing outside the office door, which had been emblazoned with the word 'AMERITRASH' in bright orange spray paint.

'Very apt,' I said to Lindi, indicating the graffiti.

Lindi greeted me, 'Howdy stranger. Long time no see. Happy New Year! How was your break?'

'Yeah, Happy New Year,' I returned. 'How was yours?' I thought I'd move the spotlight onto her. I couldn't face reliving the whole sordid story of Toby again.

'Welllll…' she said, her eyes shining. 'I met a guy. A really great guy.'

'That's fantastic,' I said, but not really meaning it. I didn't hold out much hope for Lindi's taste in men—not with her track record.

'What's the matter? Are you OK? You seem strange,' Lindi said.

'I didn't really have a great time over the break and it's got me a bit down. But why don't you tell me about this guy. How did you meet?'

'You won't believe it. It's a crazy story. I was alone at my host family's house for most of the break. They were away visiting their relatives in the south of France and Mike had gone off to Spain. It got really cold and a pipe burst. I called my host family and they told me where to find the number for their plumber—some friend of my host father apparently from his men's club. I thought it was going to be some old man and I was surprised when this gorgeous young guy showed up. It turns out the plumber was so busy because of the cold weather that he sent his assistant.'

'So did he fix your pipes?' I joked, having a feeling that I knew how the story was going to end.

'Very funny,' Lindi said. 'Well, yes, he did fix the pipe, but he was a perfect gentleman. I offered him a cup of coffee and we got to talking and ended up spending the entire afternoon just shooting the breeze. It turns out he has just come out of a relationship because his girlfriend of five years was cheating on him.'

'Uh oh, rebound,' I said.

'Anyway, we got on really well and went out on a couple of dates over the holidays. He even spent the night while my host family were away as he didn't like the idea of me being left all by myself at night.'

'I bet he didn't,' I said, sarcastically.

'What's your problem, Miss Cynical? I thought you'd be happy for me,' Lindi retorted.

'I'm sorry. I really am happy for you. I'm just in a bit of a bad mood today.'

'Why, what's the matter?'

Luckily, Gabriela joined us just then, all smiles and cheerfulness. 'Hello ladies, Happy New Year!'

'How was your trip back to the States, Gab?' Lindi asked.

'It was wonderful.' Gabriela looked pleased with herself. 'I've got something to show you.' She held out her hand displaying a sparkling diamond ring on her left ring finger.

'You got engaged?' Lindi asked.

'Yes, Jamie proposed on Christmas eve,' Gabriela gushed.

Oh great, I thought. Now we'll have to listen to her going on about her wedding plans all the time.

'Aren't you a bit young? I hope you're going to finish your studies,' I said.

'Of course, silly. We're going to get married after I graduate.'

'How did Paul take it?' I asked.

Gabriela suddenly looked crestfallen. 'Why did you have to bring him up?'

'I just know how obsessed he is with you.'

'He doesn't know yet. I haven't told my French family, for the exact reason that I was afraid of how Paul might react. I know how he feels about Jamie.'

'Haven't they noticed the ring yet?' Lindi asked.

'I take it off when I get in and just keep it in my pocket.'

Lindi and I exchanged glances.

Mike now sauntered over. 'Hey ladies,' he said in his laid back way, while licking the papers to close his roll-up.

'I hear congratulations are in order, Gabriela,' he said patting her shoulder.

Gabriela beamed and showed him her ring.

'Jamie is a lucky man,' he said.

'So, you've got to hear about Mike's little adventure. You won't believe it.' Lindi said.

'Yeah. You could say that. Adventure is definitely the right word,' Mike chuckled.

'You could've got yourself into real trouble, Mike,' Lindi said. 'I don't know how you can be so blasé.'

'Why? What happened?' I pried.

'Go on, tell them the story you told me,' Lindi coaxed him.

'I was just hitchhiking down to Spain.'

'By yourself?' Gabriela asked.

'Of course. I didn't want anyone else cramping my style. It was going really well, but then a truck driver picked me up. Everything seemed quite normal at first, but after about five hours he said he needed to rest. So he pulled over and well … he unzipped his pants, got his cock out and asked me to jerk him off.'

'Ewww!' Gabriela squealed.

'I tried to get out of the truck but he had locked the doors. He said he knew about boys like me working the autoroute. He called me a tease.'

'What the hell did you do?'

'I punched him in the face.'

'Really?' I said. Skinny, weedy Mike was the last person I could imagine punching someone in the face.

Mike laughed. 'He let me out and I didn't stick my thumb out for truckers anymore!' Mike laughed.

'The story doesn't end there,' Lindi interjected. 'Tell them what happened next, Mike.'

'OK, I finally got to Barcelona and found a cheap place to stay in the Gothic Quarter. I needed a drink so I headed for the nearest bar. It was a dark, dingy place, full of smoke and smelling of ham. A woman started chatting to me at the bar. She seemed nice enough but I wasn't interested—she wasn't really my type. Anyway, she asked if I'd buy her a drink and I didn't want to be rude, so I did. She started to get a bit touchy-feely with me. Putting her arms around me, trying to get me to dance. I was starting to feel really uncomfortable, so I said I needed to go to the toilet. When I got back to the bar I was relieved to see that the woman was gone. I had enough of that place and decide to check out a bit of the city. I put my hand in my pocket to get out my wallet to pay—but there was nothing there. I checked my other pocket and my back pockets. I took everything out of my rucksack and looked for the wallet in there. It was gone! The woman must have pick-pocketed me. I tried to explain to the barman that I couldn't pay because the woman took my money. He did not look at all pleased with my story. "You no pay—you pay with blood!" I was trying to tell him that I would pay him when I was able to get some money. Then I freaked out when I saw him wave over his friend who was built like a brick shithouse. I took one look at the guy, picked up my rucksack and ran. I had no idea where I was, I found myself in a rabbit warren of streets, with the brick shithouse chasing after me. I managed to shake him off and I stopped for a breather. I realized I was up shit creek and that I needed to find a police station. I wandered around completely lost and pissed-off for hours. I finally found someone who spoke English and pointed me in the right direction of the police station, where I spent the whole rest of the night.'

I raised my eyebrows and smirked. 'So you enjoyed Barcelona then?' I asked.

'Oh my God, Mike, that's so scary. How did you get back?' Gabriela asked.

'Luckily, my parents wired some money over, so I was able to pay for a new passport and a train ticket home.'

'But you haven't told us what you got up to. You were in Italy right?' Mike asked.

I shrugged non-committally.

'Yeah, I was in Italy for Christmas and then I came back and spent some time in Paris. My boyfriend, Toby, was over from the States for the New Year.'

'How did that work out? You mentioned that you didn't really have a great time.' Mike asked.

'Yes, tell us what happened,' Lindi pried.

Finally, I reluctantly told them the whole story about Italy, and Paris and Bruno and Toby. They all stared at me sympathetically.

'Oh no, that's dreadful. You poor thing!' Lindi and Gabriela both hugged me at the same time.

Mike handed me his roll-up. 'I think you need a smoke,' he said, and I gratefully accepted.

Snow and War

I was in my room putting the finishing touches to an essay about Verlaine that was due to be handed in later, when I heard the phone ringing in the DeClermonts' foyer. I could make out Sophie talking to someone in her fake sing-songy telephone voice. 'Siobhan,' she screeched, knocking at my bedroom door. 'Your course leader Monsieur Céleste called to say not to come to classes today.'

I opened my door to her, puzzled. *'Pourquoi?'* I asked.

'Haven't you not heard *les nouvelles? Les Américains* started bombing Baghdad and war has been declared.'

'Vraiment?' I asked, completely surprised. It was really news to me. 'But why does that mean they have to cancel classes?'

'Monsieur Céleste warned that radical students at the university were protesting against the war and threats have been made to the American office. He said to be careful and not congregate in large groups with your fellow Americans. Oh, and one more thing—*très important*. He said there is a meeting at his apartment at 5pm to discuss the fate of your study abroad program.'

I watched her walk away before scurrying back into my room to turn on the radio for some news. It was true—the USA had dropped a bomb on Baghdad. Protests were starting all over Europe.

Suddenly I felt a mixture of emotions. Fear—fear for my friends back home who might have to fight and die, and Lindi. I remembered that she was still in the Army Reserve and could be called up. I also felt anger—anger at the selfishness and greed of the American government, but also anger at the people who had misconceptions about me because of where I was born. I was pissed off at the whole human race for hating each other and for destroying our world.

I'd become used to putting up with some anti-Americanism but now it was going to get 100 times worse. I knew that many people thought they well understood the American mentality, and how they oversimplified it. I'd heard people make sweeping statements about Americans, like that they don't bother to get a passport, they think the USA is the whole world, that they are uneducated and illiterate, that their *haute cuisine* consists of McDonald's and Coca Cola. I didn't understand why it was acceptable to be overtly racist about Americans but not any other nationality.

Don't get me wrong. I was not the most patriotic, flag-waving American either—I knew there was a lot that could improve in the United States, but I also knew that you couldn't blame the citizens for the decisions their government made. I did not represent the United States and all it stood for, just as I would not blame all Germans for the Holocaust.

Despite Richard's warnings, I decided to venture out to the university. I wasn't going to let anyone scare me into submission. I phoned Lindi to see if she wanted to come with me.

I heard her intake a sharp breath. 'Didn't you hear what Richard said?'

'He just said that classes were cancelled. He didn't say not to go to the Fac at all. I need to get some books out and I'm not going to let any militants get in my way.'

'OK, alright. I also need to do some research for a project.'

We met in front of her house and as we headed to the campus I asked, 'You worried?'

She nodded. 'Yeah. I am. I'm crapping myself. They can call me up and I'll have to go and fight.'

I stopped and gave her a big hug. 'Don't you worry; I won't let that happen. If the army comes looking for you I'll hide you someplace they could never find you—like under my bed or in the armoire at the DeClermonts'.'

'I feel a lot better knowing that,' she chuckled, but we both really knew that there would be nothing either of us could do if she received her orders.

We were met at the front entrance of the library by a group of students chanting anti-war slogans and carrying placards reading '*QUELLE CONNERIE LA GUERRE*', which means 'War is bullshit', and '*ARRÊT LA BUSHERIE*' which is a play on George Bush's last name and the word for butchery in French—'Stop the butchery (Bushery)', and of course, my favorite, 'AMERITRASH'.

A girl handed us some flyers as we approached the library. We mutely nodded at her as we didn't want our accents to be detected. But just then, Gekko came out of the library and spotted us. '*Ah les belles Américaines,*' he announced a little too loudly for my liking, running up to Lindi and I and kissing us on both cheeks.

'Shhh!' Lindi hissed, looking around.

'*Nous sommes Irlandaises pas Américaines*,' I stated, winking at Gekko. The French love the Irish so it was a safe English-speaking nationality to pretend to be. He looked at me like I was crazy but then tapped the side of his nose conspiratorially.

'Do you want to come for a drink?' he asked. 'I'm meeting my new boyfriend at La Cascade.'

I looked Lindi. 'What do you say? Shall we ditch the library and go for a drink?'

'I thought you needed to get some books out?'

'Well the books can wait. I want a drink.'

'Count me out. While I'm here I'm going to do some work.'

As Gekko and I waited at the bus stop for our bus into the city center, I was aware of the temperature dropping. By the time we reached the bar, my breath froze in the air and the sky was an icy steel grey.

'Looks like it's going to snow,' I said.

'Ha, ha,' Gekko chuckled. You're mad. It hasn't snowed here for three years.'

I was grateful to get out of the cold into the warm, steamy atmosphere of the bar. It was full of people noisily chattering over the sound of the music—some waved at Gekko. It was his favorite gay bar and he was well known there. Gekko spotted his companion at a table by the window. They kissed each other exuberantly on both cheeks. Then Gekko introduced me. 'Sylvain, this is Siobhan, *ma filleulle*.'

He was an attractive young guy with spiky platinum hair and baggy jeans. As Sylvain shook my hand, I noticed he was chewing his lips and his pupils were big, black dinner plates. He already looked off his face on something.

Gekko started plying us with drinks. Sylvain whispered in my ear, 'A little beet of coke?' He surreptitiously pressed a small, white twist of paper into my palm. I nodded, smiling knowingly, and went to the toilet to snort.

When I came out, Gekko and Sylvain were all over each other. I sat around for a bit feeling like a third wheel until they finally came up for air. 'Hey,' Gekko said, pointing out the window. 'It looks like coke is falling from the sky!'

It was snowing heavily and the ground was already covered. I looked at my watch—and realized how late it was. If I didn't leave immediately I'd be late for the meeting at Richard's apartment.

I jumped up. 'Sorry guys, I've got to go,' I explained, peering worriedly out the window. It was now dark out and I couldn't believe the volume of snow that was coming down. There had to be a couple of inches accumulated on the ground already.

'Aww. Stay and have another one to warm up before you go,' Gekko said. 'I just bought you another shot.'

'I'd love to but I have to get to an important meeting,' I said, as Gekko handed me the shot glass.

I sniffed the syrupy clear liquid and wrinkled my nose. Sambuca—not my favorite—but I knew how annoyingly persistent Gekko could be and I needed Dutch courage so I downed the shot. It burned as it went down, warming my belly.

I seemed to wait forever for the bus to come. There was one other person waiting at the stop. She explained that because of the snow there was a limited service. All I could do was wait. When the bus cautiously skidded to a halt I looked at my watch. I was becoming increasingly worried about missing Richard's meeting. The bus was empty and the other passenger and I clambered on. I chose a window seat near the back, rubbed the condensation from the window and looked out at the white wasteland of deserted streets. Trees appeared like white snow monsters flailing their snow-coated tentacles. Darkened shops had closed early and everyone had sensibly gone home to their safe, warm houses. Rooftops cowered under the cold heavy blanket of snow. You could hardly see a foot in front of you. The bus driver very slowly crept up the hill toward Mont-Saint-Aignan. Soon the wheels of the bus were just spinning and it kept sliding at an angle toward the sidewalk. The driver finally skidded to a halt and announced that he would not be going any further.

I looked through my little porthole in the condensation to see if I could recognize where we were. All I could see was white. I got up uncertainly from my seat. '*Ou sommes-nous, monsieur?*' I asked the bus driver.

He said the name of a place that I had never heard of.

'Mont-Saint-Aignan?' I queried.

He shrugged that typical Gallic shrug and he pointed vaguely to his left.

I got off the bus and emerged in a white world, without a clue where I was. I was struck by the eerie silence and the strange halos of light cast by the streetlights. I shivered with both the cold and nerves, becoming aware of how drunk I was and how vulnerable it now made me feel not to be 100% in possession of my faculties and completely lost. I looked around but couldn't recognize anything to get a sense of place or direction. I squinted at the map that was posted at the bus stop to try and get my bearings. I didn't recognize any of the place names or the streets, and there wasn't a single soul in sight to ask directions—no cars, no pedestrians. I set off desolately and with trepidation in the direction that the bus driver had pointed, hoping to eventually see something that I recognized, although all landmarks were disguised under a thick layer of snow.

The snow flew into my eyes and froze my eyelashes. I walked along what I thought was the sidewalk but I wasn't sure as it all looked the same—white, white, white. I was starting to get snow blindness, feeling dizzy and disorientated. The powdery snow was up to my calves as I trudged through it. I looked around me—nothing. I thought about retracing my steps back to the bus stop and staying there for shelter until the snow stopped, but when I looked back, my footprints had already disappeared. Holy shit—I would never get out of here. Panic thumped in my chest.

I started to cry, my tears freezing to my face. I was so cold and hungry, I couldn't feel my toes and my head was beginning to throb. I felt like giving up, just throwing myself down in the snow to die of hypothermia in a snowdrift, for my body to be found in the spring when the snow melted. I had never felt so alone and desperate. At that moment, I would have thrown my arms around Sophie and would have been grateful for her scowling face, to be warm and safe in her house.

If only Bruno were here right now. I imagined seeing him appear out of the blizzard, on his clapped-out motorbike.

Then I heard the drone of a motor behind me. Oh, it couldn't be … I turned around and was suddenly blinded by the headlights from the snow plough. The driver blared the horn. I had been walking in the middle of the road and hadn't even realized it. I jumped out of the way, narrowly missing being buried under the mountain of snow the plough deposited on the side of the road.

I followed the path the plough had cleared on the road behind it, feeling a little more secure that I was at least headed somewhere that might lead to human life. I was exhausted and making slow progress. I pulled my collar around my neck and occasionally rubbed my frostbitten fingers to try and regain the blood flow.

I was almost ready to give up and turn around when I saw bright red neon tinge the snowy air. Could it be a hallucination? I squinted and could make out the sign for the Continent hypermarket—the big blue 'C' with red in the middle. I let out a sigh of relief; I finally knew where I was! Despite the lack of a defined route, I headed in the general direction of the DeClermonts' neighborhood and was able to recognize the side street where the DeClermonts lived.

For the first time since I came to France, I was overwhelmed with relief when I saw the DeClermonts' squat, grey house, tightly shuttered against the outside world, huddled under a thick blanket of snow.

I stamped the snow off my boots, throwing off my coat and relishing the warmth, rubbing my hands together when Sophie poked her head out the kitchen. 'Siobhan, you're too late for dinner.'

I sat down at the table. 'I'm so sorry I'm late. I got lost in the snow. I didn't think I'd ever get home.' I explained.

'*Quel bazar! Il y a de la neige partout*'—'What a mess! There's snow everywhere'—said Sophie. 'Take those wet things off and sit down. I'll see if there is something *rapide* I can make for you.' I smiled gratefully and sunk down in the chair. My heart sank, however, at the sight of the ham pizza that Sophie pulled out of the freezer. I couldn't believe that after all this time she still didn't remember that I was a vegetarian. I guessed I was just going to have to pick the ham off. I was so hungry I didn't care anymore.

February thaw

My life had become increasingly strange and complicated. The whole situation with the war was making me feel uneasy and putting a negative spin on everything, including my relationship with Bruno.

On Saturday he suddenly announced that he was thinking of leaving France and going to England where money would be easier to come by, and there was a great photography degree course at a university in London that he was interested in.

I was shocked and hurt but I tried not to show it. I told him that it was up to him what he did, but I wasn't going to follow him. I had to finish the semester here and then go back to the States for the final year of my degree.

He shrugged and grinned. 'Just don't be afraid to live, Primavera,' he advised me, peering over the rims of his glasses like a wise old owl.

His carefree attitude was really starting to get on my nerves. I needed to start thinking about what I was going to do with my life after I graduated from university. I couldn't drift around Europe forever, living on cheap wine and baguettes.

I was shitting myself at the thought having to find a career and make a living, and Bruno just didn't understand that. He embraced life one day at time and plans were a hindrance. He preferred uncertainty and surprise to keep him stimulated. 'Otherwise I will die like the cicada, turning into an empty husk when the summer is over,' he told me. 'Life should be eternal summer, Primavera.' Then he departed gaily to buy some tobacco and left me alone in his apartment.

Another incident made me question my relationship with Bruno: I found an earring in his apartment. One day, after he had gone out, I lay down on his bed and lit a cigarette, when I felt something sharp prick my back. It was an earring. I recognized it as belonging to Chiara, Bruno's Italian friend, who was seeing Mike.

I decided to have a little snoop around his apartment to see if there was any more incriminating evidence. In a drawer I found some photographs of Chiara sprawled across the bed wearing only some sexy lingerie, and the earrings.

When Bruno came back I showed him the earring and asked what it was doing in his apartment. He told me that Chiara had come over to talk about her relationship problems with Mike. 'She was very upset and needed consoling,' he explained.

'I bet she needed consoling. Why was the earring in your *bed*?' I asked.

'I took pictures of her lying on the bed. Nothing more.'

I went to the drawer and pulled out the photos of Chiara lounging on the bed.

'You see,' Bruno said, grabbing the photos away from me. 'She asked me to take some pictures of her.'

'In her underwear?' I asked.

'She wanted to send them to Mike to try and get his attention. He must be gay though, not to be interested in her. Chiara is a beautiful woman,' he said looking closely at the top photograph and smiling.

'You promise that nothing happened between you two?'

'Primavera, are you jealous? Of course not, I would never betray you,' he said, pulling me close to him and kissing me. 'How about I take some sexy pictures of you?'

I pushed him away. 'I'm not in the mood and I don't want you taking pictures of semi-naked women anymore.'

'Of course,' Bruno said, adjusting his glasses and heading to the door. 'Are you ready? We should leave now.'

We were going to Les Sapins, an ugly suburb on the outskirts of Rouen to see some bands playing, and Gekko was doing a DJ set. I had been looking forward to it, but was now feeling so miffed I wasn't sure that I could have a good time.

I didn't move. 'I'm not going to be that easily pacified this time, Bruno,' I said. 'I'm not so sure I can trust you anymore.'

'Come on, Primavera. You can ask Chiara. Nothing happened. I just took pictures. She doesn't interest me.'

He walked back over to me and skinned up. 'I think some of this will help you relax.' In any situation where emotions were running high Bruno always rolled a joint.

I gave in. I wanted to believe him. We smoked the joint and had a little bit of speed. I relaxed and began to look forward to a mellow evening of music and meeting up with the gang: Mimi and Patrice, Lindi and her new beau, Mike and Chiara, and Gabriela.

We didn't know where the place was and made our way just by asking people and following signs. We arrived late and just saw the tail end of a band called Les Imperverts. At least we were there in time to see Gekko's friend's band Mister Moonlight, who were really good.

In the break between sets, we found the gang and said our hellos. Lindi introduced us to Pierrot, who seemed like a nice enough guy—quite shy and quiet. He was tall, with dark curly hair, dark brown eyes and a nice smile. Lindi was beaming from ear to ear as she introduced us. He was obviously making her very happy—and if she was happy I was happy.

Mimi was with Patrice, but they didn't seem to be their usual lovey-dovey selves. I guessed that since the abortion the shine had been taken off their relationship.

I stiffened when I saw Chiara and Mike. I still had the earring in my pocket and I fingered it tensely as I approached them. 'Hello my darlings,' Chiara said in her exaggerated Italian way, embracing me. When she embraced Bruno, I scrutinized their body language. But they were both such touchy-feely people anyway that it was difficult to tell if there was a hint of a secret liaison.

Mike calmly sipped his beer and puffed on his roll-up, with his back to Chiara, ignoring her. 'Should be a good show tonight,' he said to me looking toward the stage. He glanced at his watch. 'Has anyone seen Roland? I said I'd meet him here but he hasn't shown up yet.'

Chiara rolled her eyes. 'Roland, Roland, it's always Roland, darling. You see enough of him anyway.'

Mike was so laid back that he never seemed to get annoyed, but I could see he was irritated by what Chiara said. He chose to ignore it and continued to stare at the stage.

'Hey amigo,' Bruno shouted across the crowd. 'José, come join us.'

It was Bruno's Brazilian friend. He shoved through the crowd to stand with us. He was wearing a Che Guevara t-shirt and sandals even though it was freezing outside.

He gave Bruno a hearty hug, and Chiara a kiss. He ignored me and the other Americans. 'Hey José,' I said.

'I'm sorry, did I hear something? A buzz? I don't fraternize with the enemy,' he said.

'Oh no, here we go again,' Mike said, rolling his eyes and puffing on his cigarette.

José launched into a rant about the war and how we were all terrorists. 'Man, are you still with this Yankee?' José asked Bruno.

'You better watch out brother; they're gonna try and take over Italy next.'

I wanted to tell that asshole to go fuck off, but I bit my tongue. I didn't want to seem like I was pro-American either. But I was sick of being tarred with the same brush as the warmongering, flag-waving types. It wasn't my war. I had no idea what it was about. It had nothing to do with me and I didn't appreciate people getting racist about it.

We ignored José's jibes and, after airing his views, he finally went away. I felt, though, that a negative vibe had descended on the evening.

When Mister Moonlight started playing, Lindi and Pierrot did more making out than watching the band. Mike intently observed the musicians, and looked at his watch every so often, while Chiara appeared bored.

I tapped her on the shoulder. 'I've got something of yours,' I said.

'Something of mine?' She looked puzzled.

I held the earring up in front of her face, dangling it between my fingers.

'Where did you find that?' she asked, with a hint of surprise on her face.

'At Bruno's place.'

She glanced sideways at Mike to see if he'd heard, but he was too distracted in greeting his friend Roland who had just arrived.

'Oh yes, I must have lost it when I dropped by his place the other day. Thanks, darling,' she said, pocketing the earring.

She wasn't giving anything away. I couldn't sense any guilt or furtiveness in her expression or voice. There was no mention of the photos. However, if Bruno was telling the truth about them, I presumed she wouldn't want to mention them in front of Mike. I told myself I had to stop being so paranoid and insecure, and I *really* wanted to believe Bruno. Nevertheless, I wanted her to know that I had seen the photos.

'The pictures came out well,' I said, surprising myself at how calm I sounded.

'The pictures? Ohhh … the pictures. You saw the pictures?' she said, seeming a bit startled.

I nodded, staring her straight in the eye.

She took me aside, out of Mike's earshot. 'Darling, I hope you don't mind.'

'Mind?' I was about to try to get some clarification about what I shouldn't mind, when Gekko appeared. He was wearing a fluorescent baseball cap, huge sunglasses and loads of chains and medallions in imitation of an 80s rap singer.

'*Bonsoir ma filleule*,' he sang theatrically, mincing over to me and giving me a big kiss.

That put an end to any further discussion between Chiara and me. We went back to join our circle of friends. I let the incident drop for the time being but a seed of doubt had been planted in my mind. This magnified my anxiety and insecurity and my growing sense of panic about the future. Despite all the fun and adventures I had had with Bruno, I couldn't be like him. I couldn't just live for today. I had to think about tomorrow as well.

spring trip

Gabriela and I stood at the reception desk of the Catholic Women's Center in Rome. A wizened old nun asked us for our passports. Gabriela had dual nationality and strategically pulled out her Portuguese passport. The nun looked at it and nodded approvingly. '*Si, si Portugesa,*' she said, smiling warmly at Gabriela. I handed her mine and she looked at it, disappointed. '*Americana?*' she said, looking at Gabriela questioningly, as if to ask, what are you doing with an American?

She frowned as she noted down the details and handed it back to me coldly, without saying a word.

Addressing Gabriela, she explained in halting Portuguese how to find our dormitory and what time the curfew was. Gabriela translated for me. 'The curfew is at 10pm.'

'Ten o'clock? That's too early.' Can you ask her what happens if we're late?'

'She already told me that they lock up at 10pm promptly and don't let anyone in after that time.'

'Jesus!' I exclaimed. 'How the hell are we expected to enjoy the Roman nightlife if we have to be back for 10pm?'

'No usa thata language here,' the wizened nun whispered harshly. She spoke English after all.

While we were waiting for the nuns to sort out the keys for our lockers, I rummaged around in my rucksack for a crumpled pack of 'Lookie Streek'. I'd been dying for a cigarette and lit up. I felt relaxed and was enjoying the sensation of the tobacco chemicals shooting through my bloodstream, when I suddenly heard a shrill voice shouting in Italian. I turned round and saw an enraged nun charging toward me, her habit flying behind her.

'*No fumare!*' she exclaimed, waving her hands in the air.

I quickly took another drag, before stubbing the cigarette out in the potted plant that was in the foyer. Now the nun was really furious. 'Rude American, no gooda—eh.'

Gabriela tutted. 'C'mon Siobhan have some manners; it's a house of God.'

I looked around but couldn't see anywhere I could dispose of the cigarette, so I sheepishly fished the partially smoked butt out of the plant and shoved it into my jeans pocket.

Gabriela had stalked off down the hallway, following the nun to the dormitory. I hurried to catch her up.

The corridor was long, light green, and institutional looking. I had always wondered why these types of places, schools and hospitals especially, always used green to paint their walls. Supposedly it is a relaxing color, but the bile-like hue always made me feel nauseous.

The dormitory was no more relaxing. It was a long, sparse, echoing, high-ceilinged room, with terracotta tiles and peeling, damp walls. The windows were small and set up high so that you couldn't see anything out of them. I set my bag down on a metal-framed single bed, and looked around. There were two rows of five beds. To me, it looked more like a prison or an insane asylum than a traveler's hostel.

I sat down on the edge of the bed and put my head in my hands. What the hell was I doing here?

'What's the matter with you?' Gabriela asked. 'You're not still annoyed about not going to Prague with Mike, Lindi and Mimi? You're here now so you may as well make the most of it.'

'When you told me you had found us some cheap accommodation in Rome, I expected a youth hostel or cheap hotel, not this.'

'I know it's a bit strict, but it's a bed and a roof over our heads. And besides, you don't have to pay so you shouldn't complain.'

I thought of the others going to Prague and felt envious. I'd already been to Italy, and I wanted to tick Czechoslovakia off my list of places to visit. However, Gabriela didn't have anyone else to go to Italy with and she had offered to pay for my accommodation in Rome. I hadn't been to Rome yet, so decided to take her up on her offer.

After Italy, we were going on to meet Lindi, Mike, Mimi, Anne and some of Mike's new friends, in the Alps for a skiing trip. I was really looking forward to that and just wanted to get this part of the trip out of the way.

We decided to go out and explore. Rome was beautiful, but the smell of car and motorcycle fumes made my eyes water. Cars and motorbikes wove in and out of traffic-choked narrow streets, honking their horns. We explored one of the many ruins that litter the city. It was grey with soot and the ancient steps were strewn with junkies' used needles and broken bottles. We carried on climbing up the steps to the top of a hill with a panoramic view of the city: red-tiled roofs, broken Ionic columns jutting haphazardly, cypress trees, gardens and ancient palaces. I was exhausted and sweltering in the 21-degree heat. It had been freezing when we had left France and I was wearing a sweater, my leather jacket, jeans and boots. I was about to sit down on a wall to catch my breath when a gang of five scruffy little gypsy urchins approached me. They held a ratty old newspaper up to my face and started babbling and pointing. I knew their game. I'd read about this scam in the travel guidebooks. They hold a newspaper up in front of your face so that you don't notice their grubby little hands rifling through your pockets.

Without even thinking, I karate kicked one of the thieves in the balls. That was the one thing I remembered how to do from my failed attempts at learning karate. The kid doubled over in pain and his friends all jeered and spat on me. I lashed out with another karate chop and they all started to run. I gave chase.

Gabriela shouted, 'Siobhan, Siobhan, leave them alone. They're only kids.' I stopped and went back to her, huffing and puffing. The kids had disappeared.

'The little assholes tried to steal my wallet,' I said, breathless.

'Did they get it?' she asked.

'No, luckily—I've actually got a big hole in my pocket, so everything in there falls into the bottom of the lining inside the jacket. Even I can't get anything out of there,' I laughed.

Gabriela shook her head. 'What was the need for the Kung Fu antics then?'

'It just made me angry that they thought they could get one over on me.'

'Well, we came to Rome to see the sights, not get mixed up with some little jerks. Gabriela got out her list of things to see and do in Rome and studied it. 'Let's go to the Coliseum.'

We headed back down the hill into the traffic-choked streets. Men were stopping in their tracks and wolf-whistling at Gabriela and I as we walked past. I didn't think I looked particularly sexy in my torn jeans and boots—it seemed any female could get Roman men excited. Guys were even stopping their mopeds in the middle of the street and holding up traffic to stare at us.

'These Italian men are like wolves,' Gabriela said. 'I'm scared. I wish Jamie were here right now.'

She grabbed my arm, I guessed for security, but I wasn't really sure what safety I could offer. The unwanted attention was making me feel very uncomfortable as well. I was beginning to understand the need for the women only dormitory and the early curfew.

We were having some trouble finding the Coliseum in the maze of old streets. Gabriela stood on a corner with her map open, conspicuously. Suddenly, the gang of young gypsy boys appeared from behind us. They cursed and spat at us. I stuck my middle finger up at them. The little shits were following us.

We thought we had shaken them off and finally managed to orient ourselves and found the Coliseum. There were living statues lined up along the walkway and one of them held out a giant walking stick, which he looped over Gabriela and I and dragged us toward him. I had a horrible phobia of mimes and clowns and this guy with his weird silver-painted body freaked me out. I let out a scream and yanked the stick out of the 'statue's' hands. He shouted and there was a bit of a tug of war.

'Let go!' Gabriela yelled. 'Really, Siobhan, you've got to chill out.'

I let go and we scuttled away from the mime. When we got to the entrance to the Coliseum we discovered that we would have to pay to go in. Unfortunately, the entry was too expensive for our student budgets, and we were saving our money for the Vatican, so we just took some pictures of the Coliseum from the outside.

'Well, even from the outside it's impressive,' Gabriela said.

'It looks just like a giant wedding cake,' I said as I snapped a few photos with the sun and the bright blue sky streaming through the tiers of stone arches.

Gabriela consulted her map. 'Let's go to the Forum now,' she said, leading the way.

At least the Forum was free to get in. Columns and remains of architraves stood solitary, the only remainder of the grand buildings that had once stood there. Beneath our feet the ancient paving stones were worn smooth and shiny from thousands of years of footsteps. We walked around the ancient remnants of the original city, trying to imagine what it must have looked like back in the day, with gladiators fighting to the death, the vestal virgins keeping the flames alight, people having communal shits, and prostitutes entertaining obese Romans in perfumed rooms. Rome must have been a crazy place to live back then. Come to think of it, it was still a crazy place.

I was jolted from my daydream by Gabriela tugging at my arm. 'C'mon, let's go to the Vatican now. That's what I really came here for,' she said.

As we weaved our way through the crowded Roman streets, she explained a bit about the Vatican. 'Did you know that, officially, it's not actually in Rome? It is its very own independent city, governed by its own laws.'

'Why's that?' I asked. 'Are the Pope and all his Cardinals so self-important that they have to have their own city-state?'

Gabriela gave me a withering glance, and suddenly stopped, her mouth agape as we entered the circular main plaza. It was surrounded by an impressive, curved colonnade, with hundreds of stone statues of saints perched on top, looking down at the throng of visitors. The square was full of invalids hobbling with walking sticks, or half-dead-looking people being pushed around in wheelchairs, all hoping for a chance to catch a glimpse of the Pope who might be able to cure them.

We stood in line for about an hour before we were able to get into the cathedral. Once inside, we were herded up the narrow, winding stone staircase to get to the dome and then up onto the roof. The view from the roof made it all worth it. Rome lay beneath us, spread out in all its glory, with the lazy Tiber river meandering and weaving its way around the ancient, peeling and crumbling buildings. Church bell towers soared above hundreds of red-tiled roofs that looked like they were stacked up at odd angles. You could see the hint of green in secret courtyard gardens and patios, and balconies hung with ivy and jasmine. It was breathtaking. This is what made me feel spiritual, not the Pope or any of the gold in the cathedral beneath us.

On our way back down we decided to walk around inside the cathedral. It was gigantic with so much gold and ornamentation it made my head spin. There was a big group of tourists gathered round something and a person standing in front of the group speaking. I was intrigued and pushed my way to the front of the crowd.

Inside a glass sarcophagus lay the body of a former pope, pale, and waxen, with his eyes closed, as if he was sleeping. He wore a white miter on his head and fine velvet robes, embroidered with gold trim. The tour guide explained that the pope had died hundreds of years ago but when they exhumed his body to make room for another pope's burial they discovered his body was still completely intact and undecomposed. The church declared it a miracle and kept the remains in the airtight glass box on display in the Vatican cathedral.

Gabriela was completely freaked out by it and made the sign of the cross several times, muttering prayers under her breath. She obviously believed the tour guide's spiel. But when I scrutinized the body I came to the conclusion that it was definitely made out of wax. It was so badly done as well that I was baffled as to how anyone could possibly believe it was real.

After the Vatican, we carried on doing all the normal touristy things; we walked down the Spanish steps and threw a coin in the Trevi fountain.

By then it was dusk and we realized how tired and hungry we were. The day had gone so quickly and it was already evening. It wasn't difficult to find a pizzeria—pretty much every restaurant in Rome is a pizzeria—and we went into the nearest one. The waiter immediately appeared and seated us. He put a tablecloth on the table, set out the cutlery and handed us menus. He put a basket of fresh bread on the table and took our orders. As we were on a budget, we just asked for water and the most inexpensive margherita pizzas. They seemed to be taking a long time and we were becoming more and more ravenous. I kept checking my watch. We were so hungry, not having had lunch, so we started to tuck into the bread. In the States we were used to waiting not more than 20 minutes for the food to come. In the end we had to wait over an hour. We couldn't work out why it had taken so long to make two margherita pizzas. We wolfed the pizzas down so quickly we didn't even have a chance to enjoy them.

'Siobhan, we have to get back for the curfew, or we'll be locked out,' Gabriela said, panic showing in her eyes.

'Don't worry. It'll be OK. *Il conto per favore,*' I called to the waiter.

We were shocked when we got the bill. There were three charges on there that didn't make sense. I could sort of get by with the bit of Italian that Bruno had taught me, but it was a mixture of Veronese dialect swear words and very basic guidebook Italian. I queried the extra charges, and from what I could understand of the waiter's explanation, we had to pay for the tablecloth, the bread, and the tap water.

Gabriela stood up, pushing her chair back from the table. 'He's ripping us off,' she said. She waved the waiter over. 'First you keep us waiting over an hour and then you have the nerve to charge us for a tablecloth, water, and bread that we didn't even order!'

I blinked in surprise, as I'd never seen Gabriela get angry before. The waiter then threatened to call the police unless we paid up.

It was already 9.30pm. We only had half an hour to find our way back to the hostel. We gave in, grabbed the remaining bread, left some crumpled lira on the table and dashed out.

In the darkness of the street, we fumbled with the map and tried to orientate ourselves. We realized we had no idea where we were. We heard footsteps behind us and I saw that we were being followed. My heart leapt into my throat. Rome suddenly seemed a lot more threatening in the dark.

'Let's get the hell out of here Gab,' I shouted, pulling her by the arm and running down the street. We ran until we reached a busier area.

'Shit—it's 10pm,' Gabriela said. 'We need to find the convent.'

I grabbed the map. Now that we were on a main road it was easier to figure out where we were. Sleazy men leered at us from all directions, making suggestive comments. We tried to appear confident and not lost. 'Don't make eye contact!' I commanded Gabriela.

'But I have to look up, otherwise I'll bump into someone!'

'*Le ragazze, cuanto costa?*'—'How much, girls?'—Someone said behind us.

I was fed up. Why couldn't we walk the street at night safely without these chauvinist assholes pestering us, assuming that we'd jump into bed with them for a bit of money.

I turned on my heel and faced the man. 'We're not prostitutes,' I shouted in his face. 'Leave us alone!' I was reminded of that first day I arrived in Paris and got to practice my French swearing for the first time.

We ran the last half mile, finally making it to the convent, breathless and sweaty. We tried to open the front door. It was locked.

'Shit!' I checked my watch. It was 10.20pm.

Gabriela politely knocked and we waited. There was no answer. 'They wouldn't leave us out here in the street,' Gabriela said. 'They're nuns.'

'Well my dad went to a Catholic school and he told me about the beatings that the nuns gave the pupils. They're brutal and sadistic.'

I started banging more frantically and then Gabriela started to cry. I sat down on the front steps and lit a cigarette. 'We'll just have to camp out here.'

That set her off really sobbing, and I just couldn't bear it. I had to think of something.

'Hey, let's have a look around the building and see if there's another way we can get in,' I suggested. We crept through the shadows to the side of the building where the dormitory was. There was an open window but it was too high up. We went around to the rear of the building. 'What about the bathroom?' Gabriela said, 'The window's just above the toilet.'

'But how do we get up there?' I asked frowning at the window, which was just out of reach.

We managed to drag a dumpster over. I climbed up onto the top and stuck my head in the window. To my horror, I looked down on a black habit squatting on the toilet. I quickly pulled my head back, stifling a giggle. 'There's a nun in there!' I whispered.

I held my breath, not moving, waiting for the sound of the flush. When it was all clear I strained to pull myself up onto the windowsill. It wasn't easy. I hadn't realized what a weakling I was. I went in head first and shimmied through, scraping my front along the sill and trying to get a grip onto the cistern. I tumbled down, spilling the contents of my rucksack on the floor of the cubicle.

'Siobhan, are you OK?' I could hear Gabriela saying from outside.

I gathered myself up and waved out the window, 'Yes, I'm OK. It's all clear now.'

Gabriela was having trouble trying to climb onto the dumpster. 'I'm afraid of heights,' she said. 'Can't you just go to the front door and let me in?'

'I'll try—go wait on the front steps,' I replied. I tiptoed down the darkened corridor to the heavy wooden front door. I undid the bolts as quietly as I could but the sound echoed through the sparse, cavernous foyer. Suddenly a light clicked on. The old nun stood ominously in the middle of the hallway. I felt a chill go down my spine and my heart was pounding

'Ah ha. I catcha you! You try sneaka out,' she said.

'No, no you don't understand. I'm trying to let my friend in. The Portuguese one, she missed the curfew and got locked out.'

The nun narrowed her eyes at me distrustfully. 'Your Portuguese friend? Why she-a still out and you here?'

I had to think quickly, I searched my mind for a feasible answer. 'She wanted to go to the late mass at the Vatican in hopes of seeing the Pope. She has leukemia and is desperate to be cured.'

The nun's hard-set face immediately softened a little. She still eyed me suspiciously. 'OK—letta me check you tell the truth.' She opened a small window in the heavy wooden door and looked out. Gabriela must have been sitting forelornly on the steps waiting. 'Come-a in my poor child,' the nun said opening the door. 'Goda bless you.'

'Thank you, sister,' Gabby said, looking down at her shoes meekly, expecting to be told off.

Instead the nun just said, 'May the angels sleepa with you tonight'.

Gabriela gave me a quizzical sideways glance as she entered. 'What the hell did you tell her?' she asked as we made our way back to the dorm.

From a dream to a nightmare

Another episode in my fucked up life: after doing Rome in a day we moved on to Florence. We dragged our hungry and exhausted bodies around all the tourist attractions like the Ponte Vecchio and numerous basilicas, trying to feel enthusiastic about what we were seeing. I really couldn't bear the sight of one more church or palazzo, and I was feeling shaky from dehydration and low blood sugar. We sat down on some steps in a piazza, gathering together the scraps of food we had, to make a picnic dinner. The bread that we had saved from the restaurant in Rome was sustaining us a little but it was starting to go stale and the bit of cheese I had in my bag was rancid and sweaty. Gabriela had some days-old pulverized potato chips and a warm can of Coke.

While we ate, we discussed what to do next. In a couple of days we were meeting up with Lindi, Mike, Mimi and some other students from Rouen for the skiing weekend. We'd blown the budget on the chalet and were trying to keep our spending down. 'Should we get out of Italy and head for Switzerland?' I asked. 'Maybe we could check out Bern or Zurich.'

Gabriela mulled it over. 'I was hoping to see Venice or Milan but that's probably boring for you as you've already been there before.'

'Let's get the overnight train to Switzerland; that way we don't have to fork out for another hostel. We can just sleep on the train and we've got a day and night to make our way to the ski resort.'

'Oh, I don't know,' Gabriela pouted. 'I don't feel like I've seen enough of Italy. But I guess you're right about not having to pay for another hostel. OK. Let's do it.'

We meandered toward the train station to find out how to get to Switzerland. The woman at the information desk informed us that there was a train to Milan that was going to leave soon and that we could pick up a train to Bern from there. We reserved some seats and waited, completely drained of energy. The train rolled in on time and we had some comfy seats and were able to snooze a bit. Being Italy, however, we should have expected complications. Once we arrived at Milan we looked on the board to find our train to Bern but it wasn't listed. We went to the information desk where we were told that it had been cancelled, without any notification. The first train going in that direction was at 6am the next morning.

Huge Romanesque columns rose up before us as we took the escalator from beneath the train station to the bustling square above. We wandered the streets of Milan, dragging our bags around with us, taking in the solid, Fascist-era architecture that dominated the city. Designer clothes shops lined the sidewalks and well-dressed Milanese residents strutted past as Gabriela and I sat down on the sidewalk to rest our aching backs. African street hawkers kept hassling us to buy their cheap jewelry and sunglasses. I thought we looked like dirty homeless tramps camped out on the street so was bemused as to why the sellers thought we might be promising customers.

'I'm exhausted,' Gabriela said. 'I wish we had beds tonight.'

'We could look for somewhere—get away from the hawkers,' I suggested.

Gabriela looked at her watch. 'It's already coming up to midnight. It must be too late to book into a hostel. Plus, we can't really afford to pay for a whole night for only a few hours of sleep.'

'Then let's just go back to the train station and camp out, and try to get some sleep there.'

On the station concourse we found a quiet area in a corner but we couldn't see any benches that we could lie down on; they must have got rid of them to deter vagrants.

'Eeew. It's so filthy,' Gabriela grimaced.

I flicked a cigarette butt away as I lay my head on my bag. I could feel the cold of the marble floor penetrating my clothes and I shivered. There was no way that I was going to be able to sleep. I sat up with my back against the wall and lit a cigarette, watching the strange and troubled souls drifting around me: druggies, prostitutes, vagrants, bedraggled travelers, and those who preyed on them.

An Arab-looking guy with slicked-back hair came over and sat down on the floor next to me. He smiled at me, but I didn't feel like talking to anyone so I pretended not to notice and avoided eye contact.

'*Hai fuoco?*'

'*Si*', I replied, handing him my lighter, hoping that he would go away once he got his cigarette lit.

'Where you from?' he asked in Italian.

'*La France*,' I said.

He looked relieved. '*Ah bon—je parle francais. Je suis tunisien. Je m'appelle Said*,' and he held out his hand.

Not wanting to be rude, I smiled weakly and shook his hand.

'What's your name?' he asked.

'Sophie,' I lied, saying the first French name that came to my mind.

He offered me one of his cigarettes. 'Where are you traveling to?' he asked. I didn't want to talk more. I was afraid that he would detect that I had a foreign accent.

'*Chambery, faire du ski*,' I replied.

'I am going to Paris. My train is cancelled until tomorrow morning.'

A scary-looking policeman carrying a machine gun appeared from nowhere. He nudged the sleeping Gabriela with his foot. Startled, she sat up quickly.

'You can't sleep here,' he said standing over her menacingly.

I explained that our train was cancelled and that we had to wait until morning. The policeman shrugged unsympathetically. 'Get a hotel,' he shrugged. 'It's illegal to sleep in the station.'

Then he turned to the Tunisian and said something in Italian. With my rudimentary understanding of Italian, it sounded to me like he said 'How many times do I have to warn you. Get out of here.'

We stood up and gathered our things. 'Where are we going to go?' Gabriela whined, looking like she was on the verge of tears. 'I'm so tired. I really need some sleep.'

'You come with me,' Said said. 'I know a place to sleep that is safe and comfortable, and no one will find us.'

'I think we'd rather just find somewhere on our own,' I said.

'Oh, come on Siobhan. I'm so tired. Let's go with him.'

Said looked pleased. 'Follow me,' he said with a sly grin.

The policeman had walked away and was now hassling some drunks and druggies on the other side of the concourse. Instead of heading out of the station, Said ushered us down an escalator to a dimly lit platform. He placed his hand on my back and guided me to the left. He headed toward a darkened train but carried on to another.

'The police won't see us here,' Said said, pushing us onto the train. It was dark but I could see the seats were plush and it was so quiet and warm. Gabriela and I looked at other with relief.

'Oh wow, this is great,' Gabriela said, flopping down on one of the seats.

I hesitated, waiting to see where Said would go, so that I didn't have to be near him. I sat down and put my rucksack on the seat next to me. However, Said picked up the rucksack, put it on the floor and sat down beside me.

'There are plenty of other seats. I want to stretch out here.'

'There's plenty of room for two to lie down right here,' he grinned, patting the seats between us.

I picked up my bag and moved to another seat, away from Said. I curled up and closed my eyes drifting off into blissful sleep. I dreamt about being in Bruno's arms in bed. It was so real I could feel his breath on my neck and his hands on my body. In my dream I was snuggling against Bruno's shoulder. 'Oh babes, I've really missed you,' I mumbled into his chest, moving my arms over his neck. I could feel his breathing getting more rapid against my neck. It was such a vivid dream but suddenly I couldn't breathe. Why did Bruno have his hand across my mouth? I gasped, as the world flickered into focus and I slowly came to. I realized with horror that it wasn't Bruno, and it wasn't a dream. Said was on top of me, his body pressed against mine. He had one hand across my mouth, while his other hand was shoved up my skirt. His pants were down around his ankles and he pressed against me. I could feel that he was quite excited by the situation.

I tried to scream but he pressed his hand more tightly over my mouth. He grinned down at me. 'Shhhh, it'll be all over soon,' he purred in a soothing voice.

In my sleep haze, I struggled to understand what was happening. I tried pushing him off but he was too heavy. The hand under my skirt tore frantically at my underwear and he quickly forced himself in between my legs.

'No!' I yelled, but it was just a muffled sound against the palm of his hand. I didn't try to struggle as I thought it might prolong things. It was already happening anyway. Immobile and frozen, numbing my mind to the act, I squeezed my eyes shut. Was this really what I thought it was?

When it was over, he zipped up his jeans and sat down next to me. 'Thanks,' he said, 'Did you enjoy that?'

Was he kidding? I just wanted him to fuck off and leave me alone. I tried to pull my half torn underwear back up. Did he actually think there was any way that I might have enjoyed the experience?

'Now you got what you want why don't you just fuck off,' I hissed. He looked confused. 'If you don't take a hike I'm going to tell the police what you just did.' I tried to keep my voice down, hoping that Gabriela hadn't woken up.

'The police!' he laughed, mockingly. 'Why would the police care? They see your short skirt and ripped tights, they see you sleeping on the street, they think you ask for it,' he smiled his creepy smile.

From what I had heard about the Italian police, I had to accept that he was probably right. They would think I consented. I didn't exactly put up a fight. There was no sign of a struggle. Also, I knew that Gabriela would completely freak out if she knew what had happened. I thought it best to just pretend that the incident never took place. Maybe this was karma for what I'd done to Toby.

'Well if you don't fuck off I'll kick you in the balls. I know karate,' I said sneeringly.

Said now looked agitated. He knitted his brow. 'You're angry?'

'Of course I'm angry, pencil-dick.

Gabriela roused from her sleep. 'What's going on? We haven't missed our train, have we?' she mumbled, totally oblivious to what had happened.

Said got up to go. 'Good riddance, asshole,' I said after him as he skulked out of the train car. 'Goodbye to you too,' he said. His English obviously wasn't good enough to understand my insults.

'Is it morning yet?' Gabriela asked groggily. I looked at my watch. It was nearly 5am and I figured the first trains of the day would start coming in.

'Yes, let's head back to the platform,' I said.

'Gosh, I really needed that sleep,' Gabriela said. 'Did you manage to get any Zs?'

'No, not much' I said, feeling numb.

'I'm glad that guy finally left. He was really starting to annoy me,' Gabriela said.

'I know. I finally managed to get rid of him.' I was relieved she hadn't heard or seen anything. I stopped and faced her, opening my mouth. I was about to tell her what happened and then I decided not to. I gathered my bag and walked ahead to the concourse, with Gabriela running behind me trying to put on her coat.

'Are you OK Siobhan?' Gabriela called after me.

For a minute I thought I caught a glimpse of Said hanging around the tobacco kiosk, but when I looked again there was no one there.

We checked our train time on the board and luckily it was due to arrive in half an hour.

I felt like I needed to speak to Bruno. 'I'm just going to make a phone call, Gab,' I said. I scraped together all my loose change and inserted the coins one by one into the pay phone to call him in Rouen.

'Pronto!'

'Hi, it's me.'

'Primavera! How are you? How is my country?'

'Well, actually, I can't wait to get out of here. It's not the same without you to fend off the predators.' I managed to choke back the tears but I couldn't disguise the quaver in my voice. Shock at what had happened was beginning to take hold.

'Primavera, are you OK? You sound strange.'

Just then my money ran out and the call cut off.

'C'mon,' Gabriela said, pulling at my arm. 'Let's get on the train and get a seat.'

Ghost train

In true American style, Gabriela and I 'did' Bern in a day. We
trailed around, taking in the sights and the architecture in a
mechanical, tourist daze. Switzerland was as tidy and clean as a
cut made by a Swiss Army knife, and it operated as flawlessly as
a Rolex watch. The cleanliness of the streets, and the perfection
of the mannequin-like people that graced them, made me feel, by
comparison, like a greasy McDonald's burger wrapper blown in
from a giant, stinking dump somewhere far away, marring the
sidewalk. I felt disgusting, and knew I must have looked disgusting
too, not having been near a mirror for a couple of days. I tried to
enjoy myself, but all I could think about was a hot bath of luxurious
bubbles to wash away the dirt, grime and unpleasantness of the
night before. Then it would be bed, sweet bed.

It must have been pure adrenaline that kept my body in
motion. I had experienced a few all-nighters in my time, but the
tiredness that I was experiencing was extreme. I was so tired that
I was beyond being tired. Not sleeping was becoming a state of
normality. I now knew it to be fact that zombies existed—I had
become one.

Although it was March, it started snowing and it became very
cold. We decided to go back to the train station and get out of the
weather while waiting for our train. We were due in Chambery
in the early hours of the morning, where we had to catch another
train to Bourg-Saint-Maurice, and from there on to our ultimate
destination, a ski resort, where we were sharing an apartment
with some others from the American group.

For once our train was on time. I put my head back on the
seat and closed my eyes. Gabriela was stressing out. 'We can't
fall asleep in case we miss the stop,' she said. 'Here, have this,'
she was holding two styrofoam cups of coffee she'd bought for
us to get wired up on. I knew there was no chance of sleep. 'It's

really important. The train gets in to Chambery at 3am, so we must stay alert.'

'OK, OK, Gab,' I grumbled, grabbing the coffee and sipping it. It was all very well for her—she'd actually got some sleep the night before. She chattered incessantly throughout the journey— all about her plans to get married to Jamie, her career plans, her plans for a family. As her voice droned on and on, I nodded blankly, ruminating about my own aimlessness and lack of direction.

After what seemed like an interminable journey, we finally reached Chambery at the scheduled time. Our train to Bourg-Saint-Maurice wasn't due to leave for half an hour, but Gabriela was very anxious to be the first to get on it and get good seats, so we went to the designated platform to wait. There happened to be a train stopped there.

'It must be ours,' Gabriela said.

However, as we got on, I noticed something strange about the train. There were no other people on it, no lights on and no heating. 'We must be the first people on,' Gabriela said chirpily, as we settled down in the dark with our bags. I was just about to relax and shut my eyes, when the train jerked forward and groaned into motion.

I looked at my watch. 'This can't be our train, Gab. It's not due to depart yet.' We both shot up from our seats, gathered up our bags and ran like hell through the shadowy train car to the exit. I heaved the sliding door open and we looked out as the train speeded up and the station disappeared into the distance. The snow was really starting to come down now and the tracks were beginning to get covered.

'Shit!' Gabriela shouted. I could see tears beginning to well up in her eyes.

'It'll be OK, Gab,' I said, even though I wasn't feeling it myself. 'We'll just have to get out at the next station.' I tried to appear confident and unworried, for Gabriela's sake, although I was, in fact, shitting myself.

We stood at the ready with our bags by the exit, as the train slipped through the darkness. All around we could see the jagged white peaks of mountains, and pine forests, but there was not a single streetlight in sight, not one tiny hint of civilization— only the icy, white wilderness. Suddenly we were plunged into total darkness as the train entered a tunnel. Gabriela let out a scream. I felt in my pocket for my cigarettes and a lighter. With a trembling hand I lit the cigarette and was grateful for the momentary light. Gabriela was practically hysterical.

The train emerged from the tunnel and the whiteness of the snow outside once again illuminated the interior of the carriage. I thrust my head out the window, looking around for a sign of life. 'Where the hell do you think we are?' I said with an edge of panic in my voice, puffing manically on my cigarette.

'Somewhere in the Alps I guess, but I wonder where on earth we are going to end up?' Gabriela sobbed and sniffed, wiping her running nose with her sleeve.

'Please not back to Italy!' I gulped.

'This has got to be the most fucked up thing I've ever done!' Gabriela wailed, holding her head.

'Well, if it makes you feel any better, I've done worse,' I replied.

'Really? What could be worse than this?'

'Never mind. I've got an idea,' I said. 'Let's go as far to the front of the train as we can and see if we can alert the train driver that we need to get off.'

Gabriela nodded and sniffled. She wiped away a tear and followed me through the door that led to the next carriage. We made our way through a couple more carriages until we could go no further. The last door was made of thick iron, and locked shut. We banged on it and shouted, as the train slowly trundled along the snowy tracks. Just then the train started to slow down.

We ran frantically back down through the carriages to where we had left our bags and stood anxiously poised by the door.

'Do you think we can jump?' Gabriela asked, frozen with fear.

The train was now moving at a slow crawl but it would have been difficult to jump out with the bags.

'I don't think it's a good idea, Gab.' We both stared despondently at the whiteness going past. Then the brakes began to squeal and the train creaked to a standstill.

'Come on let's do it,' Gabriela stood on the edge, clutching her bag tightly to her chest. Suddenly, the train jerked back into motion and crept into the tiny train station of Albertville, in the middle of the mountain wilderness, where it finally stopped. We tossed our bags out onto the tracks.

'Get off, get off!' I urged, and we both jumped out into the snow, trying to run with our bags across the tracks to the platform. A uniformed train worker came toward us, shouting, '*Arretez!*'

In an outpouring of garbled French, punctuated by sobs, Gabriela recounted our story to him.

'Can I see your passports and tickets please, Mesdemoiselles?' he asked.

Gabriela showed him her Portuguese passport, which seemed to immediately earn his trust and sympathy. He just looked down his nose at my passport. 'Why are an American and a Portuguese travelling together?' he asked, perplexed, as if it were the strangest thing he had ever heard of.

'University,' Gabriela piped up quickly, before I could blow her cover as a fellow stupid American. I was really fed up of her goody-two-shoes Portuguese Catholic girl act.

He nodded, satisfied with that answer, and reassured Gabriela that we were actually going in the right direction. We both heaved a huge sigh of relief as our train pulled in two minutes later.

Feeling like a couple of complete nitwits, we finally got on the right train, which arrived into Bourg-Saint-Maurice at 6am. We were ravenous and were lucky to find a little kiosk selling hot croissants and coffee. There was also a nice warm waiting room where we settled on a bench and managed to catch a couple of hours' sleep.

When we woke up we realized that we needed to find out where to catch our bus to Vallandry, where the chalet was. We walked all around the front of the train station but there didn't seem to be any information about buses—there didn't even seem to be a bus stop.

We finally asked at the information desk and I couldn't believe my ears when we were told that we were at the wrong station and we needed to go back to Landry, the station before. I was seriously fed up now.

We returned to the platform and waited for a train to take us in the direction we had just come from. I was beginning to wonder if this nightmare was ever going to end; I felt like whatever I did I just never seemed to make any progress, and every step I took was like trying to run through deep water.

We made it to Landry just in time to see our bus pull away and disappear out of sight.

'Shit!' I said, throwing my bag down on the ground and kicking it. 'What the hell are we going to do now?' I could feel my eyes brimming with hot tears.

'Hey, Siobhan, honey. Don't get upset,' Gabriela said, putting her arm around me. 'The next bus is in a couple of hours.'

All I could think of was a hot bath and a warm bed. My hair was so greasy it smelled like a wet dog and Said's disgusting remnants remained. 'I can't wait that long, Gab,' I said, sticking my thumb out. 'There's only one way we're going to get there any time soon.'

Determined, I started to walk up the narrow and snowy road that led up the mountain. 'Let's hitchhike,' I said sticking my thumb out at a passing car. 'It's the only way we're going to get there any time soon.'

'But Jamie told me not to hitchhike. It could be dangerous. What if some madman picks us up?' Gabriela said anxiously.

'At this point I don't care, as long as I get to sleep.'

Gabriela reluctantly followed me along the road. The incline was getting quite steep and I was feeling really short of breath due to the high altitude. We seemed to be walking forever without a single car passing by.

After about half an hour there was the sound of a vehicle approaching from around the bend behind us. I stuck my thumb out and a four-by-four pulled over up ahead. We scurried toward it as the passenger door swung open. We jumped up into the front seat and squeezed in side by side, with our bags at our feet.

'*Vous allez ou?*' the driver asked in strange-sounding French. I explained that we were going to Vallandry.

'Me too,' he said, in perfect North American English. 'Where are you from?'

The driver was a Canadian ski instructor. We were so happy to meet a fellow native English speaker and we babbled on all about our journey, grateful for someone who could understand us and offer some sympathy. He knew the resort well and delivered us right to the front door of our chalet; he even helped us with our bags.

We were the first ones to arrive at the chalet. The others were coming from Prague and were expected in later that the evening. As soon as we dumped our bags I rushed to the bathroom and locked the door. I peeled off my clothes, which could have stood up by themselves by that point. Not wanting to touch them I picked my underwear up off the floor using my thumb and forefinger. I found my lighter in my jacket pocket and held the flame to the torn cotton. I threw it into the sink and watched with satisfaction as it burned.

I then ran a bath, as hot as I could bear and eased myself into the scalding hot water, feeling Said's odious touch burn away.

Mountains

The apartment was small—much smaller than I had imagined it would be. It was supposed to be a two-bedroom accommodation to sleep six at a push. There was a double bed in one of the bedrooms, a double sofa bed in the open-plan living room/kitchenette, and a couple of bunk beds in what was supposed to be a bedroom, but which was actually in the entrance area to the apartment. The narrow space had no windows, but was also the thoroughfare to the bathroom. The apartment would clearly not accommodate EIGHT people without there being some bed sharing. I was desperate to get some sleep before the others arrived. Gabriela had already conked out on the sofa. I wanted to ensure that I wouldn't have to share with anyone, so I chose the single bottom bunk. I collapsed onto the bed and fell asleep as soon as my head hit the pillow.

A loud hammering on the door roused me. It felt like I had only been asleep for a few minutes, but according to my watch it had been a few hours, and now the others had arrived. I couldn't face them. I didn't feel ready for a party yet. I left Gabriela to answer the door, pulled the cover over my head and closed my eyes, plunging back into the black hole of unconsciousness.

What woke me up next was a feeling of being suffocated, with Said's hand over my face again. I realized it was just the covers on my head and my pounding heart began to slow. The room was dark. I could smell cooking and hear animated chatter and laughter.

I was still trying to gather my wits when Lindi burst into the room and handed me a cocktail. 'C'mon sleepy head. We're all here now and dinner's on the go.'

I took the cocktail and had a sip. It was so good it cheered me up a little, giving me courage to get up and face the world. I followed Lindi into the open-plan kitchen. There were six people sitting round the table sipping cocktails: Mike and his friend Roland; Mimi; Gabriela; and, to my annoyance, the two inseparable sorority girls, Natalie and Sara. They seemed to have Gabriela enthralled, as they both talked a mile a minute about their time in Prague. I chose to join Lindi, who was standing at the stove, stirring a pot of chili.

'How was Italy?' she asked me.

'Tiring,' I said. I feel like I could sleep for a week. I yawned and knocked back the cocktail. 'Is there any more of this? It's great,' I said.

'It's my own special margarita recipe,' she informed me proudly, as she poured me another glassful from the pitcher on the table.

I sat down resignedly at the table with the others. Gabriela was telling them about Vatican City and the Roman Coliseum.

'What did you think of Milan?' Mike asked me.

'I hated it,' I said despondently.

He raised his eyebrows at me. 'Really, why's that?'

I was rescued from having to answer by a sudden, loud knock on the door that startled us all.

'I didn't think we were expecting anyone else,' Sara said.

'No, I don't think we are,' Mike replied.

Then I heard the strains of Perez Prado's 'Guaglione' being whistled through the keyhole.

'Bruno?' I gulped.

Sara flashed me a cutting look. 'There's not enough room for anyone else; we have to share beds as it is.'

'Why did you invite him?' Natalie asked, accusingly.

'I didn't, I swear! I have no idea why he's here.'

Another knock, more persistent this time. Nobody moved. Everyone was looking at me, presumably to see what I would do. I got up and went to open the door.

Bruno's beaming face greeted me. '*Ciao bella!*' He held out a wilted bouquet that looked as if it had travelled all the way from Rouen with him.

'Bruno, what the hell are you doing here?'

'Now is that a way to greet the man you love?' he said, giving me a swift kiss. Then he leaned back and studied me with a serious expression. 'You sounded so strange on the phone before we got cut off and I was so worried that something happened to you, Primavera.'

Standing next to Bruno was Chiara. She shoved both Bruno and I out of the way and barged into the apartment. 'Michael, dahling, I hope you don't mind me just showing up like this. Bruno needed someone to keep him company on the long journey.'

'I bet he did,' I mumbled under my breath.

Mike squirmed uncomfortably. Roland glared at him and Mike shrugged.

The two Italians plopped their rucksacks down on the floor.

'Ah, I see that dinner is almost ready,' Bruno said, sniffing the air. 'I'm starving after such a long journey.' He rubbed his hands together and sat down at the table. 'May I?' he asked as he reached for the pitcher of margarita and poured himself one.

'Can you pour me one too?' Chiara cooed, as she sat down on Mike's knee and threw her arms around his neck. Natalie's mouth dropped open in disbelief and Sara pursed her lips and crossed her arms, watching the Italians making themselves comfortable. 'I hope that you two are going to contribute something. We have all brought some food and drink to share,' Sara scolded.

'Of course,' Bruno produced a skull-shaped bottle of tequila from his bag. 'Get some glasses, Primavera. We are going to celebrate our arrival!'

'I don't like tequila,' Sara said, sticking out her tongue in disgust.

'Me neither,' said Natalie. 'And where do you two think you are going to sleep? There are only enough beds for six and now there are 10 of us.'

'*Calma*,' Bruno said. 'Of course, I will share with Primavera.'

'And I will share with Michael,' Chiara chirped, gazing lovingly at Mike.

Roland shifted uncomfortably in his seat and frowned. '*Puis-je parler avec toi?*' he whispered loudly to Mike, springing to his feet and yanking Mike's arm, pulling him away from the table. They marched to the door and exited with a dramatic slam.

We could hear the sound of muted arguing through the door. After a few minutes they came back in, tense-shouldered and looking pissed-off.

'Lindi and I can share then, I guess,' Gabriela suggested. 'And Sara and Natalie can share, if you two don't mind, seeing as you're best friends.'

'That leaves only Mimi and Roland, and one bed.' Natalie said. 'It won't be fair that she has to share with a guy she doesn't know very well.'

Chiara pouted. 'I'm sure Mimi is used to sleeping with men she doesn't know very well anyway. What's the big deal?'

'I don't mind camping out on the floor by myself,' Mimi offered, good-naturedly, Chiara's insult going completely over her head.

'That's not fair! Then Roland gets a bed all to himself while the rest of us have to share,' Natalie griped.

'Mimi and I can take turns sleeping in the bed, then,' Roland said.

'Hold on, hold on,' Mike interrupted, holding his hand in the air. 'I see the most logical solution here. Why don't the two ladies, Mimi and Chiara share and then Roland and I can share, as I am the one who invited him along. That way no one has to sleep on the floor.'

'Ah, yes. Great idea!' Roland agreed, his furrowed brow relaxing.

'But darling, Michael, I thought…' Chiara simpered.

Mike shrugged and popped a cigarette in his mouth. 'Needs must!'

Now that the sleeping arrangements had been sorted, Mimi and Gabriela pulled up a couple of extra chairs from the patio, so everyone had a seat.

'I propose a toast,' Bruno said, standing up theatrically with his glass held high. 'To great friends and a great life. Cin cin. And to my Primavera.' Throwing his arm round me, he pulled me close, proprietarily. I thought I would find his closeness comforting, but instead his possessiveness felt stifling and annoying. I looked around at everyone at the table. My two best friends, Lindi and Gabriela, were smiling and chatting to each other. Mimi and Mike were laughing at something Roland was saying. Natalie and Sara were looking prissy and uptight. When my eyes settled on Chiara, I found her gazing at Bruno and I, with a mischievous glint in her eye. I suddenly felt on my guard, and snuggled in closer to Bruno.

Quickly, I swallowed my cocktail and Bruno attentively poured me another one. I could feel the alcohol starting to go to my head, but I didn't want to stop. I felt desperate to get the image of Said's face out of my mind.

'Shall we go out for some fresh air, Primavera?' Bruno said, his arm feeling more and more vice-like round my shoulders.

We went out to the balcony and Bruno pulled me to him in an amorous embrace. He kissed me forcefully, just like the first time he kissed me up in the Ferris wheel, but this time, instead of the lights of Rouen, it was the white, jaggedy landscape of the Alps that lay beyond us. It was cold, and as I didn't have my jacket on I shivered and snuggled close into Bruno's shoulder. I closed my eyes, the sleepiness taking hold once again. Then, all of a sudden I saw a horrible image of Said's face and felt the sensation of his body pressed up against me. 'No!' I found myself saying as I pushed Bruno away.

'What's the matter with you?' Bruno stepped back and observed me, his eyes narrowed in suspicion.

I sighed and hung my head. 'I'm sorry, I don't know. I'm tired. The trip here was a bit trying. I haven't slept much in the past few days.'

'Come here, Primavera,' Bruno said, holding his arms out to me. 'Maybe we should go to bed. You know what I mean?' he said, winking and trying to pull me to him again.

I felt really weird and I went rigid. The feeling of violation had still not left me and I didn't feel quite ready for any intimacy. He just didn't get it. It was always about him and what he wanted—namely sex.

'You have been with someone else. I can tell,' Bruno said accusingly. 'That's why you sounded so strange when I spoke to you on the phone. You are hiding something from me?'

'No, it's not like that at all. I promise,' I said. I thought for a moment about telling him about what really happened but then decided against it. From all that I had learned so far about Italian men and their attitudes to women, I knew that even if I explained, he would think I was to blame.

'What's the matter then?' he persisted, pulling me to him again.

'I told you, I'm really tired. I just want a cuddle and to take it easy tonight, OK?' But I knew that Bruno never took 'no' for an answer, and I mentally prepared myself once again to put on an act for the sake of pacifying a male ego.

Black diamond

Bruno jumped chirpily out of bed. 'C'mon, Primavera. We have to get up early to be on the slopes before they are too crowded.'

I groaned and pulled the duvet over my head. 'It's still the middle of the night. It's pitch dark outside!'

'It's 6am,' he said. 'I'll make some espresso. That should wake you up.'

I was going to need something stronger than espresso to wake me up. I was going to need rocket fuel. I hadn't slept very well in the cramped single bed, with Bruno's arms in a suffocating, vice-like grip around my middle and his lanky frame pressed up against my back. To make matters worse, Sara and Natalie were in the bunk above and they had both been up and down repeatedly in the night to use the nearby bathroom, at times puking and shitting in stereo.

I rolled over and looked down at the pancake of pinkish vomit on the floor next to the bed. I remembered that at one point Natalie couldn't get down in time and had vomited over the side of the top bunk.

'Can't you just go without me?' I said, rolling over and hiding my head in the warmth of the duvet to escape the smell.

Bruno whipped the cover away, leaving me shivering. 'The early bird catch the worm,' he sang in his quirky Italian-accented English.

I heard moaning from above. Natalie's crumpled face appeared over the side of the bunk 'Keep it down, we're trying to sleep up here.'

It seemed like a no-win situation, so I dragged myself out of bed, carefully stepping over the puke-cake. My head was pounding with the mother of all hangovers. I figured that the earlier we got out, the earlier I could return and go to sleep again.

I headed into the bathroom only to be confronted by a horrific sight—the sub-standard French plumbing obviously couldn't cope with the deposits of 10 people who had just consumed a very hot chili and very strong margaritas.

On my way out, I collided with Chiara who was also heading into the bathroom. She was wearing one of the boys' t-shirts, which barely covered her pert bottom.

'I come skiing as well this morning, darling,' she purred in her sleepy Italian morning voice.

My head was still hurting so I crawled back to bed while Bruno made some coffee. I must have drifted off again and was woken by a strong cup of espresso under my nose. Both Chiara and Bruno where dressed and ready to go. Chiara was wearing a chic pink ski outfit with a matching hat. Bruno was wearing some old ski pants and a worn-out parka, both of which looked like they used to belong to his granddad. He looked ridiculous as usual, but not as ridiculous as I was going to look. I didn't have any skiing clothes and was just going to have to layer up with tights and thermals under my jeans.

'C'mon, Primavera. Get dressed. We are going,' Bruno said.

I knocked back the strong shot of espresso and got dressed. Although all I really wanted to do was to catch up on my sleep and for Bruno to leave me alone, I wasn't prepared to let him go alone with Chiara.

'Darling, don't you have any waterproof clothing? You are going to get soaked,' Chiara said to me.

'I'm not really much of a skier and never invested in the gear,' I said. I had been skiing once before back in the States, on a family trip to New Hampshire. I'd had a few lessons, but spent more time on my butt than on the skis.

'Don't you worry, darling. We look after you,' Chiara said.

The three of us headed down to the ski rental and got fitted for ski boots and skis. I struggled to squeeze my feet into the tight plastic boots. They were heavy and clamped so tightly round my feet that I felt like I was stuck in cement. Then it was on to the slopes. I followed Chiara and Bruno and stood in line for a chair lift.

Bruno saw me struggling to attach my skis. 'Let me help you, Primavera,' he said. The three of us stood shoulder to shoulder, waiting for the seat to swing in behind us. The chair lift came up behind us and scooped me right off my feet. My legs and arms were flailing. Luckily my poles were strapped to my wrists but my skis were slicing around in the air like blades and got crossed with Chiara's causing her to lose her balance and fall off the seat before the safety bar could be pulled down.

'*Porca Madonna!*' she shouted, as she lay in a pink heap below our rising chairlift. The operators had to stop the chairlift so that Chiara could get up without being knocked down by another lift. It was really not a good start.

Bruno started swinging his legs to make the chairlift rock as we rose higher and higher up the mountain, above the tops of the lush pines. I grabbed the safety rail, my head spinning and the nausea rising. 'Please, Bruno, stop. I'm going to be sick in a minute.'

He took the opportunity to engulf me in a romantic embrace. He always liked to throw me off guard like that, when I was at my most vulnerable.

I looked down and around and noticed how far away the bottom of the mountain was. It didn't look like the beginners' trail to me. Below us, skiers swooshed and slalomed elegantly. We were now well above the tree line and I could see the top of the trail a few meters ahead of us. 'Is this an easy slope?' I asked.

'Oh, yes. This one is quite easy,' Bruno said. 'You should be able to do it, no problem.'

Getting off the chairlift was even trickier than getting on it. 'Get ready, Primavera,' Bruno said, lifting the safety bar. 'Now, now, now,' he shouted as the chair slowed a bit at the top of a mound.

I must have put my feet down a bit too early, as the seat hit me in the back of the legs, gave me a little shove down the slope and I ended up face-first in the snow. There were other people getting off the chairlift as well, who couldn't stop in time to avoid me, so every time I managed to get upright, I was knocked over again by someone colliding with me.

Bruno was pissing himself laughing as he finally helped me to get up. 'I hope it wasn't yellow snow you ate,' he joked. I righted myself and felt like a newborn foal with my feet slipping and sliding in all directions.

'C'mon, follow me,' Bruno said, holding out his hand. 'Stick together and you'll be fine.'

I noticed the other skiers, all decked out in their professional-looking gear, looking like they were born on skis. I held Bruno's hand, but our poles got entwined and threw me off balance. Down I went again. When I got up I tried to remember what I had learnt in my skiing lessons. I kept my skis parallel and slowly made a big zigzag going from right to left. 'Hey, I'm getting the hang of it,' I said, proudly.

'C'mon, let's go!' Bruno launched himself down the hill. I went to follow him with my slow zigzag technique, but the slope soon became incredibly steep. I picked up speed, which made me feel out of control. Skiers were shooting past, like streaks of color, from all sides. One whizzed past me on my left and virtually sent me spinning in his wake. I landed on my ass, but kept sliding down the hill. One of my skis caught on something and came off

I got up and tried to clamber back up the slope, slipping and sliding, to find my skis. The tightly clamped ski boots were almost impossible to walk in and I was sure I was walking like Frankenstein. A couple of times I had to dodge people careening toward me in a flurry of French expletives. I found my ski lodged in the brambly branches of a shrub and managed to put it back on. I looked ahead as I prepared myself to set off again, but the bottom of the slope was nowhere in sight. I was still above the tree line. I hadn't got very far at all. The slope was getting steeper and steeper, and there were jumps and twists and turns, way beyond my skill level. This was no beginner's slope. I could see a signpost at the side of the piste, with a black diamond clearly indicated. I could have killed Bruno and Chiara for bringing me onto a piste with one of the highest difficulty levels.

I couldn't stay where I was, however, so the only thing I could do was to try and ski down. I pushed off tentatively and skied a bit before I fell again. I just couldn't manage to stay upright. I'd stand up, ski two feet and end up on my ass being showered with snow from the other skiers. I felt so hopeless that I took the damn skis off and decided I was going to walk down. I just couldn't go on so I loosened the clamps on my boots and gathered up my skis and poles. All I could do was make my way to the side of the piste, out of the way of the skiers zipping past, and then start to trudge down, slipping and sliding through the deep snow.

'Whoo, hooo!'

I looked up and saw Bruno and Chiara waving at me from the chairlift above, going up for another go. 'What happened, Primavera?' Bruno yelled down.

I stuck my middle finger up at them, humiliated, pissed off and aching. I collapsed in the snow to have a rest, trying not to think about how cold I was and how long it was going to take me.

Sooner than expected, Chiara whooshed past me. Then Bruno slid to a stop alongside me, creating a thin wave of snow. He took one look at my humiliated tear-stained face and took pity. 'Primavera, what's the matter?'

'I'm scared shitless to ski down this hill. Why the hell did you bring me to the Black Diamond trail? I told you I was a beginner.'

'C'mon, don't be scared. Treat the mountain like life. Just get up and go. I help you.' Bruno helped me put my skis back on and watched as I skied about a yard before falling over.

'I can't do it!' I cried. 'Why don't you just fuck off and find Chiara.'

'Primavera, what are you saying. I don't care about her. She's a friend. Nothing more. She's just using me to get to Mike.' Bruno gave me a big hug and I could smell the odor of mothball coming off his old-fashioned ski jacket.

I smiled. 'Where did you get the ski outfit? Did you raid your granddad's wardrobe?'

'I bought it in a charity shop,' he said proudly.

'Here, you hold on to me and we go very carefully down the hill.'

I positioned myself behind him, my arms round his waist and my skis outside of his. Just like that first time on his motorbike, I held on tightly and let him propel us. After a while I felt like I was getting the hang of it, snaking smoothly from left to right across the piste in a controlled manner. I finally felt confident enough to let go and I was able to ski on my own. I suddenly felt exhilarated and free, the cold mountain air filling my lungs and the vastness of the landscape enveloping me. I saw Bruno waving at me from the bottom of the hill.

It suddenly occurred to me that I was going quite fast and didn't know how I was going to stop. Bruno jumped out of the way just as I hit a patch of ice and went careening into a circle of beginner skiers having their lesson.

Amid shrieks and shouting, a large American woman said, 'Don't you know how to stop?' As I lay in a heap on the ground in the middle of their circle, with furious faces peering down at me, I made a vow never to go skiing ever again.

spring in the air

Back in Rouen, I sat at my desk, with Toby's letter open in front of me. I had a pang of guilt as I looked at the calendar on the wall and realized his birthday was about a week ago. The only reason I was reminded of it was because he mentioned it in the letter, which was the first communication from him since he had gone back to America a couple of months earlier.

After he had spent a few weeks in the hospital, he was well enough to be able to fly home. The doctors said he had been lucky not to have had more serious injuries. He had suffered a broken leg and a concussion. The driver of the motorbike he had stupidly jumped in front of had only had a few scrapes and bruises, and had decided not to press any charges, even though the motorbike was pretty banged-up.

Toby, being Toby, did not have any travel insurance and his grandmother ended up having to pay a fortune for his medical care in the French hospital. I went to visit him a few times when he was there, but since he'd gone back to the States I hadn't heard from him. I could only assume that everything was totally off between us.

Then his letter arrived and my light spring mood was smothered by a heavy horse blanket of guilt. He gave me an ultimatum, adding another weight on to my shoulders. I couldn't believe what he had written. It was pure manipulation.

Dear Siobhan,

It's my birthday today and I realize I am not getting any younger so I've been doing a lot of thinking about us and about what happened when I was in France.

This is what I have decided: I am willing to forgive you for cheating on me with Alfonso. And the reason for this is that I

realize that I am still in love with you. I want to get married after
we finish our degrees, and have some kids.

I realize that you are in a foreign country and you slipped up,
but I'm willing to forget it if you dump him and come back to me. I
understand that you need to finish your studies so I will wait that
long. However, if you decide you don't want to get back together, I
never want to see you again, and I expect you to stay away from all
my friends and family.

With love,
Toby

I did need to decide very soon about when I would return to the
US. My gut feeling was that I wanted to remain in Europe as
long as possible. I didn't want to go back to Toby. Maybe I could
suggest to Bruno that we move in together? I could find a job and
earn some money, at least until September when I knew I had to
return to the University of New England to finish my degree.

But was I really in love with Bruno? I just knew I felt 'in love'—
especially after the past weekend we had spent together. He had
picked me up on his motorcycle and we had visited the picturesque
seaside village of Honfleur, with its picture-postcard perfect seaside
cottages standing vigil over the little boats in the still harbor. On
our way back to Rouen, we rode through the green and blooming
Normandy countryside along a path lined with sweet-smelling
flowers, their buds beginning to burst open. We had stopped off in a
remote field for a little picnic. Bruno had spread his white raincoat
on the ground and we had lain side by side, listening to the wind
and birds. Under the shade of the cherry blossoms, my heart had
felt so happy. I gently put my hand on his. We were alone in the
vast countryside. Silence was followed by feverish love, as Bruno
pulled me against him and we melted into the golden grass and the
blue sky, our feelings left unspoken.

I reread Toby's letter. Did I really know what the emotion
of love was? At one time I had believed I loved Toby, and now, I
thought I might be in love with Bruno, or was I actually just in
love with being in Europe?

I was just hoping that fate would take its course and answer
my question for me. I assumed that this must be part of life's
responsibilities, facing unpleasant realities and having to make
tough decisions. Like Bruno always said, 'Life is truly beautiful
but sometimes it can kick you in the ass.'

I decided to write back to Toby. I owed that much to him. I
sat at my desk with my pen poised. *'Dear Toby,'* I wrote. *'It was*

nice to hear from you after such a long time. I hope your leg has healed.' Then I stopped and scribbled out the word 'nice'. I stared at the page then crumpled it up. I started again. '*Dear Toby, I was surprised to get your letter after all that has happened. I hope you can...*' I hope you can what?

I was startled from my writing by a noise outside my bedroom window, like someone rattling the shutters, which were bolted shut from the inside. I assumed it was probably Bruno, although I hadn't been expecting him. Or it could have been Thierry, my host father. He sometimes knocked on the window for someone to open up the garage so he could drive the car in.

I opened the window and flung open the shutters. There was a man standing there—a dark-skinned man who I didn't recognize. I froze with fear. He had the same swarthy look of Said.

After a moment, he ducked down and disappeared into the shadows. I banged the window closed, locked the shutters, then, my heart pounding, I ran to find Sophie. She was knitting in the living room.

She looked up. 'What are you doing? You gave me a fright,' she snapped.

I tried to get my breath back and gushed, 'There was a man, Sophie... There was a man at my window!'

She dropped her knitting and jumped up. 'Who? Who was it?'

'I don't know. Some guy. I heard a noise and opened the shutters.'

'What did he look like?'

'He looked uh, dark-skinned, dark-haired.'

'*Oh mon dieu!* An Arab. Maybe they hear that we have an American living here. Why did you open the window?'

'I ... I don't know. I thought maybe it was Bruno, or Thierry?'

'Maybe he wants to rob the house. *Mon dieu!*' She rushed to the front door, threw it open and peered out into the night.

'*Qui est la?*' she shouted into the darkness.

I nervously peered out over her shoulder, hoping that the stranger wouldn't jump out of the shadows. 'There's no one there. He's gone,' I said.

Sophie slammed the door and rounded on me. 'Don't ever open the window to anyone ever again. And don't tell anyone you are American. You make this house a target!'

I skulked back to my room, curled up into a ball on my hard, thin mattress, and started to cry. I'd felt alone many times but never as much as now. A feeling of homesickness overcame me. I had not spared my family a single thought the whole time I had been in France. I remembered how eager I had been to get away from them—from the pressure to excel at school, from their middle-class competitiveness and keeping up with appearances. I really missed being back in a familiar bed, listening to the sound of crickets in the Connecticut woods. I missed the smell of wood smoke, and blue jay calls echoing through the tall trees.

Remembering home made me think about Toby and the guilt about the way I'd treated him returned. No wonder Sophie couldn't stand me. I couldn't stand me either. I was rotten and despicable, and to top it all off, American. The most detested nationality on earth. I despised myself to the core and I deserved all of the shit that I got.

I might be in love with an annoying, big headed, chauvinist womanizer, I thought, and I had ripped the heart out of the man who really loved me. I deserved to die.

I felt so alone and thought about asking Bruno to come over, but I was reminded of the time when we were in the Alps and I had just needed a hug, and all he had wanted to do was have sex. I doubted that he would be of any comfort.

My tears became uncontrollable and I sobbed my self-loathing. I grabbed an earring off my bedside table and plunged it into my wrist, wincing with the pain, but relishing it at the same time. Like lancing a boil to relieve the pressure, I scratched and gouged at my skin, feeling a kind of liberation as I watched the red streams and slashes of blood contrasting against my insipid white skin, like a Jackson Pollack painting.

I suddenly jumped up, concerned that I would drip on the sheets. I wasn't even capable of killing myself. I was just too much of a wimp, too scared of making Sophie angry. I ran my wrist under cold water and bandaged it up, crawling desolately into bed.

Film party

Sophie and Thierry sat down alongside me on the edge of my hard bed. Thierry looked serious but embarrassed and Sophie's mouth was a wire-tight line. I could tell that what they were going to tell me would not be good. Sophie listed off several incidents including the unlocked door blowing open in the night, the nail polish spilled on the bedding, and me opening the windows to anyone and everyone, endangering her family. She had really blown it all out of proportion and my lack of fluency in French prevented me from really defending myself.

'I don't know how you live in the United States, but here in France your guests call at the front door.' Sophie was referring, of course, to Bruno's quirky habit of knocking on my window, and the fact that I had opened the window to a threatening stranger as a result. 'That man could have robbed us, or killed us, who knows,' Sophie said, disdainfully. 'I also heard from the neighbor that you had some friends stay over when we went away. I hadn't said anything before, but now I think that maybe these people were strangers coming into my house. They could have been anyone you met on the street.'

She went on to say that she found my attitude aloof, that I couldn't be bothered with the children and that I showed them a bad example with my multiple boyfriends and drinking.

I hung my head. I felt really horrible about the whole thing, because in a way, Sophie was right. It was my fault that I didn't really make an effort with the family. I was after a good time and couldn't be bothered with hanging out with the DeClermonts or their kids. On the other hand, I was paying them rent and I didn't know what they expected of me. It wasn't really anyone's fault and all this bad feeling was just a result of crossed wires and different expectations on both parts.

Sophie and Thierry hadn't asked me to move out, although I really didn't want to stay there any longer. They knew and I knew that it was too late in the academic year for the university to find me different accommodation. I would just have to stick it out and stay at Bruno's as much as possible from now on.

That familiar old horse blanket of depression once again dropped its heaviness on my heart. No matter how strongly the magnet of fun and adventure attracted me, the horse blanket somehow always eventually smothered it.

I had to find a way to escape from the house. I started to put a few things in my bag to go down to Rouen, when the phone rang.

Sophie knocked on my door and wordlessly left the phone on the chair in the foyer. I was relieved to hear Mimi's voice.

'Hey you. How's it going?' she drawled in her dusky voice.

'To be honest, I can't wait to get out of here. My French family are such a drag. What are you up to? Is there anything going on?'

'I met this really interesting guy at Morrison's the other day and he said he's having a party tonight and to bring as many people as I want.'

'Count me in!' I said. My mood immediately lifted.

'Great, meet me at Morrison's at eight and we can go together.'

I hurried to get changed and put on some makeup. I heard the phone ring again in the foyer followed by a terse knock at my door.

'For you again. It sounds like the Italian,' Sophie remarked, holding the phone out to me as if it were a dirty diaper.

'Primavera, I come to get you tonight, no?'

'Mimi has invited me to a party tonight. I'm sure it's OK if you tag along. She said to invite people.'

'OK, I come get you soon,'

'Can you do me a favor and knock on the door this time, instead of my window. Sophie's got a bug up her ass at the moment.'

'Si, si, of course. *Ciao mi amore.*'

Half an hour later, there was a tapping at my window and the familiar Perez Prado tune being whistled.

I opened the window and saw Bruno standing there puffing on a cigarette. 'I asked you not to do that,' I said.

'I know, I just didn't want the wicked witch to open the door,' Bruno said, tossing his cigarette into Sophie's roses.

I passed Sophie in the hallway on my way out. 'I'm going out now, Sophie. I won't be in for dinner,' I said breezily.

***

Mimi was seated by the window of Morrison's, her beautiful, pale face framed by her big cloud of dark curls, her sensuous lips, dragging lazily on a roll-up. I was dismayed to see that Sara and Natalie were standing at the bar ordering their drinks.

'Hi Mimi. Where are the guys?' I asked.

'Mike is out with Roland tonight. They didn't want to come.'

'What about Lindi and Gab?' I asked.

'I think Lindi is out with her new man. Gabby's got a cold.'

'I guess it's just us then?' I asked, looking at Natalie and Sara flirting with the barman.

'I must take a photo of you.' Bruno stood back and aimed his camera at Mimi. 'Beautiful!' He said as he gave her a big hug and a kiss on both cheeks.

'Where's Patrice?' I asked Mimi, trying to divert Bruno's misdirected attention to the fact that Mimi had a boyfriend.

'Oh, he's out of the picture right now. Things haven't really been right between us since you know what.'

'So who's this guy who's having the party?'

'Oh, I met him here, in Morrison's, last weekend. He's a bit older but he seems cool. His name is Jean-Sebastien and he is a filmmaker.'

'And he said we could all come to his party?'

'The more the merrier apparently,' she said tossing her curls away from her face and taking a drag on her cigarette. I noticed with annoyance that Bruno was still snapping away.

Natalie and Sara wanted to get going. 'C'mon, drink up everyone. We've got a party to go to,' Sara said after finishing her drink and slamming the glass drunkenly on the table.

I rolled my eyes. She really didn't know how to handle her alcohol. I dreaded to think what she would be like later on.

We all drank up and headed to Mimi's new friend's apartment. It was right in the center of the old city, in a grand Renaissance-style building. We waited outside the gate to be buzzed in and we entered the house through a courtyard. The floor was made of black and white marble in a checkerboard pattern and a worn old stone staircase with an ornate black iron banister spiraled upwards several floors. We trudged up the steps, our footsteps and voices echoing through the vast stone stairwell. Jean-Sebastien's apartment was right at the top.

We arrived breathless and dizzy with alcohol. A man stood at the open doorway and our eyes met. He looked familiar. I tried to think where I had seen him before.

'*Bienvenue mes amis. Entrez,*' he said showing us the way into the apartment. My eyes were dazzled by a bright white light reflected by a white umbrella-type thing.

'Wow!' Bruno said. 'You have your own studio!' He circled around the equipment, inspecting it and nodding his head, obviously impressed.

Jean-Sebastien stood by, looking cool and proud in a Serge Gainsbourg kind of way.

'Oh, I see you come finally,' Jean-Sebastien said, looking at Bruno and I. 'How was Paris?'

The penny suddenly dropped. Of course! He was the guy who had given Bruno and I a ride to Paris when we were hitchhiking. I remembered sitting in the back of the yuppie jeep, and kicking a whole load of S & M magazines under the seat.

'I would like to introduce you to Sandrine and Maria,' Jean-Sebastien said indicating two 40-something women in low-cut tops who were sitting on the sofa, sipping martinis.

One of them was a bleached blond with a swept-up hairdo and lots of eye makeup. The other one had long dark hair streaked with filaments of grey, olive skin and a shock of bright red lipstick. They looked intimidating. I didn't know any women who looked so grown-up, womanly and sophisticated. They looked hungrily at Bruno, licking their lips like lionesses getting ready to attack their prey.

'Can I offer you all a drink?' Jean-Sebastien said, walking over to a fully stocked bar. He opened a bottle of Veuve Cliquot, popping the cork with a guttural *thwock*. He began pouring the fizzing liquid into glasses. Mimi was the first to grab one. When we each had a glass we raised a toast.

'I also have a little something else,' Jean-Sebastien said, standing at the bar, and cutting up lines of white powder with an Amex Gold card. 'It helps to lower the inhibitions,' he said with a wolf-like smile.

He held out a straw to Bruno, who snorted a line. He handed it to me and and then Bruno and Mimi each did a line as well, followed by Sara and Natalie.

Mimi and I sat down on the comfy sofa, feeling relaxed and buzzing. Jean-Sebastien put on some free-form jazz and went to stand behind one of his cameras. Aiming toward us all sitting on the sofa, '*Santé, les filles,*' he said, getting us to lift our glasses.

As usual, Bruno had his ridiculous vintage camera hanging round his neck. Sandrine and Maria seemed very interested in it and were stroking the camera's contours, oooing and ahhhing over it.

'Will you show us what that camera can do?' Maria warbled in a husky, sing-songy Spanish accent.

Bruno immediately started chatting away to her in Spanish. I never knew that he could speak Spanish. He began taking pictures of Sandrine and Maria, and whatever he was saying to them, they were lapping it up, posing and crossing and uncrossing their legs suggestively.

'So when are the other people coming?' I asked Mimi, trying to play it cool and not show myself up by being the jealous girlfriend. 'I thought this was a big party. We seem to be the only guests.'

Mimi shrugged. 'I dunno, maybe we *are* the party,' she said grabbing me by the hand and pulling me up from the sofa. 'C'mon let's dance,' she said, doing a weird hippy kind of dance to the unrythmic jazz.

Then there was a knock on the door. Finally, some other guests had arrived. A couple of guys came in. They looked to be the about the same age as Jean-Sebastien, around 40ish. Jean-Sebastien poured them some drinks as well and they settled on the sofa next to Natalie and Sara, watching Mimi and I dance.

I didn't feel much like dancing. In fact, I felt a little queasy.

'I feel funny,' Natalie said, slurring her words. She and Sara must have already had quite a bit to drink, they were acting really ridiculously, lolling about, woozily. The two French guys seemed amused and quite pleased to offer a comforting shoulder for them to pass out on.

I was beginning to feel very strange myself and put it down to the combination of fizz and coke. I stumbled back onto Bruno's lap and Mimi fell on top of us, hugging us. Bruno put his arms round us both, laughing.

'*Parfait, parfait*,' Jean-Sebastien said, snapping his camera at us, before turning back toward the bar to fill some more glasses that were lined up on the bar. 'More champagne?'

We all accepted and raised another toast.

I suddenly felt really dizzy and sick. 'I need the bathroom,' I said, trying to stand up.

Natalie also wobbled to her feet at the same time. 'Me first!' she slurred, as she shoved me out of the way and stumbled ahead to find the bathroom.

She got there first and immediately began being sick. With Natalie's head down the toilet, I fell on my knees at the bidet. Kneeling next to each other we were like two faithful worshippers, retching our praises to the great porcelain god.

I broke out in a cold sweat. The spots before my eyes multiplied to a grey fuzz. I felt myself falling and I blacked out.

I woke up with the cold tile caressing my cheek. I managed to stand up and I splashed some cold water on my face. Natalie was asleep on the floor and I just left her there.

Seeing double, I gingerly made my way back into the living room. Sara seemed to be face down in the lap of one Jean Sebastien's friends, possibly sucking him off, while the other guy was removing her shoes. Mimi was doing a stumbling, drunken striptease dance around the room while Jean-Sebastien filmed her. It was all too weird, like one of Bosch's paintings of hell.

I stood over Bruno, who was flanked by the two women, touching and caressing his chest and thigh, perilously close to his already bulging crotch. 'I don't feel well. I need to go now,' I demanded.

Maria looked annoyed. 'But darling, we are having such an interesting conversation,' she said.

'Well I can't speak Spanish, and I feel sick,' so I'm going now, and I need MY boyfriend to take me home.' I tugged at Bruno's hand and he finally got up.

'Let's get out of here,' I whispered in his ear. 'These people are weird.'

I grabbed Mimi by the hand and pulled her away from Jean-Sebastien. 'C'mon, put your top back on and let's get away from these freaky swingers.'

Before either of them could protest, I dragged them both out the door. 'We're going to buy some cigarettes,' I announced, and we shut the door behind us and ran dizzily down the spiral staircase, hanging on to each other.

'Thank God we got out of there when we did,' I said once we were out in the street. 'I think that guy put something in our drinks.'

'Do you think so?' Mimi said, 'Maybe that's why I feel so strange.'

'You should thank me, Bruno. You had a lucky escape from the clutches of that old hag. She was all over you.'

'Older women have always found me attractive,' Bruno said with a swagger in his step.

'What about Natalie and Sara?' Mimi asked. 'Maybe we should go back and rescue them too. They might get mad if they realize that we just left like that.'

'Nah,' I said. 'I'm sure they can handle themselves. They love that kind of thing. I'm sure they can boast about how they were in this really cool homemade porno film.' We all laughed at the thought of the two stuck-up sorority girls appearing in a low-budget blue movie.

We decided to go back to Morrison's for a nightcap and to discuss the weirdness of the evening's activities.

Je ne regrette rien

Over the next few days I kept my head buried in books, trying to cram in as much information as I could. I was determined that I would pass my final exams with flying colors. I avoided seeing Bruno or anyone else outside of classes. I went back and forth to the university, going to lectures and then coming home, shutting my bedroom door and studying.

I took five exams over a period of five days: Monday, translation; Tuesday, literary theory; Wednesday, French art history; Thursday, phonetics and pronunciation, both written and oral; and on Friday it was business French. By Friday afternoon, having taken them all, I walked out of the Fac confident that I had done my best and that I had passed everything. The further away I walked from the university, the more buoyant and liberated I began to feel.

I met up with the gang to celebrate at Big Ben's, the English pub we used to drink at in the early days of arriving in Rouen. It was the place where I had first met Bruno. We all sat around the tables outside and talked about our plans for the summer.

Gabriela's fiancé, Jamie, was flying over from the USA and they were going to spend the time in Paris. Lindi was going to stay on in Rouen for a bit longer with her new beau, Pierrot. Mike and Roland were going to spend the rest of the summer travelling around Scandinavia. Mimi was going to work on a commune in the south of France, picking grapes, and Sara and Natalie were going to Wimbledon to watch the tennis.

Suddenly, Bruno roared up on his motorbike in a cloud of dust. Gabriela and Lindi coughed and Mike put his hands over his ears.

'Look what I got, Primavera!' he shouted as he revved the engine to the annoyance of all the customers trying to enjoy their drinks outside the bar. 'A Moto Guzzi. The best type of motorcycle you can buy—Italian of course!'

I ran up to him and waved my hand to try to clear the bluish smoke that spewed from the exhaust pipe.

'It doesn't look so new to me,' I said, eyeing the scratched paintwork and tatty seat.

'I bought it from my friend Vincenzo. He made me a good price.'

I recalled Vincenzo from one of Bruno's parties: a haggard guy with teeth missing, who looked like a heroin addict. 'And where did Vincenzo get it from?' I asked, although I assumed that the bike was stolen. I walked it, sliding my hand along the dusty metallic body.

'Now you are finished with exams I take you back to Italy with me,' Bruno said, beaming.

It was the chance I had been waiting for and I wasted no time in accepting his offer. I flung my arms round his neck. '*Si, si, si*— take me to Italy with you!'

'Hey lovebirds, sorry to interrupt,' Lindi said. 'We were wondering what to do after this. Siobhan, do you have any ideas?

I thought for a second and then remembered that Sophie had said that the family were going away overnight on a church retreat. 'Yeah, sure. My host family are away for the evening. Why don't you and Pierrot come over? Come back for a quiet nightcap. They have a sofa bed in the living room, so you two can stay over.' I knew that Pierrot still lived with his parents and they didn't have a place to go to be alone together.

'Oh really, could we?' Lindi's eyes lit up. 'That would be great.'

'*Oui, ma chérie,*' Pierrot said, tipping Lindi in a theatrical romantic embrace, much to her squealing delight.

I had only really intended for Bruno, Lindi and Pierrot to come over for a quiet nightcap, but when Gabby heard about it, she asked if she could come too. Her host mother was also away at the same church retreat as the DeClermonts, and she didn't want to stay at home alone with her creepy host brother, Paul. But then I felt bad as Mimi was all by herself, so I invited her too, but she ended up flirting with the English bartender, so he, of course, had to come along as well. After closing the bar, the bartender, whose name was Ian, grabbed a bottle of rum and some mixers from the storeroom.

We trudged up the hill toward quiet, suburban Mont-Saint-Aignan, whooping and hollering all the way. I couldn't stop laughing, looking at our rag-tag group.

As we approached the DeClermonts' house, I turned to look at the boisterous group and held my finger to my lips. 'Shhhhh, we don't want to wake the neighbors.' The dog was in its kennel outside and it started going berserk, barking and jumping around. 'Shit,' I said, as I fumbled in the darkness to fit the key in the lock. I could hear stifled sniggers around me. I just hoped that the barking would not rouse the curiosity of the neighbors. I hurried them all inside and quickly peered out to see if any curtains were twitching, then I shut the door. The dog had settled down and all seemed fine.

Bruno began going from room to room, turning on lights, opening doors, cupboards and drawers. Everyone else tramped in behind him.

'Look what I found!' Bruno proudly produced the bottle of Courvoisier from the drinks cabinet.

'We can make creamsicles!' Lindi announced. She used to work in a bar and knew lots of cocktail recipes. I just need some orange juice and milk. When she opened the fridge she let out a shriek. 'There's a body in there!'

We all peered into the fridge at the plucked corpse of a quail, legs, head and all, with a few spiky feathers clinging to its purplish, pimply skin. Its glazed, beady eyes stared out at us from its grotesquely twisted head, beak agape.

Mimi wrinkled her nose. 'Eeew. That's gross.'

Bruno grabbed the corpse and started making it walk across the table like a marionette. 'I'm coming to get you!' he put on a squawky bird-like voice and began chasing after me with the dead quail, its wings flapping and floppy head bobbing.

I screamed, laughing so hard, and running through the living room, when I crashed into a side table next to the sofa. A vase full of flowers toppled over and smashed on the floor. I stopped in my tracks, staring at the shattered porcelain. 'Oh shit! Sophie is going to flip!'

Lindi grabbed a cloth and started mopping up the mess. 'Don't worry, we'll clean it up.'

I turned on Bruno. 'Now put the quail back in the fridge and stop fucking around before something else gets broken,'

'Don't blame it on me. You're the one who knocked over the vase,' he said in the bird voice. I couldn't help but crack a smile, and everyone started to laugh again. I decided to deal with the aftermath later.

Next, Bruno and Pierrot were playing catch with the quail. 'Didn't your mother ever tell you not to play with food,' Gabriela scolded the guys.

Lindi emerged from the kitchen with the creamsicle cocktails. We each took one and clinked glasses.

After downing a few and losing track of what time it was, we all eventually stumbled to bed. Bruno and I went to my room, Lindi and Pierrot slept on the pull-out sofa in the living room, Mimi and Ian in Sophie and Thierry's bedroom, and Gabby in the kids' room.

The next morning, I had a hazy recollection of the previous night's mayhem. 'We can have a nightcap,' were the last words that I vaguely remembered saying. I looked over at Bruno sprawled next to me. I was surprised that he wasn't awake yet. He was usually up with the sun. I decided to rise from the dead and survey the damage, hoping that I would be able to get everything back in order before the DeClermonts got home. They would absolutely freak out if they walked in at that point.

I padded into the living room, where Lindi and Pierrot were asleep on the sofa bed. I hadn't been able to figure out where Sophie kept the bedding, so they were lying on the bare sofa bed mattress, their naked bodies barely covered by their coats and a throw.

In the cold light of day, I surveyed the chaos. Flowers lay trampled on the floor; there were shards of porcelain that we had missed picking up, muddy shoe prints across the terracotta tiles, pictures hanging at lopsided angles, and people passed out in nearly every room. I noted the open door on the drinks cabinet and the half-empty Courvoisier bottle.

I went to the toilet and when I looked down I realized it was blocked by something. On closer inspection I saw to my horror that it was the quail. 'Bruno, what the hell!' I shouted.

Bruno came shuffling in. 'What's all the shouting, Primavera?' he said innocently, his hair sticking up all over the place.

I pointed into the bowl. 'Did you do that? Get it out.' He was squinting because he didn't have his glasses on.

Bruno stuck his arm in and yanked out the corpse. Luckily there was nothing else in there with it. 'Sophie's going to go nuts. What the hell can I do?'

He winked at me and tapped the side of his Roman nose. He dried the dripping bird off with a tea towel and put it back in the fridge. 'No one will ever know,' he said, grinning.

I was so glad to be a vegetarian, and not be in any danger of having to eat the offending bird.

I put some strong coffee on and woke everyone up with a steaming bowl each of café crème, as bribery to help me get the place cleaned. Once everyone was wired enough, I rounded them all up, and with military precision I orchestrated a massive clean-up. I handed Bruno a broom, Mimi a mop, Pierrot a plastic trash bag and Lindi and Gabriela washed the dishes. I went around tidying up the beds, straightening the pictures, placing objects back where they belonged and picking up bottles and cans from behind and under furniture. I was determined not to leave a single clue of what had gone on.

Finally, it was all perfect and I stood back and inspected the result. Everything was just right. I would just have to tell Sophie that I knocked the vase over by accident and that I would buy her a new one. It looked cheap and ugly anyway.

Everyone had scattered like cockroaches back to their homes. I sat down at my desk, opened a book and breathed a sigh of relief.

When the DeClermonts arrived home, Sophie was in good spirits. 'Did you have a nice weekend?' she asked me, even managing to crack a smile.

Then I remembered something. I never replaced the bottle of Courvoisier. I hoped that it would go unnoticed until I could go out and get one. It wasn't as though Sophie and Thierry were hitting the bottle every night. I felt certain that I would get away with it.

At the Continent hypermarket, in the spirits aisle, I took a sharp intake of breath at the price of a bottle of Courvoisier. I didn't have that amount of cash on me, and since it had been stolen in Paris, I didn't even have the American Express card to fall back on for emergencies. I visualized the scornful and accusing look that Sophie would surely give me when she discovered that the bottle was missing, and me squirming and trying to think of a lame excuse. I would just have to water it down.

I quietly entered the house, quickly grabbed the bottle and filled it up at the kitchen sink. I looked around and everything seemed silent. It didn't appear that anyone was around and I figured it would be an opportune moment to slip the bottle back into the drinks cabinet.

I tiptoed into the living room and placed it gently inside the cabinet. Just as I closed it, I heard someone come in the front door. I quickly turned on the TV and sat down, trying to make it look like I was watching television.

Sophie marched in and stood in the middle of the living room with her arms folded. 'I was just speaking to the next door neighbor and he mentioned that he saw you come home very late last night with some friends. Did you have some friends over?'

'Oh yes, just my friends Mimi and Lindi came over because they were too scared to walk home alone so late at night.'

'Mm, hmm, is that so? Not that Italian boy then? The neighbor thought that he could see a tall man enter the house.'

'Oh yes, and Bruno as well. He thought it would be best if he walked us all back together. But he didn't stay.' Sophie obviously had spies and I thought that even if I didn't tell the whole truth, a partial truth might be acceptable.

Her eyes immediately darted to the empty table next to the sofa. 'And who broke my Limoges porcelain vase? That was a family heirloom.'

Later that evening as the family all sat down around the dinner table, I gulped when Sophie produced the steaming roasted quail from the oven.

'Too bad you are a vegetarian, Siobhan,' Thierry said. 'You won't have the pleasure of tasting the quail that I brought back from my latest hunting trip.'

I grimaced as he carved it and gave each member of the family a small piece. 'Oh don't worry about me. I'm very happy with my salad,' I said, as I watched Sophie place the quail meat in her mouth and start chewing.

After finishing the meal, Thierry said, 'That was so delicious, I'm now in the mood for a little *digestif*. Would anyone else like to join me in a little glass of Courvoisier?'

He poured both Sophie and I a little glass of the liqueur. He took the first sip and spat it out in the sink. 'We have had this bottle for so long it must have gone off. It tastes terrible,' he said, grimacing.

Not-so-easy rider

I didn't even look back as we zoomed away from the DeClermonts' house in a cloud of dust.

'Italia here we come,' Bruno shouted over the roar. I held on tightly to his waist, as we sped through the cobbled city streets of Rouen, past Monet's ruined cathedral, past the Gros Horloge, past the Joan of Arc church. Soon the stone and concrete gave way to green rolling pastures and country lanes lined with trees and hedgerows.

We decided that on our way down to Italy we would take in some of the famous sights in France, so that I could experience them before I had to go back to the USA.

First on the list that I wanted to see was Mont Saint Michel, an ancient walled island commune, with a medieval monastery at its heart. The island can be accessed on foot by walking across the sandy bay when the tide is out. Mike had told me how amazing it was.

I could see the squat conical shape of the island, sprouting up from the sand, as we came around a bend on the coast road. Bruno pulled the bike over to the side of the road and we gazed out across the bay. We were lucky in our timing; it looked like the tide was completely out, and we would be able to walk across the bay on foot, avoiding the crowds that took the causeway that linked the island to the mainland.

Bruno parked the motorbike, and we took off our shoes, rolled up our jeans and set off across the vast expanse of bay toward the impressive spire of the abbey, which appeared to pierce the sky.

I read aloud from the guidebook as we walked. 'It says that it is a UNESCO World Heritage site, *"boasting the spectacular and well-preserved Norman Benedictine Abbey of St Michael."* It also says, *"WARNING: Attempting to reach Mont Saint Michel on foot can be dangerous. It is not unheard of for tourists to drown after being cut off by the tide, and the deep mud and quicksand surrounding the island can be treacherous."* Do you think we should be doing this? Maybe we should just drive across on the causeway.'

'Don't be silly, Primavera. There will be too much traffic on the causeway. And besides, it will be more picturesque walking across,' he said, as he fiddled with the lens on his camera. 'It will be hours before the tide comes in again.'

The fine, damp sand squished between my toes. It seemed quite firm underfoot and I was reassured by Bruno's confidence that the tide would be out for a few more hours, so I relaxed and sauntered casually. Bruno was snapping away with his camera, trying to get photos of me walking across the bay from every angle. He was often fiddling with the camera settings for ages, trying to get the right light and position. I had to stop and wait for him a few times to catch up with me.

I looked toward the mount, which I expected to be getting closer, but I guess we had overestimated the distance. It seemed like we had been out in the bay for hours and we still had quite a distance to go. I noticed the sand was beginning to feel wetter, and I could see a slick film of water forming on top of it. I started to walk through the centimeter-deep water, but with each step it seemed to rise, and was soon swirling around my ankles. I looked behind me and could see the water creeping closer and closer in smooth ebbing sheaths. I saw that Bruno was far behind and he was sloshing toward me through ankle-deep water.

I decided not to wait for him and began walking more and more quickly. The water was now above my ankles and creeping up my calves. My feet seemed to be sinking deeper and deeper and I recalled what the guidebook had said about quicksand.

'Bruno, come on, or else we might get cut off by the tide!' I shouted urgently.

'Don't panic, Primavera, it's only a little water.'

I stayed focused on the nearing mount. Soon the water was just below my knees. I looked back at Bruno who was trying to catch up, splashing and getting drenched but holding his camera above his head to keep it from getting wet. I ran toward the stone steps that ascended from the lapping water. I was exhausted by the time I reached them and I dragged myself up out of the water with a gasp of relief. I looked way above my head at the rocky cliff face and the steep steps trailing upwards toward the village.

Bruno hauled himself up after me. 'Wow, what an adventure!' he whooped, throwing his arms wide in exhilaration. 'I got some great photos.'

We wound our way to the top, stopping every so often so that Bruno could try to get photos of the seagulls flying below us, against the backdrop of the long jaggedy shadow of the mount. I didn't mind, as it allowed me to catch my breath.

Once we made it to the top, what we found was a real disappointment. The place was a total tourist trap, absolutely heaving with people crowding the narrow, cobbled lanes. There were loads of cheesy souvenir shops selling plastic figures of the mount. We were thirsty and hungry but all of the cafés and restaurants were really expensive. All we could afford was a bottle of water and a couple of chocolate bars.

We decided to leave and get back on the road. I looked back at the bay filled with gently lapping waves. 'I think we are going to have to walk across the causeway and back along the road to get to the motorbike,' I said.

The causeway was about a mile long and we must have parked at least another mile up the road, so we decided to hitch a ride back to the bike in order to save our legs. It wasn't too difficult to find a ride with the high volume of cars and buses streaming out of the parking area and we got back in the nick of time, and without getting wet!

Back on the bike, we consulted the map. Our next port of call was Giverny to see Claude Monet's house and gardens, the place that inspired his most famous impressionist paintings. It was about a three hour drive back inland, which seemed to breeze by, now we were on dry land and not having to wade through waves.

When we got to Monet's house we walked toward the gardens expecting peace, serenity and beauty to reveal itself. However, we turned the corner and were hit with chaos. The line of eager tourists snaked up and down in cordoned rows leading up to the ticket window. Bruno whistled through his teeth. '*Porca Madonna!* What a queue.' It always amused me when he used quaint British words for things, like 'queue', which I learned meant 'line'. 'Should we give it a miss?'

I was disappointed and it must have shown on my face. 'But we came all this way. We are so close now. Can't you just stop being an impatient Italian and wait for 10 minutes to get in?'

He gave in and we joined the line, moving at a snail's pace and being herded with all the other tourists through the maze of cordons.

When we finally arrived inside the garden it was incredibly crowded, but nevertheless you could see its breathtaking beauty. Monet's paintings came alive right before my eyes. There was the iconic footbridge arching lightly over the emerald lily pond. There were roses and wisteria and nasturtium adding strokes of color to the dappled water and the lush greenness.

Inside the house there was just as bold a use of color and shapes and patterns. The dining room floor, tiled with diamond-shaped terracotta and ivory tiles, seemed to jump about joyfully, and everything was painted a bright, sunny yellow—the table and chairs, walls, cupboards, and even the ceiling. The sitting room soothed the eyes in shades of blue and Monet's bedroom exploded with a bold mixture of colors inspired by the spectacular garden view, which was the focus of the room, like a masterpiece framed by the central window.

Our next destination, Versailles, contrasted acutely with the rustic domesticity of Giverny. It was also beautiful, but the most over-the-top, mind-blowing circus of ornateness. Everything was carved with swirls and leafed in gold. Immense mirrors and impressive paintings of generations of French royalty lined the long galleries. The gardens were a riot of neoclassical sculptures, of cupids and spouting water fountains gushing and bubbling all around.

My head was spinning and I was exhausted but we had to get back on the road. As we zoomed along the autoroute I smiled and closed my eyes as I clasped Bruno's waist. Images of Japanese bridges, swathes of flowers, beautiful scents, imposing abbeys and ballrooms spun around in my head, replacing the vision of the French countryside swirling by. Rouen and the DeClermonts were distant memories. Toby was a distant memory, and all that was on my mind was the future and what adventures lay in wait.

After we had crossed the Massif Central and camped out in various little hamlets, we decided to head to Provence. I had heard so much about this part of France and how different it was to the north.

From the back of the bike, I could see the landscape changing. Green rolling hills and tree-lined lanes gave way to dusty trails, mountains and orange-hued rocky outcroppings. The light became yellower and more intense, heating my leather-clad back. Even the air changed. The smog of the north was far behind and now the air was tinged with the scent of lavender.

We had been very lucky with the weather. It had been warm, dry and partly sunny since we had started out from Rouen, and as we made our way south, the clouds diminished, leaving a vibrant and startlingly empty blue sky. However, on leaving Nice, the humidity began to build and the clouds gathered ominously.

We were heading to Monaco and hoped that we could get there before a thunderstorm broke. We were zooming along at top speed in the fast lane and I was watching the grey clouds collect into huge dark grey billows when the motorbike started juddering. Still doing top speed, Bruno pulled across into the slow lane. He managed to steer the motorbike into the breakdown lane before the motor choked to a sudden halt. He turned the bike violently, causing it to skid, and we both ended up on the ground with a mouthful of gravel.

Bruno scrambled up and dusted himself off and then proceeded to check his camera. '*Grazie Dio*, the camera isn't broken!' he announced.

I was a bit stunned and lay still for a moment, trying to determine if I was OK. The bike had fallen on my foot and I could feel a jolt of pain.

'The bike's on my foot,' I said, just as the first heavy rain drops started to smack me in the face.

Bruno lifted the bike up and tried to get it going again. It wouldn't start. The rain had become absolutely torrential and explosive thunderclaps followed white flashes of lightning. In the meantime, I tried to stand up on my throbbing foot. I took off my Doc Marten boot to have a look at it. There was already some swelling and I could tell that tomorrow it would be bruised as well.

'C'mon Primavera, we'll have to push it,' Bruno said as he started walking up the road with the motorbike.

'Slow down!' I yelled, as I limped after him through the downpour, feeling like Quasimodo, my hair plastered over my face.

'Why the hell did you have to buy such a cheap old piece of shit that couldn't make it to Italy? I'm soaked to the skin and smell like a wet dog, my foot is killing me, and now we have to walk for God-only-knows how many miles to find a garage!' I wailed.

'It's an adventure, Primavera. You can write about it in that diary of yours. Don't worry, we will find help and get the bike fixed. And everything will be OK again when we are back in Italy—the best country in the world.'

I shook my head, and looked at the muddy ground as we trudged along. Sometimes I wondered what the hell I was doing and how I ended up in the shit situations that I always found myself in, when my friends back home all had normal jobs and normal boyfriends.

After what seemed like hours of plodding through the rain, with the greasy road spray infiltrating every pore of our bodies, we found a small garage. Being a Sunday evening it was shut and there was no one around.

'We will have to wait 'til the morning,' Bruno said. 'We can camp here overnight.'

I sat down on an embankment, shivering and in pain, to rest my foot while Bruno put the tent up. The rain wasn't letting up and we were both soaked to the core, sitting in the damp, smelly tent listening to the sound of raindrops splattering on the canvas. I had had some pretty horrendous nights in the past year, but this one really did take the cake for ultimate discomfort. I had no idea how Bruno could remain so obstinately cheerful.

'Have we got anything to eat?' Bruno asked.

I remembered that I had a single chocolate bar in my bag. We both shared it, savoring the small, chocolatey morsels, knowing that was all we had. It wasn't enough to stave off the hunger, however.

'I know what will help,' Bruno said as he produced some hash from his pocket and started rolling a joint. The tent soon filled with a choking cloud of weed smoke.

'Gimme some of that,' I said desperately grabbing for the joint. Maybe I could just dope myself up so I could actually sleep in this miserable environment.

We woke in the morning to a baking heat beating down on the tent. The moisture evaporating from our clothes turned the inside of the tent into a steamy fug. I flung open the tent flaps gasping for air.

Thankfully there was someone opening the garage. Bruno approached them and explained what happened to the motorbike. Hopefully it would be an easy repair.

A surprise proposal

We ended up having to camp out in the gas station parking lot for two days, having been told by the mechanic that he had to order a part from Italy. So much for Italian motorcycles! We had to survive on chocolate bars and soda, the only refreshments that were available in the gas station. My teeth became coated with a sticky fur and felt like they were going to fall out from all the sugar. To top it off I felt sick to my stomach and spent most of the time retching in the filthy toilet. Needless to say, I was extremely pissed off and Bruno was becoming increasingly irritating.

'*Tranquilo*, Primavera,' he said when I became angry and started shouting at him that I was sick and needed to be in bed. I was tired of all his stupid quips and platitudes about taking an easygoing approach to life in the face of adversity. He actually seemed to be enjoying himself, joking with the mechanic. I didn't understand how he could be so unsympathetic to my need for a shower, a warm bed and some decent food.

When we were finally back on the road, Bruno drove like a maniac around the winding roads of Monaco, inspired by the fact that it was where the Grand Prix takes place. Nevertheless, I was starting to feel a bit better as I contemplated the view of the sparkling blue sea in the bay below us—until Bruno ran a red light and cut off an unmarked police car. He tried to argue with the cops, which resulted in them issuing him with an extortionate fine. As soon as the police drove off, he dropped the ticket down a drain in the road and we zoomed off again. I found myself looking forward to my flight back to the USA, and living a normal and predictable existence again.

By the time we reached Italy, the sun was shining brightly in an intense blue sky and I perked up again. The road we were now on hugged the coast of the Ligurian Sea before heading northwards to Lake Garda.

'We go somewhere special for lunch today, Primavera,' Bruno shouted back to me. We ascended the mountain, going round countless hairpin turns. I was dizzy with hunger and excitement as the lake appeared below us, a vision of sparkling blue-green. Bruno pulled into a little pizzeria with a canopy of grapevines covering a patio perched on the edge of the hill, overlooking the lake. This place epitomized everything I loved about Italy: the warmth of the sun, a little pizzeria tucked away down a narrow mountain lane, delicious pizza and wine. A feeling of happiness and contentment returned.

I was sooooo hungry for proper food I wolfed down my pizza and sat back with my glass of wine to contemplate the view. And in that moment, I felt I could live there forever.

Suddenly Bruno grabbed my hand. He got down on one knee in front of me and said, 'Primavera, will you marry me?'

It all seemed to happen so quickly that I wasn't quite sure what he had actually said.

'Sorry, what did you say?' I asked.

He rummaged around in his jacket pocket and pulled out a worn little box.

'Primavera, marry me,' he said, presenting me with a very old and ornate diamond ring, far too gaudy for my taste.

I gulped. This was always Bruno's strategy. He distracted me first— be it dangling high up in a Ferris wheel, whizzing through the night on a speeding motorcycle, or here, being seduced by a magnificent vista in the Italian lake district, and having eaten a delicious meal after days of deprivation—then he would swoop in using the element of surprise.

'Mama wanted you to have it. It was my Nonna's when she got engaged to my Nonno,' Bruno said earnestly, bringing the ring closer to my face.

I had been hoping that fate would determine how I could come back to live in Europe. If I married Bruno then I could stay in Italy. I could get a job teaching French or English, I could live amongst old Roman ruins, and grape vines, and I could eat al fresco, and walk down cobbled lanes while ancient church bells chimed.

Then I realized the situation I was in. I had been swept away on a whirlwind motorcycle tour around Europe, on Bruno's whim, only to end up nearly drowning at Mont Saint Michel, and having to camp out in a gas station, hungry and sleepless for two days. I remembered being stopped at the German border when Bruno had slyly stashed his drugs, which could have got us sent to jail. I remembered the humiliating experience of meeting his friends for the first time, when Matteo had come on to me and then I had unintentionally asked one of Bruno's friends in Veronese dialect if he wanted to fuck, all to the amusement of Bruno. And then there was Chiara's earring in the bed.

Did I really want to end up like Bruno's mother, cheated on by her arrogant, philandering husband, and still doting on him like a king because that's what Italian women were supposed to do?

'Bruno... this is a really big deal, and I, I need some time to think about it.'

He looked deflated and confused. He obviously hadn't expected that response.

'Please, take it, Primavera,' he continued to hold the ring out. You keep it.'

'But I haven't made a decision yet, Bruno. I can't accept it just yet.'

'But you're just in shock I think. I give you some time. But have it until you reply me.'

His quirky English made me smile, and he smiled back, his glasses crooked on his Roman nose, and his hair sticking up—the Bruno I fell in love in with.

But I slowly shook my head and repeated that I need some time to think about it. 'I have to go back to the States and finish my degree, so I can't rush into things.'

'That's OK. If we get married I will come to the USA and you can finish your studies.'

'Bruno, you've never even been to the USA, how do you know you'll like it?'

'No problem. I will go anywhere in the world, for you, Primavera.'

We rode back to Verona in silence and my thoughts raced in confusion, as the motorbike sped dangerously round endless bends through the Italian countryside.

Verona revisited

The weather was beautiful for the rest of my week in Italy, and Bruno made sure that our days were filled with excursions: around the lakes, to restaurants, parties and even a short but exhilarating jaunt on a friend's sailboat. We wound our way around the countryside on the Moto Guzzi, past holy shrines of the Virgin Mary tucked in alcoves in the stone walls that lined the little roads, past cemeteries with intricate wrought iron gates, past vineyards, gardens and fountains. And I fell ever more deeply in love with Italy. Increasingly, I wanted to stay here. When I thought about having to leave to go back to France and pick up my stuff from the DeClermonts', and then get a long-haul flight back to the USA, my heart sunk. I knew that with one little word, I could change all that forever. Just one little word.

Bruno surprised me by being quieter than usual. He decided that he wasn't going back to Rouen with me. He was fed-up with France, and with me leaving there was nothing to keep him there. I expected him to be his usual persistent self and to incessantly needle me until I gave in and said yes to his proposal, but he didn't. Instead he tried to woo me through his country.

On my last weekend, he took me on a motorbike ride on a narrow mountain pass through the pre-Alps, way, way up to a tiny, incredibly ancient and remote village. From there we progressed on foot through a forest to see some waterfalls. They were spectacular and beautiful, and I should have felt happy and privileged to experience so many beautiful sights at such a young age, but something was holding me back.

There was a raging conflict inside my heart. I felt the heavy, thick smoke of depression choking my happiness, which seemed to be imprisoned and trying to escape. Despite all the fun I was having, I couldn't shake off an underlying dread of making a mistake, and ruining my life.

Retracing our steps back to the village, the dark and foggy woods matched my mood. We were going to meet some of Bruno's pals, and all go on to their friend Marco's birthday party.

The party was in the only restaurant in the village, a large, spacious stone building with rough-hewn wooden beams and long wooden tables set up in rows. There was already wine on the tables when we arrived. As more people turned up, the food was brought out—massive amounts of food—enough to feed the whole nation of Ethiopia. There was a starter plate with pasta, then about five meat plates, two plates of vegetables, cheese, more wine, and a delicious cake afterwards with champagne to accompany it. The main attraction—and the most curious custom I've ever seen—was the coffee. It was served flaming in a carved wooden pot with a round opening in the center and four spouts around it. Four people drank the coffee from the same pot, through long straws stuck in the spouts. The coffee itself was exceptional. It was made with grappa, sugar and lemon. It was very strong and I was pretty lit afterwards.

I already had experience of Italian parties, and knew how out of control they could get, this one being no exception. People were shouting, singing and throwing things across the room, including chairs! I had to duck out of the way a couple of times, to avoid being hit by a piece of flying birthday cake. After dinner, at 1am, we all staggered out of the restaurant into the village to play a game that was like tag/hide-n-go-seek. The group scattered as they all hid themselves away in places around the village, and Marco, the birthday boy, covered his eyes and counted out loud to 100.

An eerie fog penetrated the narrow passageways and played tricks on my eyes. I was too frightened to hide on my own, so Bruno and I stuck together and we looked for a suitable hiding place. We crept silently down a dark alley, keeping to the shadows. A decrepit old outbuilding, with a peeling old wooden door hanging crookedly from one hinge, loomed in front of us. 'This looks like a good place,' Bruno whispered, as he pushed open the creaky old door. I was hit by a strong smell of goats and chickens.

It was pitch dark and as soon as we entered something feathery squawked and flew into my face. I let out a little yelp and Bruno put his hand over my mouth and said, 'Shhh, Primavera.' He pulled me close and although I couldn't see a thing, I could feel the warmth of his body, and I could hear his heart beating against my ear. I nestled my face into his chest and inhaled his scent, the scent of Italy: strong tobacco, basil and wine. As we held each other in the silent darkness, I realized how much I would miss him when I went back to the USA. In my mind I said, 'Yes, yes, I will marry you.'

Suddenly, the rickety door of the outbuilding swung open and someone shone a flashlight in our faces. Marco. He laughed, '*Li ho trovato—gli amante!*'

We all ended up back in the village square to say goodbye, which in Italy takes a long time, as you have to chat to everyone present and kiss them on both cheeks. Then, as drunk as anything, they all got in their cars, or onto their scooters and motorbikes, and headed down the winding roads through the fog.

As expected, it was a hair-raising journey on the back of the motorbike. Italian drivers are maniacs at the best of times, but these guys were beyond mental. They raced each other down the mountain, passing each other, then slamming on brakes, tooting their horns and hollering obscenities at each other. I guessed it was a macho thing—trying to see who was the most daring and who could outsmart who—but I thought they were all just plain stupid. I clenched my eyes shut and gritted my teeth, certain that the finish line for this race was in the cemetery.

I should have felt lucky that we made it back to Bruno's mother's apartment alive, but a feeling of dread descended as I realized that it was actually the early hours of Monday morning and I would have to catch a train to France later that evening. I wasn't sure I would be able to give Bruno an answer to his proposal before I had to leave. In bed, I lay awake, mulling the situation over and over again in my mind, weighing up the pros and cons of becoming the next Signora Calibri, listening to Bruno snoring next to me, and watching the light creep in under the blind as the sun rose.

By the time I got up, my mind was still reeling. I was packing my things when Signora Calibri came over and threw her arms around me. 'I will be so proud to have you as my daughter-in-law,' she said.

I didn't have the heart to say that I hadn't made up my mind yet. Instead I just said, 'Thank you, Signora Calibri. You've been very kind to let me stay here.'

'Please, call me "Mama".' Now next time you are back in Italy, when you are finished with your studies in the USA, we can start planning the wedding,' she said beaming. 'I make you something for your journey,' she said, handing me a bag filled with carefully wrapped parcels of food. 'I can't let my future daughter-in-law go hungry.'

'*Grazie*,' I said smiling a half-hearted, embarrassed smile. Fred the pink cat twirled his plump, furry body around my legs, purring. The smell of pasta sauce cooking on the stove and the warmth of the late afternoon sun squeezing through the slats in the shutters suddenly gave me a warm, longing feeling. I didn't want to leave. For a split second I thought that maybe I could extend my stay just one more day, but realized that if I didn't get the overnight train I might miss the final farewell party at the university back in Rouen.

Suddenly the doorbell rang. Signora Calibri answered it and Matteo and his girlfriend came in through the door like a whirlwind.

'What are they doing here?' I asked Bruno. 'You know I've got to go to the train station.'

'Don't worry. They wanted to come and see you off.'

'My parents lent me the Mercedes,' Matteo said. 'I will drive you to the train station.'

Signora Calibri stood waving at the door as we descended the steps and headed out toward the convertible. Matteo opened the trunk and produced a bottle of champagne. 'Before you go we have one last celebration up on the Roman ruins.'

'But I really need to get to the train station,' I protested, although from all I had learnt about Italians, I knew that there was no use arguing.

We piled into the car and wound our way up to the ruins above the city. I remembered the first time I went up there with Bruno and Matteo and the German/Australian couple that we had met. I recalled the exhilaration, the happiness from being in such a beautiful place.

We parked and Matteo popped the cork. He passed the bottle to me and I took a big swig. When the bottle was empty, Matteo opened another.

'We have something to announce,' Matteo said. 'Andrina and I are getting married.'

His girlfriend squealed and leapt at Matteo giving him a big, sloppy kiss. Then she shoved her hand in front of my face to show off the enormous rock on her finger. I thought it looked like a hideous lump of gaudiness on her manicured hands and I recoiled.

'Maybe we have a double wedding and a wife swap,' Matteo said lasciviously, as he winked at me. 'Maybe you have some news as well?'

Andrina stared expectantly at me. I smiled awkwardly and shrugged my shoulders. 'I really need to get to the train station now,' I said unenthusiastically.

Andrina looked disappointed for a second and then ran over to Matteo, flung her arms around him, and started kissing him again.

'OK, let's go,' Matteo said, getting into the car.

When we got to the train station I found out that my train had been cancelled due to a rail strike in France. I felt secretly relieved that I was able to spend a little bit more time in Italy with Bruno, and I would have more time to make a decision before going back.

Bruno and I ended up joining Matteo and Andrina for dinner to celebrate their engagement, drinking more champagne and enjoying a lavish meal. It really couldn't have been a more perfect evening. I thought, I could wine and dine like this all the time if I lived here—if I became Signora Calibri.

The next morning, when the time to board my train to France had finally come, Bruno and I sat in his mother's old, red Fiat 500 in the train station parking lot.

'You haven't answered me yet, Primavera. Is there something wrong?' Bruno pressed. 'You are coming back to marry me aren't you?'

I burst out in tears, threw my arms around him and buried my head in his shoulder. 'I can't decide yet,' I sobbed. 'I'll miss you so much but I can't make a decision like that right now. I want to finish my studies and that's all I can think about right now. Why don't you come to see me in the USA?'

'I will. Just remember, *ti amo*, Primavera. Come back to me. I don't want to lose you.'

Bruno walked me to the train, helped me to find my seat and put my bag on the luggage rack like a perfect gentleman. We stood kissing and holding hands on the steps of the carriage, until the conductor blew his whistle and Bruno jumped off. As the train pulled away I hung out the window and waved as Bruno ran alongside, trying to keep up.

'*Ti amo*, Primavera,' I heard him shout as the train pulled out of the station and he disappeared from sight.

The last supper

I wasn't even going to bother to unpack my things when I arrived in France. I would be leaving for the USA in two days anyway and it didn't seem worth it. Our French 'mentors' were having a farewell dinner and party for the American group and their host families that evening. Gekko would, of course, be DJing. The party was being held in a restaurant in the center of Rouen. I was surprised that the DeClermonts said they would go. I suppose they wanted to schmooze a bit with the other families. I was looking forward to seeing Lindi, Angie, Mimi and Mike, and finding out how their summer had been.

I still had a whole load of Italian lire and I needed to change them for francs but as the banks were closed I would just have to get some money out on my cash card. I first went to the ATM machine at the Continent hypermarket, but when I put my card into the slot and typed in my PIN number, a message came up saying my card was rejected and the machine spat it back out at me. Confused, I tried again. Maybe I had put the wrong PIN number in. No, it still didn't work. I figured it was just the machine, so I made my way to another cash machine at the university.

However, the second ATM I tried also rejected my card. I made my way to the party, cashless and a bit worried about what was going on with my card. I might need a bit of money at the airport the next day, but luckily, I wouldn't need any money that evening—the food and drink at the party were paid for already, and the DeClermonts were driving down to Rouen, so I didn't need to catch a bus.

At the party, the host families congregated at one side of the room, while the students huddled together on the other side. I could hear Sophie's whiney, ingratiating voice from across the room. She was such a middle-class wannabe. I had heard from Richard that some of the families hosted foreign students as a status symbol, because if they had room for a student to live with them for a year, their house must be large with lots of superfluous rooms, and it showed how cultured and open-minded they were to have rich foreign students living under their roof. Sophie was definitely one of those. She didn't care about the fact my mattress was an inch-thick piece of foam that hurt my back, or that I always had to pick the meat out of my 'vegetarian' meals that she prepared, or the fact that her daughter used my bedroom for piano practice, or that we intensely disliked each other.

I'd been to some of the houses where the other students were lodging and some of them lived in their own little annexes in the roofs of grand Haussmann houses, or in huge old, rambling barn conversions. By contrast, Sophie's place was a little, bland, characterless, newly built box, in a dull development not even in the city. I had definitely drawn the short straw with Sophie's place.

I felt a tap on my shoulder and turned to see Lindi smiling brightly. 'Long time no see,' she said. 'Where have you been?'

I told her all about my whirlwind tour of France down to Italy on the back of Bruno's motorbike.

Lindi had stayed in Rouen with her beau, Pierrot. 'Guess, what?' she said, beaming ear to ear. 'He popped the question!'

'No way, really? What did you say?'

'What do you think I said, silly?'

I looked at her blankly.

'I said yes,' she said.

Gabriela came running up to us and gave Lindi a big hug. 'Congratulations. That's wonderful news. Can I see the ring?' she asked.

Lindi presented a modest little band. 'Have you planned a day yet?

'Well, actually,' Lindi's fair skin flushed pink. 'We kinda, sorta, are already married.'

'What?!' I said in disbelief. Gabriela was speechless for once; her jaw was practically dragging on the ground.

'We did it in secret, sorry guys. I would have invited you all to the *mairie*, where we actually had the service but it all happened so quickly. Pierre wanted to get it done as fast as possible so that he could apply for a green card and come back with me to the States. He's going to try to find a job while I finish the last year of my degree.'

Alarm bells began ringing in my brain. I knew that Lindi made terrible decisions regarding relationships. I didn't think she'd thought it through and I immediately had suspicions that

Pierre was just in it for the passport. I didn't say anything but smiled weakly and gave her a hug. 'Well, I hope you are both happy together.'

I turned to Gabriela. 'How's your summer been?'

'Apart from having to fend off my crazy host brother, things have been OK. He started to send me love letters, slipping them into my coat pocket or into a bag if I left it lying around. He even left one in my underwear drawer.'

'Gosh, that's so creepy,' Lindi said. 'He's not coming tonight is he?'

'I hope not, but I wouldn't be surprised if I found him spying on me from behind the curtains or disguised as a plant or something, eavesdropping on my conversations,' Gabby said, looking around anxiously.

Gekko arrived with his bag of records. He came over to us with a flourish of his smoking Gauloise, kissing us all before rushing off to set up his decks. I was going to miss that crazy Frenchman and his unique style.

Mike and Roland also arrived at the same time. They seemed to always be together, like they were an item or something, and I started to wonder. I remember Bruno had once said to me that he thought Mike was gay. He said he could tell a gay guy when he saw one, although I totally didn't see it. I didn't think it was possible as he dated women.

'Is Chiara coming?' I asked Mike.

'No, we broke up.'

'Oh what a shame,' Gabby said. 'She was such a nice girl. What happened?'

'She was a bitch,' Roland said venomously, and we all looked surprised at his outburst as usually he was so quiet. I could only assume that perhaps there was some love rivalry. Maybe Mike would finally come out of the closet.

'Where's Mimi?' I asked hoping to hear her carefree, joyous laughter and smell that lingering scent of patchouli that she always left in her wake.

'Oh, didn't you hear?' Lindi said.

'No, what?' I asked.

'She just ran off with some weird German guy. We think she's joined some cult and is living in a commune in the south of France.'

'You're kidding me!?' I was genuinely worried about her. She was so trusting and giving of herself. 'Does anyone know where she is?'

Mike shook his head. 'We just know it's some place near Lourdes where people live in caves. The weird German guy was telling us about it. Then she just disappeared one day.'

I suddenly felt sad, remembering the first day when we'd all arrived off the bus in Paris, trying to blend in and look cool, the promise of adventure hanging in the Parisian air. Now it was over and we were all taking different paths in life. I didn't know if I would see Mimi again, and Lindi and Gabby would be married, and Mike, well he was so aloof anyway. I would be all on my own, stuck in the ass-end of Connecticut.

I still hadn't given Bruno an answer to his marriage proposal. He was planning on coming over to visit me in the USA in a few months. He wanted to see New York City and was planning on buying a new camera there.

Gekko grabbed me in a big bear hug. 'Farewell my *filleule*, I hope you never forget your uncle Gekko. And I have to tell you that I'm glad you dumped that Italian, he was so wrong for you.'

I was about to tell him that I hadn't dumped him when he whispered in my ear. 'It's such a shame too about your girlfriend, Mimi. I think you could have had something there.' Gekko winked at me and then flitted off to change the record.

It was starting to get late and the host families were all starting to put their coats on. I was getting up early for my flight so I decided to head home with the DeClermonts.

'See you all in September back at NEU,' I said as I waved bye to everyone.

Au revoir

The alarm woke me up with its loud, abrasive buzz. I numbly got up, brushed my teeth, had a bath and got dressed, putting the last few toiletries in my case and zipping it up. I took a look around the room, at the antique wardrobe, the rickety desk, the uncomfortable bed and the piano. Even though I was not looking forward to going home, I would not miss this dour room, or the boxy concrete house, or the DeClermonts for that matter. But I would miss Europe and seeing it through the eyes of an outsider. I lugged my cases out into the foyer and went into the kitchen to have my breakfast. The family was already sitting at the table.

'My flight is at 11, Sophie. I was wondering if you would be able to drop me off at the airport?'

'Oh dear, I'm afraid that we are going to church. Can't you get the train?' she suggested, as she poured milk into her bowl of coffee, without even so much as a glance in my direction.

'No. I don't think I can do that,' I said indicating through the doorway to my luggage in the hallway. 'My bags are just too heavy. I couldn't manage it all.'

'Well you can phone for a taxi then,' she said, finally looking up at me, a false smile shaping her thin lips.

I really couldn't believe that she could be so horrible. A taxi would cost an absolute fortune and all I had were some Italian lire and a cash card that didn't work.

'But I'm not sure that I have enough money to pay. My card isn't working and I haven't been able to get any cash out from the machines.'

'Haven't you been to the bank to get some money?'

'I just got back from Italy. I haven't had any time and the banks are closed today, it's Sunday. Would you be able to lend it to me?'

'I'm afraid that we don't have that much cash on us right now. Why don't you try getting some money out at the bureau de change at the airport?'

I phoned for a taxi and asked how much it would cost to go to Charles De Gaulle airport. It would be about 250 francs. I did some swift calculations in my head and worked out that if I exchanged all my Italian money I would still not have quite enough. I just had to hope for a good exchange rate. I booked the taxi and stood waiting by the door. The DeClermonts seemed indifferent to the fact that I was leaving. When the taxi arrived, Sophie gave me the '*bises*', kissing the air on either side of my face. I had a warmer hug from Thierry and the children who waited at the door, waving as the taxi driver helped me to load up my luggage. I imagined I could hear a collective sigh of relief from the family as the taxi driver shut my door and we set off.

On the way to the airport, the driver tried to make small talk and chit chatted inanely about his niece who was going to study computer science in California. He was worried about how she would get on in America where everything was so un-French. I interrupted his monologue to explain my money situation and that on arriving at the airport he would have to wait for me to run in and get the money for the fare. Fortunately, he didn't mind.

There were several bureaux de change inside the terminal but they all had a terrible rate of exchange. I changed the lire, but as I expected, I was still about 50 francs short of the fare. I attempted to use my card to get some more cash but the woman behind the desk shook her head. 'It is invalid, I am afraid,' she said, handing the card back to me. 'Do you have another one you could try?' she suggested.

I wished I still had my emergency American Express card that had been stolen in Paris. If ever there was an emergency this was it.

I tried another two bureaux de change but it was the same story—my card was just not working. I looked at my watch and realized that the taxi driver had been waiting about 20 minutes and would probably add that to the fare. I began to worry that if I wasn't able to pay the full amount he might just drive off with my stuff.

I sheepishly made my way back to the taxi and handed the driver the cash that I had. He counted it and then asked, 'Do you have 50 francs more, Mademoiselle?'

I apologized and explained my situation. His friendly, chatty disposition suddenly changed. He did not look at all happy and glared at me as he dumped my bags in a heap on the sidewalk outside the terminal. 'I'm sure the people at the house where you picked me up from wouldn't mind paying you the rest.'

I wrote down Sophie's name and phone number and handed it to him. If they were going to leave me in the lurch I figured I had the right to drop them in it as well.

I had spent a bit longer than I had planned trawling around the airport in search of money and I was now pressed for time. I arrived at the check-in desk, sweaty and frazzled, about five minutes before they closed it. I was relieved to see that I wasn't the only one. There were a few other stragglers ahead of me in line. As I waited, I collapsed onto my luggage, trying to catch my breath after racing through the terminal pushing my overloaded cart, the adrenalin from the stress beginning to subside.

I suddenly felt a tap on my shoulder. I span around.

'Are you OK?' a dark-haired man asked me.

There was something familiar about him. It was his eyes. He had the most amazing blue eyes that were made all the more striking by the contrast of his dark olive skin.

It took me a minute, but then I recalled an overnight train journey from Paris to Italy. 'It's Ivan, isn't it?' I said, smiling and holding out my hand.

He beamed. 'You remember?'

'Yes, of course. You showed me your drawings.'

'You never called me or came to visit.'

'I know, I'm sorry,' I shrugged. 'Are you on this flight?'

'Yes, I'm going to visit my family in Argentina and I have to change flights in New York to go to Buenos Aires.'

At this point I reached the check-in desk. 'Are you two travelling together?' the assistant asked, noticing that Ivan and I were talking to each other. I looked back at him and he smiled and stepped up beside me.

'Yes,' he smiled.

'I can show you some of my new sketches,' Ivan said, touching my arm.

My stomach did a flip-flop and I smiled inwardly as we wove our way through the security check and past the duty free shops, talking like we had known each other forever.

We boarded the plane and he helped me put my hand luggage up in the hold, and then we settled down in our seats, side by side. Ivan looked out the porthole as the plane lifted up into the sky, then he turned to me and said, 'You should come to Buenos Aires to see me. I can show you around. It could be an adventure.'

Fin

Author biography

Linn Parker is a writer, editor and linguist, born in New York, raised in Connecticut and now living in Brighton, UK. She has had her share of creative pursuits from writing poetry and songs, to playing bass and singing in a band that once did a Radio 1 John Peel session, to writing stories for *Thomas the Tank Engine* and teen magazines. Linn works as a freelance writer and editor, and when she gets time off she combines her passion for travel and writing in her blog: lifeslittleadventurestravelblog.wordpress. com. *Ameritrash* is Linn's first novel.

https://www.facebook.com/linnparkerauthor/
https://twitter.com/linnparkernovel

www.ingramcontent.com/pod-product-compliance
Lightning Source LLC
Chambersburg PA
CBHW070614130626
46556CB00001B/362